All Caught Up

SOPHIA SHAW

Dafina
Books

Kensington Publishing Corp.

http://www.kensingtonbooks.com

DAFINA BOOKS are published by

Kensington Publishing Corp.
119 West 40th Street
New York, NY 10018

All Kensington Titles, Imprints, and Distributed Lines are
available at special quantity discounts for bulk purchases for
sales promotions, premiums, fund-raising, and educational or
institutional use. Special book excerpts or customized print-
ings can also be created to fit specific needs. For details,
write or phone the office of the Kensington special sales
manager: Kensington Publishing Corp., 119 West 40th Street,
New York, NY 10018, attn: Special Sales Department, Phone:
1-800-221-2647.

Dafina and the Dafina logo Reg. U.S. Pat. & TM Off.

ISBN-13: 978-0-7582-6527-2
ISBN-10: 0-7582-6527-1

First mass market printing: November 2011

10 9 8 7 6 5 4 3 2 1

Printed in the United States of America

ALL CAUGHT UP

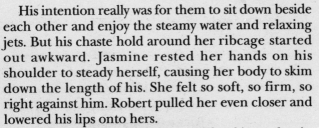

His intention really was for them to sit down beside each other and enjoy the steamy water and relaxing jets. But his chaste hold around her ribcage started out awkward. Jasmine rested her hands on his shoulder to steady herself, causing her body to skim down the length of his. She felt so soft, so firm, so right against him. Robert pulled her even closer and lowered his lips onto hers.

It should have ended there, with a kiss stolen in the heat of the moment. But Robert couldn't stop. It was like a fire had ignited inside of him, sparked by the taste of her mouth, and the feel of her full breasts pressed against him. He kissed her harder, deeper, his lips tasting hers, his tongue dipping into her wetness. And through the fog of his raging desire, he felt her response.

Jasmine arched her back and ran her hands from his shoulders up his neck to cup the back of his head. Robert froze, trying hard to regain his composure and understand what she was trying to tell him. They stood there for long seconds with the sounds of their labored breathing bouncing off the walls. Then she pulled his head closer to hers and took his bottom lip between her teeth, first nibbling it, then bathing it with her tongue.

"Jasmine," he whispered harshly as his hands swept over her back and his mouth covered hers again for another long series of deep, hot kisses.

Robert finally grasped the firm curves of her bottom, squeezing its fullness and pulling her hips up against his. Then he lifted her up by the backs of her thighs and wrapped her legs around his hips. Jasmine gasped, gripping his shoulder again.

"What if someone comes in," she stammered breathlessly.

"Then they'll walk back out," he whispered harshly.

Also by Sophia Shaw

Published by Dafina Books

If I was as beautiful as I am ambitious,
I would be too stunning to look at.
People would have to cover their eyes when I walked by.

Dr. Iris D. Thomas

Acknowledgments

Writing ALL CAUGHT UP was so much fun! The beautiful, diverse city of Key West was the inspiration, and I can't wait to go back. Everything else just fell into place.

To my baby sister, Natasha Jackson—thank you for, once again, being my sounding board and unofficial editor. I really couldn't do the process without you.

To my agent, Sha-Shana Crichton and editor, Mercedes Fernandez—thank you both for your ideas and encouragement through the creative process. We make a great team!

To my fiancé, Scott Henderson—thank you so much for being my resource for all things hockey and jock related. Who would have thought at the beginning of the 2010/11 NHL season that Vancouver and Tampa Bay would come so close to facing off in the finals?

Love always,
Sophia

Chapter 1

May in Miami Beach was usually sunny and comfortably warm, great weather for being out-side before the stifling summer heat kicked in. But on this day, the sky was heavy with rain clouds and the humidity in the air was almost visibly thick.

Jasmine Croft walked up to the railing at the edge of her loft bedroom and looked out at the At-lantic Ocean through the patio doors on the main floor of her apartment. She frowned at the gray weather, biting the side of her mouth as she rethought her plans for the day. Turning away from the view, she headed to her bathroom, switching on the radio next to her bed along the way. It was a quarter after eight o'clock on Satur-day morning, and she had a few minutes to wash up and get dressed before heading to the gym for a nine o'clock Pilates class.

When Jasmine left the apartment a few minutes later, she was dressed in an athletic tank top over a heavy-duty sports bra, knee-length yoga pants and flip-flops. Her thick, shoulder-length hair was covered and tied back with a bright colored scarf to protect it from the damp air and potential rain, her gym bag was slung across her back. She was a member of a large, full-service fitness club located a couple of blocks away from her building near the heart of Miami Beach's famous South Beach district. The street was already busy with activity—people of all ages running, biking, and rollerblading, or walking their dogs in the warm, sticky morning air. Jasmine was sweating by the time she stepped into the overly air-conditioned club after the brisk walk, but had ten minutes to spare.

"Hey, sexy," greeted the young man at the front desk as he flashed her a big smile. His youthful face was tanned a deep bronze and his white teeth sparkled. Stunning green eyes looked at her keenly.

"Hi, George," Jasmine replied cheerfully as she handed him her membership card.

"Are you taking Mark's class?" George asked. "I saved you a spot just in case."

Mark Santiago was one of the best instructors in South Beach, drawing members from all over South Florida to his Pilates classes, which were always so packed that they had to turn people away.

"Yup. You're the best," she told George with a flirty look.

He laughed while blushing slightly and handed back her card.

"See you later," he added.

Jasmine walked away with a bounce in her step.

While she was certain George O'Toole was no more than nineteen years old and definitely not her type, he had an amazing body and was beautiful to look at. Their regular flirting was always fun and harmless.

"Hey Jay!"

Jasmine had said hello to several people as she made her way through the entrance of the gym toward the change rooms, but the call had come from behind her. She turned to find a pretty woman with coppery brown skin and short-cropped natural hair rushing to catch up to her. It was her best friend, Madison Cooper.

"Hey, Madie, I thought you weren't going to make it today." Jasmine replied, stopping to wait for her.

"My plans got cancelled," she stated with a twist of her mouth.

"No way. He cancelled again?" asked Jasmine.

The women continued walking and entered the women's change room, choosing lockers in their usual spot at the back near the showers and counters.

"Yeah, can you believe that?" Madison said. "He sent me a text message this morning saying something's come up and he'll call me later. That's the third time. Well that's it, then. That's the last time I'm making plans with him. In fact, I'm not even going to reply to his message."

"Wow," stated Jasmine while shaking her head. "I'm sorry, Madie. I know how much you liked him."

Madison sighed. "I did like him, and it started out so well. We seemed to have a connection and had a great time together for a few months. Then suddenly, he takes days to return my phone calls, and starts cancelling plans last minute. Typical story, right?"

Jasmine nodded sadly.

"Anyway, I know the signs, so I'm not going to waste any more time on him."

"Well, I'm glad you're here. I'm going to the spa after class for a mani-pedi. Do you want to come? We can hang out for the afternoon, do some shopping."

"Sure, why not. A little retail therapy sounds like good medicine," stated Madison with a dry laugh. "I was thinking about going into the office to drum up some business, but your suggestion is much better."

Madison was in real estate and did most of her work in South Beach.

"Good. I have a meeting at twelve o'clock at Mango's Café, but it won't take long and we can stay for lunch," Jasmine suggested. "We can go to Lincoln Road Mall after."

"Sounds like a plan. You're meeting a new client?" Madison asked.

"No, it's an interview with a writer for the *Miami Weekly* for an article on dating services. Maya Jones set it up and they want to talk about the services that Croft Connections provides to its clients."

"That's great!"

"I hope so," replied Jasmine. "It could be great marketing for my business."

Once they were ready, and carrying their mats, they joined several other class participants and headed to the studio for the intense one-hour power Pilates class. Mark Santiago was waiting at the front of the room with a slow Latin ballad playing softly in the background. He was a short man, about five feet six inches, with a thin build but ripped beyond belief with long lean muscles everywhere and next to zero body fat. As usual, he ran the class like a drill sergeant, pushing everyone to the limit and leaving them dripping with sweat. Everyone cheered at the end, and he bowed with a cheeky grin.

"God, I'm exhausted!" exclaimed Madison still lying on her back. "I could fall asleep right here."

Jasmine laughed and stood looking down at her limp friend. She felt the same way, but knew the tiredness would fade quickly and an energy boost would kick in the minute she stepped into the shower.

"Well, you better get up quick. My appointment at the spa is in thirty minutes."

Madison rolled onto her knees with a groan.

"Uggggh! You're always on a schedule, Jay!" she grumbled. "It's Saturday. Relax a little."

Jasmine was used to the ribbing from her friends about her tightly managed timetables, so she ignored the comment. She rolled up her mat and headed out of the room, assuming that Madie would eventually follow along. Mark, the instructor, was standing near the exit of the studio and gave her a friendly smile as she approached.

"You did great today," he stated, his voice flowing with a distinctive Puerto Rican accent.

"Thanks," replied Jasmine. "It was a great class."

"I'm glad you enjoyed it. See you again next week?"

"Definitely," she stated firmly.

"Good," he added with sincerity.

Jasmine smiled and continued out the door.

"Wow," whispered Madison as she stepped close behind Jasmine.

"What?"

"I told you he was into you! You should have seen the way his eyes followed your tush as you walked away. It was like he couldn't help himself."

Jasmine gave her friend a glance that clearly said, *Oh please!*, causing Madison to laugh.

"First poor George, and now our famous instructor. That body of yours should require a license, Jay. It's dangerous."

"Don't be ridiculous. The instructors flirt with everyone, especially George. Why do you think there are so many female members?" said Jasmine dismissively. "And the place is full of Miami babes with unbelievable bodies, including yours. I could do a million more crunches and would still never have a hint of the six-pack you do."

"Yeah, well, these abs have never put a man into a hypnotic trance like your deadly combo of T&A," teased Madison, still grinning.

Jasmine ignored her and continued to the change

room. But once they were ready for the showers, she couldn't help feeling embarrassed, wrapping the towel around her naked body a little tighter than usual. While others thought she should proudly flaunt her more than necessary curves, Jasmine secretly hated them, and the unwanted attention they always attracted. While almost every woman in Florida was addicted to push-up bras and silicone implants, Jasmine dreamed of a reduction. Under the spray of hot water in the private shower, she looked down at the plumb swells of her breasts, wishing instead they were normal-sized B cups. And it didn't help that her behind was a little too full and round to ignore, clinging to the fabric of everything she wore.

Jasmine and her sister, Jennifer, were raised in Fort Lauderdale by their Cuban-Jamaican mother. While growing up, they learned an appreciation for both cultures, including the many shapes and sizes of Caribbean women. Both sisters had similar smooth, nutmeg-toned skin. But Jennifer, who was four years older, seemed to inherit everything else from their mother's side of the family, like her naturally lean, athletic figure. Apparently, Jasmine was the spitting image of their father, with his smooth square-shaped face and rounder body. Since Clifton Croft had disappeared out of his daughters' lives when Jasmine was three years old, the descriptions and comments about her resemblance to him were almost never positive or flattering. She grew up feeling as though her body was a curse and she was stuck with all her physical attributes. It was pointless to try and change genetics, so why bother to try.

As a teenager, she was chubby, and became completely overweight while in college. Then two years ago, when she thought seriously about starting up her personalized dating service, it became essential to take better care of her body. Her early research into the business and consumer market indicated quite quickly that single, eligible men and women would not trust her to find them a partner unless she looked the part—someone whom women wanted to be seen with or men would want to date. It was the motivation she needed to get in shape.

Eight months later, with the help of a personal trainer, a rigid workout schedule, and a complete overhaul of her eating habits, Jasmine dropped over forty pounds. While her new body was firm and toned with a flat abdomen and lean legs, her bustline hardly budged. And, to her dismay, as the rest of her body slimmed down and was redefined, it only made her breasts appear larger. Jasmine was thrilled with her new body, but it did create a whole new set of issues, like the relentless and unwanted attention from men.

After showering, the women were dressed again in about twenty minutes. While Madison changed into jean-shorts, a T-shirt and flip-flops, Jasmine left the change room wearing a pretty linen sundress in a light tan color and gold-tone sandals adorned with polished stones the color of topaz.

Her meeting with the magazine writer was at noon, and there wouldn't be time to stop at home after her spa appointment to change again. She combed out her hair until it fell smoothly around her shoulder in a long bob.

They took their purses and walked to the club spa at the front of the building, leaving their gym bags and workout clothes in their lockers. Jasmine spent the next hour getting pampered until both her hands and feet were silky smooth and finished with French manicure polish. Madison opted for a facial instead and was waiting in the front reception area drinking tea when Jasmine emerged to pay for her services.

"Do you want to walk or take a taxi?" asked Madison once they were outside.

It was just past 11:30. The sky was still cloudy, but the sun was starting to peek out.

"We can walk. We have time and it's only a few blocks away," Jasmine replied.

When they arrived at Mango's Café, Madison decided to stop at the drugstore across the street so Jasmine could have her meeting privately. Jasmine secured a table outside on the sidewalk and still had a few minutes to spare. She took out her mobile phone to check for messages. There was a text message from her friend, Maya Jones. Jasmine knew immediately what it was regarding, and could not help rolling her eyes.

The message read: **Everything all set for tonight?**

Jasmine quickly tapped out a response: **So far so good.**

She looked up at that moment and recognized the young woman who turned into the café patio from the street. The hostess greeted her, then pointed to the table where Jasmine was seated. Jasmine used the next few seconds to type up another text message in reply to Maya: **I'll call you a little later with details.**

Chapter 2

"Jasmine Croft?"

The woman standing over her was tall, slender, and very blond. Her sky-blue eyes had a friendly sparkle.

"Yes," Jasmine replied as she stood up and extended her hand. "Hi, it's Amanda, right?"

"Amanda Bryant, with *Miami Weekly*," she replied while accepting the handshake.

She sat back down, and Amanda took the seat across from her. A waiter approached their table at that moment and took their orders for coffee. The women exchanged polite conversation about the weather as they waited for their drinks to arrive.

"Thank you for taking the time to meet with me," Amanda stated as they sipped their hot drinks. "As I mentioned on the phone, my article is about the surge of online dating services and how it's changing the dating scene and nightlife in South Florida. I recognize that your firm is not strictly an online service, but I was intrigued by what you are offering and think it's worth including in the story."

"It's my pleasure, Amanda," replied Jasmine with a bright smile. "An article like this can help highlight what makes us different from those Web sites and hopefully help us reach some potential clients who don't realize there are other kinds of dating solutions."

"Great. So let's get started."

Amanda then proceeded to pull a digital micro-recorder out of her purse, turn it on, and place it between them on the bistro table.

"Your Web site says you started Croft Connections three years ago. What made you decide to go into the dating business?" she asked Jasmine

"It was a combination of a few things, but mainly my experience and the right timing. My first job out of university was in the sales department of a larger online service. I was only there for about nine months, but I learned a lot about membership services and gained some knowledge about the industry and our competitors. I left there to take a position as a corporate recruiter for a marketing and communications firm. That's when I realized that I had an intuitive ability to assess people and identify the best candidate for our positions. It was a great job, but the company went through a merger and my position became redundant. Around that time, I happened to introduce two people who were acquaintances of mine from different circles. They were friends of friends who I saw regularly at parties or get-togethers, and they hit it off right away.

"Thinking back on it now, I really had no intentions other than the impulse to see two single people meet each other based on what they said they wanted in a partner and relationship. Then I did it a few weeks later, again with great results. By then, I was unemployed and getting anxious about finding another job quickly. That's when it occurred to me that I had all the tools to start my own dating services," Jasmine recalled with a modest smile. "Necessity forced me to accept another recruitment position, but the idea stuck in my head and grew as I thought about the perfect business model. The next time I offered to set someone up, I asked for a fee. That was four years ago. I established the company about a year later, but didn't quit my recruitment job until last year."

"Wow, that's a very interesting start-up," Amanda said. "So, what can clients expect from Croft Connections? What services do you provide?" she quizzed.

Jasmine paused for a couple of seconds before responding. Her mission statement was available on the Web site, but she wanted to convey more than that.

"The short answer is that we offer access to an exclusive private approach to connecting single people in South Florida. It would be too simplistic to say that Croft Connections is a dating service. We're much more than that. Yes, we help people meet each other, maybe for casual dating, maybe for serious relationships. But our approach is what makes us different from other companies and online services. We take the time to meet every new member to the Connection and recommend matches based on our personal knowledge of the individuals, not a computer program."

"And at a very steep price," added Amanda pointedly.

"Our fees are an investment," Jasmine replied without discomfort. "We do not provide the cheapest service, nor is it the fastest or most convenient. But that's part of the reason we are so effective and successful. Our members are very serious and committed to the process of meeting the right person, unlike many of the people that use a free Web site, or low-cost competitors. I can assure you that all of the happy couples we have brought together over the last three years see the value."

Amanda smiled, nodding. "Can you walk me through the process a new client would go through? What would I need to do and what can I expect?"

"Here is one of our brochures," Jasmine told her as she reached into her purse and pulled out a glossy color pamphlet. "It describes our three memberships and outlines the process. But, in the end, it boils down to what our clients are looking for. Part of the reason the personal dating solution works so well is that it's not the cookie-cutter approach of dumping everyone into a database and letting them sort through pictures and brief, superficial self-descriptions. We are able to give each client the experience they are seeking."

"That's interesting," Amanda said with a raised brow. "Can you give me some examples of what different people want, and how you provide it?"

Her tone made Jasmine laugh. "I'm not referring to anything indecent! But we first help our clients to understand what they are looking for in a partner, and what their interpretation is of dating. We end up with people looking for one end of the spectrum, which is the occasional dinner date a couple times a month, to someone who wants to get married within the year, and everything in between."

"So how can you possibly meet those expectations?"

"We don't promise to. All we can do is introduce you to someone who claims to want the same things, in addition to having an acceptable number of matching attributes on their lists of wants and needs. The rest is out of our control."

"That sounds pretty logical," Amanda stated.

"It is, particularly since most people make very illogical and emotional dating decisions."

"That is so true."

There were a few minutes of silence as Amanda looked through the Croft Connections brochure.

"This has a great deal of information, so I think that covers it," she finally told Jasmine. "I should be able to include the article in our July edition."

"That's great! I'm excited to read it. Thank you again for reaching out to me, and let me know if you need any more information."

"It was my pleasure. As a recently single woman,

I can identify with lots of what you have told me about your company. In fact, the concept for the article began with my personal research into how I can meet new people and get out into the dating world. When I told Maya about it, she was pretty adamant that I talk with you," Amanda added as she turned off her recorder and put it in her purse. "She told me that she knows a few people who've hired you and had great success."

"That's great! Does that mean that we can set up some time for a consultation?" asked Jasmine with a teasing smile.

Amanda laughed. "We'll see. I'll let you know once the article is published."

"Sounds good," Jasmine agreed with a firm nod.

The women both stood up to shake hands and say good-bye.

Jasmine sat back down and watched her walk away, feeling excited by how well the meeting went. She also made a mental note to get Maya something special while out shopping later to thank her for her constant support.

"I take it by the giant smile on your face that the interview went well?" said Madison as she sat down.

"Hey, where did you come from?" Jasmine asked, surprised by her sudden appearance.

"I got here a few minutes ago," explained Madie. "Are we still staying to eat? I'm starving."

"Sure. I'm pretty hungry, too."

"Good. I asked them to bring us a couple of menus. So, how did it go?"

Jasmine told her all about it as they ate lunch. About an hour later, they grabbed a cab up to Lincoln Road Mall, a street lined with high-end stores and boutiques. Jasmine took the opportunity to call Maya Jones during the ride as she had promised in her earlier text messages.

"Hi, Maya, it's Jasmine," she stated after Maya's greeting.

"Hey, girl! How's it going?"

"Not bad. How about you? Are you feeling better?"

Earlier in the week when the two friends last spoke, Maya had been trying to get over the flu.

"I'm better, thank God! Still pretty tired, but at least I can now keep some food down. So, today is the big day."

"You mean the interview with Amanda Bryant? We met earlier this afternoon," Jasmine confirmed. "It went really well, I think."

"Oh, yeah!" exclaimed Maya, caught off-guard. "I completely forgot about that. Amanda is great, isn't she?"

"Yeah, she seemed really nice. But I can't thank you enough for your endorsement, Maya. She also suggested that she is interested in becoming a client," Jasmine added with a big smile on her face.

Maya chuckled. "Perfect."

"If you keep it up, Maya, I'm going to have to introduce some sort of referral bonus," teased

Jasmine, causing Maya to laugh even harder. "So, if you weren't referring to the article interview, I guess you were referring to the big date tonight for our favorite writer."

"Yup, that would be it," Maya confirmed.

Over four weeks ago, Maya had referred one of her clients, a writer named Robert Rankin, to Jasmine. He very quickly became the bane of her existence. Not only was he impossible to reach, he was reluctant and skeptical of her services from the beginning. Then, when they finally connected, he was only willing to do so by instant message, and had very specific and unrealistic expectations. Jasmine was almost sure he would prove to be a waste of her time, but then he paid her highest membership fee, so she felt obligated to pursue his search. His first date was tonight.

"Well, so far so good on my end," Jasmine told her. "His date, Carole, is to meet him at the hotel at seven o'clock this evening. I sent Robert an e-mail last night to touch base, but as usual, he hasn't responded. I have to assume that he's still confirmed."

"He's confirmed," Maya stated after a long sigh. "I spoke with him this morning. I know I've already apologized for him a few times already, but I swear he's not as big an ass as he acts sometimes. He's working on finishing up the new novel, and I guess he doesn't handle distractions very well. But I really appreciate how difficult it has been for you to work with him. In fact, why don't we just call it even between you and me, no need to pay me any referral fees any time soon."

Jasmine laughed and agreed. "It's a deal."

She ended the call as the cab pulled up to an intersection near the outdoor mall. After paying the fare, Madison joined her on the sidewalk and they linked their arms together.

"So where do we start?" she asked Jasmine as they started walking.

"Well, I'm running low on bath products," Jasmine told her. "And, I'm desperately in need of a new dress. It appears that weekly wedding invitations are an occupational hazard I hadn't anticipated."

They continued walking down the street into the heart of the outdoor mall at a leisurely pace, stopping in stores as items in the display windows caught their eyes. Two hours easily went by while the clouds thinned out, finally unveiling blue skies and the Florida sun. Eventually, they ended up at a women's clothing store. While Madison was trying on several pairs of skinny jeans, Jasmine browsed through the jewelry section near the register. Her cell phone rang, and she recognized the number right away.

"Hi, Carole," she said when she answered the call. "How is it going?"

"Hi, Jasmine, sorry to bother you," replied Carole.

Her voice, tense and stilted, alluded to something ominous. The smile on Jasmine's lips wavered.

"That's okay. Is everything alright?" she asked Carole.

"No, actually. I'm so sorry, Jasmine. But I won't be able to make it for the date tonight."

Jasmine froze. "Why? What happened?"

"I'm not exactly sure, but it looks like I've fractured my wrist," Carole explained.

"Oh, my God! Are you okay?"

"It was so stupid! I was running across the street at an intersection, and I heard a car horn blow just as I was about to get on the sidewalk. But I guess I missed a step when I turned to look around, or something. Anyway, I just remembered going flying and landing hard on my right hand."

"Oh, Carole, that's horrible! Do you need anything?" Jasmine asked.

"No, I'm okay. I'm at the hospital now and they're doing X-rays to see if I need a cast."

"Okay. Will you need a ride home after?"

"No," Carole replied. "My sister is on her way, so I should be okay. But I'm really sorry to cancel on you at the last minute, Jasmine. I know how hard it was to arrange this first meeting. I was really looking forward to it."

"Don't worry about it, Carole. These things happen. Just take care of yourself, and I will let Robert know what happened. Give me a call next week and let me know if you would like me to try and reschedule the date."

The women exchanged a few more words before they hung up.

"What's wrong?" Madison asked as she walked

out of the change room and found Jasmine staring off into space.

"Oh, nothing," she replied sarcastically. "I just have to call the worst client I've ever had to tell him his date that is supposed to happen in less than three hours is now off."

Chapter 3

"Uncle Rob, can you fix the television for me? The channel won't change."

Robert Rankin looked up from his laptop at his seven-year-old nephew, Alex, who now stood just inside the doorway of his office. He was a slender kid, a little tall for his age, and his bronze skin and curly hair revealed his mixed cultural heritage. While Alex had the remote control is his hand, the look on his face was curious and eager. Rob knew the look well. It meant Alex was looking for some attention and had found the perfect excuse.

"Alex, I thought we agreed that you were going to play outside while I worked?" Robert asked in a quiet but firm voice.

"I know, but Sam and Quentin had to go home. Then Mary made me come in for lunch."

"Okay, so go and eat your lunch. And ask your nanny to fix the TV for you."

Robert turned his attention back to the computer, attempting to end any further conversation with Alex. But the boy was not put off. Rob closed his eyes for a couple of seconds as he heard his nephew walk across the room and around the large desk until he was leaning against Robert's chair.

"Uncle Rob, why can't I go to Uncle Matthew's party tonight? I want to go for a ride on your boat."

Robert let out a long sigh, letting go of the possibility that his nephew would just go away.

"Alex, we've talked about this already. Tonight is an adult party. There won't be any other kids there. I'll take you out on the boat tomorrow, I promise. Then, next week, we'll all go up to Canada for Matthew's wedding. The whole family will be there, okay?" Robert explained. "But tonight, you need to stay with Mary. Your mom and I will be back tomorrow. Why don't you invite one of your friends over for a sleepover?"

Alex frowned for a brief moment and then looked up at his uncle with a spark in his eyes. "I'll ask Quentin. Can we rent movies and have popcorn?" he asked eagerly.

"Are you going to let me work for the rest of the afternoon?" Robert replied.

Alex immediately nodded.

"Okay, then tell Mary what movies you want and ask her to call Quentin's mom," said Robert.

"Thanks, Uncle Rob!" Alex yelled while hugging his uncle.

His nephew then ran off, yelling his nanny's name at the top of his lungs. Robert could not help smiling at the youthful energy and enthusiasm for the simplest pleasures. He then turned his attention back to the manuscript he was working on, trying to recapture his thought process in order to continue writing. It was almost one-thirty in the afternoon, so he had about three hours left to get some work done.

Robert was right in the middle of writing his third suspense novel, still untitled. According to his agent, Maya Jones, it was the long-awaited sequel to his first bestselling book, *Dead of Night*. He considered it to be the most ambitious project he had ever agreed to, and was starting to wonder if he had bitten off more than he could chew.

The idea of being an author was still new and strange to him. When Robert wrote his first two books, he was at a crossroads in his life and between careers. It had been a pretty easy process, more of a therapeutic pastime with no pressure or deadlines. His younger brother, Matthew, had been the only person to read the manuscripts and he talked Robert into finding an agent.

That was over three year ago, and before a lifetime of changes.

One month, he was celebrating his first book deal; the next, he was burying his wife after a deadly car crash. While his books were being released, gaining market share and a loyal fan base, Robert was lost in a stupor. He emerged from the hellish fog several months later with a completely new path in life and a burgeoning writing career. But along with his very impressive publishing contract, there was also a list of expectations, commitments, and aggressive deadlines all outlined in the fine print.

When Robert finally pushed his chair back from his desk, he was satisfied with his progress but running behind schedule. He should have stopped writing about thirty minutes earlier, but couldn't until he finished the current chapter. If he rushed, there was a chance he could make up the time. So he quickly headed upstairs to his bedroom to shower and get dressed.

Robert lived with his younger sister, Cara, and her son, Alex, in a suburb of Key West, Florida, at the southernmost point of the Florida Keys. Mary Jacobs was their live-in housekeeper and Alex's nanny during the week, and stayed the occasional weekend when needed. Tonight was the pre-wedding celebration for the youngest Rankin sibling, Matthew, so Mary was staying the weekend to take care of Alex. As the maid-of-honor, Cara had planned the party at one the most posh waterfront hotels in Miami, where Matthew lived with his fiancée, Rosanna Brooke. She had flown to Miami yesterday to finalize all of the arrangements and remain there for the weekend.

It was almost five o'clock when Robert made his way downstairs carrying a small overnight bag. He found his nephew and the nanny in the backyard. Alex was splashing around in the swimming pool while Mary read a book, reclined on a padded lounge chair under the cabana. She quickly stood up when she saw Robert walking toward her. She was a tiny woman with a red-brown complexion and long wavy hair pulled into a bun.

"Hi, Mr. Rankin, you look very nice," she stated pleasantly with a melodic Trinidadian accent.

He smiled politely, noting the surprise on her age-lined face. This was likely the first time in her six months of employment that she had seen Robert in anything other than shorts and a golf shirt. He was barely recognizable in a tailored gray suit and sky-blue shirt, his standard scruffy beard shaved into a slick mustache and goatee. His copper-flecked eyes sparkled against his smooth brown skin.

"Thanks, Mary. I've left the hotel information in the kitchen, but call me on my cell phone if you need me for any reason," he instructed. "I should be back around noon tomorrow."

"Yes, sir," she replied. "Why don't you just stay at your apartment in Miami?"

"Cara is using it, and so are several of Rosanna's friends that live farther away," he explained. "So it's just easier for me to use a hotel for one night."

They both looked over at Alex as he did a cannonball into deep end of the pool, creating a big splash that sprayed water onto the stone deck.

"Is his friend, Quentin, going to sleep over?" Robert asked.

"Yes. His mom said he can come over after dinner."

"Okay, that's good."

"Did you see that jump, Uncle Rob?" demanded Alex as he pulled himself out of the water and sat at the edge of the pool.

"I did. It was pretty impressive," Robert told him.

"Watch. I'm going to do an even bigger jump. Maybe even a belly flop," he exclaimed.

"Sorry, buddy," said Robert as he bent down to be closer to eye level. "I have to get going or I'm going to be really late. You can show me tomorrow, okay?"

"Alright," Alex conceded, his shoulder slumped to demonstrate his disappointment. "But don't forget your promise. You'll take me out on your boat tomorrow, right?"

"I won't forget. Be good for Mary, and I'll see you tomorrow."

Robert gave his nephew's wet hair a gentle rub, then stood up.

"Bye, Uncle Rob,"

He heard another big splash as he headed toward the wooden pier behind the pool area.

Miami was about one hundred and fifty miles northeast from Key West. It was a quick flight, but over three hours driving. Robert preferred to travel by water. For him, the best feature of his ocean-front property was the ability to dock his boat and have immediate access to the Gulf of Mexico. In his thirty-nine-foot blue and white Top Gun cigarette boat, a decent cruising speed would get him to Miami in about an hour and a half. And the breath-taking scenery was just a bonus.

Robert threw his bag into the sleek watercraft, the name POKERFACE scripted in dark blue across the stern, then prepped for the departure. Once he turned on the powerful twin engines, he took his iPhone out of his inside jacket pocket and turned it on for a final check of the weather forecast. It had been overcast for most of the day, but the clouds had moved out over the ocean, leaving clear skies and calm waters. The weather report promised light winds through the evening. He then tucked the phone back in his pocket, not noticing the missed calls or message indicator.

It was about five-thirty when Robert carefully pulled away from the shore, maintaining the posted speed through the shallow waters between Parrot Key to his right and the Key West Naval Air Station to his left. The water was busy with all types of vessels from fishing boats to sailboats and a few luxury yachts. All around them, small packs of water-skiers zipped nimbly about, leaving long wakes behind them.

Once he passed under the Overseas Highway, the only road that linked the many islands that formed the Florida Keys to the mainland, he headed out into the Gulf, steadily increasing his speed until he reached a comfortable ninety nautical miles per hour. The boat engine hummed smoothly, nowhere near its top racing speed.

At thirty-two years of age, Robert had experienced and accomplished more than most men twice his age. He grew up in Minneapolis, Minnesota, in a normal middle-class Midwest family, with his parents and two younger siblings. Like every other boy he knew, Robert played sports at school, then road hockey in the streets for fun.

Then, when he was nine years old, his dad, Arnold Rankin, started watching ice hockey on television and instantly fell in love with the excitement of the game. That winter, he signed his two sons up for hockey lessons, completely unfazed by the early morning practices or by being the only black people at the rink.

Within three years, Robert was playing in the local junior league and making a name for himself in the state as the goaltender to beat. He had developed a natural ability for the game that would eventually take him to the pinnacle of success and to the depths of pain and despair.

By high school graduation, he was a member of the USA national junior hockey team. Four years later, at twenty-one years old, Robert stepped on the ice in Miami as a backup goalie for the Florida Panthers. He spent the next eight years in the NHL with unflappable focus and drive on the ice, and then partied equally hard during the off-season. The world was like his personal ice rink, and he played in it with the heroes and icons of the sport. For those years, fun meant wild parties and over-indulgence. He bought stuff and did things simply because he could, without any appreciation of the value or experience. At the peak of his madness, wasteful extravagance felt normal and the middle-class moderation he knew as a child seemed to belong to someone else's memories.

Robert met his wife, Lakeisha Clarke, during his fourth NHL season at a hotel club in Detroit after an away game. There were very few black women who followed the hockey scene, so when she walked into the room with her light, hazelnut skin and long straight hair, she caught his eye right away. Robert bought her a drink and they hit it off immediately. She was smart, sophisticated, and gorgeous. For him, at twenty-five years old, it felt like love at first sight had hit him hard. He proposed to Lakeisha three months later and they were married that summer. It was a tumultuous relationship from rushed beginning to tragic end.

As Robert handled his speedboat with practiced ease, skimming over the water along the southern Florida coastline, he barely remembered the arrogant and misguided young man he had once been. The entitled world of professional sports had lost its appeal years ago. He had traded in the rush of game night and the deafening roar of the fans for quiet nights and spectacular sunsets when he retired from hockey.

Robert reduced speed as he entered Biscayne Bay, the waterway between Miami to the west and Miami Beach to the east. The hotel for the party was a waterfront property on a small exclusive island in the bay with a marina attached. He pulled up to the mooring area and slowly docked his boat.

His phone rang as he walked past the outdoor pool and patio toward the rear entrance of the hotel. He could hear the music from the party.

"Hello," he answered without checking the caller.

"Where are you?"

Robert recognized Cara's voice right away.

"I'm just about to go into the hotel," he told her.

"What took you so long? You were supposed to be here an hour ago."

"Cara, the party started at six o'clock. Why do I have to be there the minute the doors open? Is Matthew even here yet?"

"I just spoke with Rosanna. They're going to be here in about fifteen minutes," she stated.

"Good, then I'm right on time."

"Whatever," said Cara dismissively. "Just hurry up."

"I'm going to check into my room; I'll be there in a few minutes."

"Okay. We're set up on the beach just to the left of the pool. Follow the music."

He hung up and checked his watch and cursed. It was fifteen minutes after seven o'clock. Not only was he technically late for his brother's pre-wedding party, he was also late for his first real date in almost seven years.

Chapter 4

"This is a nightmare," Jasmine whispered.

Madison stepped closer to her, barely able to hear Jasmine's response. "What happened?"

"This is a disastrous nightmare," repeated Jasmine, this time loud enough for several people near them to hear.

Madison looked around the store, then back at her friend. "Okay, let's get out of here; then you can tell me what happened."

Madie had a pair of jeans over her arm, but tossed them on a nearby display table and wrapped a supportive arm around Jasmine's waist to guide her toward the front entrance. Jasmine hesitated.

"What are you doing? Don't you want to buy those?" she asked her friend.

"Nah, I don't really need them. And I'm not sure about the color. Come on, let's go."

They walked outside.

"Okay, what exactly happened?"

Jasmine's shoulders visibly slumped. "Sorry, it's nothing serious. One of my clients slipped and injured her wrist this afternoon," she explained.

"Ouch. That's too bad. Is she okay?" asked Madison.

"Seems so. She's at the hospital but should be okay."

"But now you have to cancel the date with the other client, right?"

Jasmine rubbed a few fingers across her forehead, as though to ward off an emerging headache.

"Right," she replied. "Normally it's no big deal. I would just call the other person to explain and rebook if needed."

"But . . . ?"

Jasmine let out a long exaggerated sigh. "Madison, this guy has been just so difficult to work with! He doesn't respond to my e-mails or phone calls, his expectations are unrealistic, and it's obvious he has no respect for what I do. It took me three months just to set up this first date and that's after he's canceled at least four others."

"So, why is he using a dating service at all?" asked Madison.

"Right! That's what I wondered. Other than his bad attitude, he's not a bad catch. At least on paper anyway. He's a successfully published writer and decent looking from his pictures. Looks a bit like Boris Kudjoe, now that I think about it. And my friend Maya Jones is his agent and says he's usually a pretty nice guy," Jasmine explained.

"Boris? Yum! You haven't met him? I thought that was one of the key steps in your process?"

"It is, and I've always insisted that it's mandatory for everyone who signs up. But I couldn't make it happen. At first he was traveling, and then he was writing and working toward a deadline. And he lives in Key West, so I couldn't even arrange a quick meeting over coffee. I wasn't even able to get him to talk to me on the phone, to be honest. It was ridiculous," exclaimed Jasmine, using gestures with her hands to express her frustration. "Anyway, I just figured that I would arrange a first date and then walk away."

"I don't get it. Why did he sign up for a dating service at all then? It doesn't make any sense."

"I know, right? But according to Maya, he has a family function to go to tonight and for some reason has decided to bring a plus one," Jasmine explained. "So now, after all that, I need to tell him that I can't deliver at the last minute."

Both women looked at each other.

"Any chance you can find him another date?" Madison asked.

Jasmine let out a sharp, sarcastic snort. "Sure, if it was anyone else. I could think of at least five women who would be happy to go on a last-minute date on a Saturday night, especially with a tall, good-looking man. But none of them are going to meet his requirements."

"What requirements?"

"Ah, let's see . . . She has to be smart, educated, and professional. No more than about five feet five inches, great body, must have some curves but not too fat. She needs to have a really pretty face, but not be conceited or pretentious."

"You're kidding, right? He was that specific?" Madison asked incredulously.

"Oh, it gets better. She can't be too loud, demanding, or opinionated. And to top it off, she needs to have a happy, cheerful personality. But not too cheerful, because that's annoying."

Madison just blinked.

"So, I've been looking for a smart bombshell who is happy but doesn't speak and who is looking for a distant, unavailable, arrogant prick."

Her friend giggled at the description.

"It's not funny, Madie! It's been hell."

Madison continued to chuckle.

"So maybe canceling is not such a bad thing. Then you won't have to deal with him anymore," she suggested.

"Trust me, I've thought of that many times. But I don't want to let Maya down. For some reason she is really close to him, almost protective. She's been so supportive of Croft Connections, always referring clients. I'm not going to let this idiot damage my reputation with her."

"Okay, then you're just going to have to call him . . ."

"Wait!" exclaimed Jasmine, cutting Madison off mid-sentence. "What about you?"

"What about me?"

"You can be his date tonight, Madie," she explained, her eyes bright with the possibility. "Why not? You're available, and gorgeous."

But Madison was already shaking her head. "Jay, you're out of your mind! I'm nothing like his wish list. Forget that my personality and big mouth are the complete opposite of what he asked for, I don't think an ultrapadded push-up bra describes the curves he wants."

Jasmine slumped like a deflated balloon and bowed her head in absolute defeat. "You're right. I should just call him and face his wrath. What's the worst that he could do to me?"

"Or send him another date."

"Madie, I just told you, there is no way for me to find another woman for him now that comes close to his requirements."

"Jay, I'm talking about you."

"What?" she demanded, clearly confused.

"You, Jay. Why don't you go as his date?"

Jasmine was speechless for several seconds.

"That's crazy! I can't do that."

"Why not?" Madison insisted.

"Madison, he's my client. He's paid for my services. I can't show up as his date. That's . . . That's unethical."

"Oh please. Are you going to get kicked out of the Dating Service Association?"

Jasmine frowned at the sarcasm, crossing her arms aggressively.

"Look," continued Madison in a softer tone, "you said that you've never met him, right? So you show up as his date, satisfy his requirements for this family function, and everyone's happy."

"It's not going to work. I sent him a picture of Carole, and we look nothing alike. How do I explain that? I can't lie and pretend to be her," Jasmine insisted.

"Jay, you're overthinking it. Just introduce yourself and be you. Even if he thinks your name should be Carole, he's not going to question you on it in case he's wrong. And nobody looks like their picture in person. I'm telling you, it's the perfect solution."

But Jasmine was shaking her head, completely uncomfortable with the plan. "No. You were right the first time, Madie. I'm just going to call him and tell him what happened."

Madison shrugged, gave her a smile for encouragement, and watched as her friend walked a few steps away to make the call in private. Jasmine returned a few seconds later with a frown on her face.

"There was no answer, as usual. I just asked him to call me as soon as possible."

Three hours later, Jasmine was still trying to reach Robert Rankin to let him know his date with Carole was off.

She and Madison walked around the outdoor mall for a little while after her first attempt to reach Robert, but neither was able to regain any interest in shopping. They shared a cab back to the fitness club to pick up their gym bags. Outside of the gym, they hugged before parting, with Madison insisting on an update as soon as possible.

Jasmine walked back to her building and it was almost five o'clock when she entered her apartment. She turned on the radio in the living room, then unpacked the gym clothes from her bag. Then she called Robert's cell phone for the fourth time. It still went straight to his voice mail. Jasmine disconnected quickly, not wanting to leave another message.

Trying not to worry, she sat down on her couch and attempted to do some work on her laptop. It was fruitless. Jasmine could not stop thinking about the problem and debating with herself about what to do. She thought about calling Maya and enlisting her help in reaching Robert. But then Jasmine remembered their last conversation just that afternoon, when she assured Maya that everything was under control. Her pride would not let her admit that it had all fallen apart.

Jasmine's home phone rang while she was still pondering what to do. It was her older sister, Jennifer.

"What's up?" she asked after they both said hello.

"Nothing really, I'm just at home with the kids. What are you doing?" Jennifer replied.

"Not much. Just a little work."

"On a Saturday? That's too bad."

Jasmine shrugged even though her sister couldn't see it.

"Any plans for tonight? A hot date, maybe?" continued Jennifer.

"Not really. I think I'll just stay in."

"Really? You're young and single in a big city, Jasmine. You're supposed to be out dancing, meeting new people. Not just sitting at home working and watching television."

Jasmine snorted. "Well, I wish it was that simple, Sis. I don't really have a lot of time for all that."

"Are you seeing anyone new?" her sister pressed.

"No, not really."

"Come on, Jasmine. Your life can't be that boring. It sounds like I'm getting more action than you are. And that's very sad," Jennifer teased.

"I'm sure you are, Jen. Isn't that why people get married? So they can have some regular action?"

"Well, that might be the plan originally, but I'm pretty sure it never works out that way."

They both giggled.

"How are Emily and Neil?" Jasmine inquired about her six-year-old niece and nine-year-old nephew.

"Busy as usual. Literally, all I do is drive them around to all their events and parties. It's insane."

"What are you guys doing tonight?"

"The usual. Ted's out playing golf, so I'll probably just order a pizza and watch movies like we normally do. It's become our Saturday ritual."

"That sounds nice. Too bad you live so far away or I would join you guys."

"Well, why don't you come up for a visit soon? We haven't seen you since Christmas, and the kids really miss you."

"I know. I'll try to come up soon for a weekend. Or maybe you can come down to Miami? You're always talking about how much you need a break. Come down and stay with me for a few days. I could take you to the spa, then a nice restaurant. We might even go dancing so you can see what you're missing as a married woman."

"That sounds wonderful, Jay. But what would I do with the kids? If I bring them, it kind of defeats the purpose of a getaway," Jennifer teased.

"Leave them with Ted," insisted Jasmine. "What's the worst he can do in a couple of days?"

"Yeah, well, that's easier said than done. He works hard during the week and he uses his weekends to wind down. Leaving the kids with him would just be chaos."

"It can't hurt to ask, Jen. You never know. He might surprise you and enjoy spending more time with Emily and Neil."

"*Hmm*," her sister replied vaguely. "I know it sounds weird, Jay. But it's almost as though Ted has no clue what to do with the kids. He used to be great with them when they were babies. But as soon as they started talking and really developed their own personalities, he lost interest. It sounds bad, and I don't mean it that way. I know he loves them and would do anything for them."

"See, that's why I think you should take some time away for yourself. Then Ted will have no choice but to talk to them, do stuff."

"I try to talk to him and get him to see that it's important that he does more things with them. You know, help me out a little. But he just keeps saying that he doesn't know what I'm talking about."

"Jen, that doesn't sound very good."

"I know. I'm getting more worried about it. Especially now that Neil is getting older."

"Well, you'll just have to keep trying to talk to him. And don't do everything yourself. Maybe part of the reason he does less than he should is because he knows you will do it all anyway."

Jasmine had had very similar conversations with her sister over the past few years, and knew it was a sensitive topic. And though Jen was a smart woman, she still continued to do the same things in her marriage and yet expect a different result.

"Anyway, thanks for listening, Jay. Even though I'm starting to think talking about my problems is the most fun you've had all week."

Jasmine laughed out loud. "You know, I was perfectly fine with having no plans for the evening. And now, I feel like a total loser. Thanks, Sis. I'm so happy we had this conversation."

The sisters giggled some more before promising to talk again soon and hanging up.

Jasmine then checked the time and saw that it was almost six o'clock. Robert Rankin had not called her back, so there was really only one solution. Despite how difficult he had been to work with, he had paid for her services in full. There was no way that she could allow him to show up at an important family event expecting a date, only to be stood up. She was going to have to tell him about the cancellation in person.

Chapter 5

Robert entered the hotel and started toward the front desk. According to the confirmation details from Croft Connections, his date, Carole, was to meet him at the entrance of the hotel bar at seven o'clock. His original plan had been to arrive in Miami with enough time to check in and drop his bag off in the room before they met. But that wasn't going to work now, not unless she was also running behind schedule.

It had been three months since he started this embarrassing process of looking for a date. Robert still could not explain why he let his agent, Maya Jones, talk him into this whole thing. The idea was pretty simple at first. He only wanted to make his parents stop worrying about his single status and reclusive lifestyle. Bringing a date to Matthew's wedding seemed like the best solution. The only problem was that Robert had no idea how to meet a woman these days, particularly in a sleepy vacation community like Key West. There were plenty of attractive local women who worked in various restaurants and bars in town, but most were just too young for him to seriously be interested in. The rest that he met were already married or quite desperate to be soon. Robert tried very hard to stay away from both those types.

There had been a few women over the last couple of years that he had connected with casually, but they had all been tourists staying in the area for a week or two. Those brief liaisons lasted only as long as the ladies were on vacation, despite any conversations suggesting they wanted something longer with Robert. While he enjoyed their company in the short time they were in town, he was also content to let them go once they went home to their regular lives.

It was Maya's idea to use a dating service or a matchmaker. She then insisted Croft Connections was the best—very professional and confidential. Robert finally agreed, assuming she would make the arrangements. He had just figured he would give her a picture, answer a few questions, then spend a few minutes looking through profiles to find someone who looked decent. It didn't quite work out that way.

In retrospect, Robert really did not have a clue as to what dating was all about when you weren't a sports star. The last time he was single and available, there were more beautiful women than he could count, all wanting to catch his eye. Almost every situation where he was out in the public was an opportunity to meet a new woman, and none of them asked what he had to offer or wanted in a partner. They certainly did not make him answer a long series of questions about his likes, dislikes, religious affiliations, or political allegiance.

Very soon after signing up with Croft Connections, these were the things he was asked to articulate and evaluate, and Robert quickly realized he had few answers. The whole process made him uncomfortable, reminding him of those shallow years in his youth when he made decisions with his ego and his money. It was only dating, and arguably long overdue, but it should not be so difficult. He just wasn't prepared for how much time and thought it was going to require.

Now, weeks later, he was about to have his first date. As Maya had promised, Croft Connections was very professional. His contact, Jasmine Croft, really did her best to make him happy, trying repeatedly to find him someone with whom he might have a connection, even though he had to cancel on more than one occasion. The date with Carole came together at the last moment, just in time for Matthew's party. Robert did not have any expectations from the evening, but hoped it would at least be pleasant. However, it seemed pretty unlikely that she would be the right person to accompany him to his brother's wedding next week in Canada. His mother was going to be so disappointed when he showed up alone again.

The bar was near the front of the hotel lobby and Robert was able to see the entrance as he walked across the polished marble floor of the lobby. There did not appear to be anyone waiting there. He slowed his steps and looked around, suddenly wondering if he had gotten the directions wrong. Was there another bar?

He checked his watch again and looked back at the front of the hotel. Finally, Robert took out his iPhone, wondering if he had missed a message with an update. Immediately, he noticed that he had a new voice-mail message. According to the missed calls list, it was from Croft Connections, left earlier that afternoon. He was about to listen to it when something caught his eye as he looked across the lobby again.

A woman stepped through the front doors, paused for a second to look around, then headed in the direction of the bar. Robert watched her for a few seconds, struck by her confident posture and the purpose in her stride. She wore a light-colored dress in a tailored fabric that hugged the curves of her body. The skirt ended at midthigh, revealing bare legs that looked silky and firm, even from a distance.

The woman looked around again as she approached the front of the bar and then stopped when she saw Robert. He couldn't see her face, but felt a tingle of anticipation that she might be Carole, the woman he was there to meet. After a quick pause, she changed direction and started walking toward him at a slower, less determined pace. Robert put his cell phone away and went to meet her.

As he got closer, it began to occur to Robert

that he may have made a mistake. The dating service had sent him a picture of Carole a couple of weeks ago. Robert had looked at the photo along with the general description of her background, appearance, and personality before he agreed to meet her. Though he had found her fairly attractive and her information acceptable at the time, he honestly could not remember exactly what she looked like. But he knew for certain that he would have remembered the likeness of the woman that stood in front of him now. Her square face was highlighted by bright brown eyes with an enticing slant and hidden depths. She smiled slightly, hesitantly, drawing his eyes to her coral-toned mouth. It was well defined with a curvy shape and a full lower lip. They were covered with a sheer gloss that made them seem sticky and wet.

Robert was certain he would have remembered this face.

"Hi," she said with her hand extended. "Robert Rankin, right? I recognize you from your picture."

He shook her hand, but was now uncertain of who exactly she was. Maybe the photo they had sent him was just a bad shot? Lots of people didn't look like their pictures.

"Yes, hi. It's Carole, right?"

"Actually, no. Carole was unable to make it. She had an accident this afternoon."

"Oh," Robert replied, still confused. "Nothing serious, I hope."

"No, she's fine now, but has a wrist fracture."

"*Ahhh,*" he replied with a smile. "There's a message from Croft Connections on my phone. Now I know what it's regarding."

She smiled back politely.

"Sorry about the last-minute notice," she added.

"No worries. I had my phone off all day, unfortunately. But thank you for coming instead."

Robert was about to ask her name when he heard his name shouted from across the lobby. He turned to see Matthew walking quickly toward them with a big, joyous grin on his face.

"Excuse me," Robert stated before turning to greet his brother a few steps away.

They hugged for a few seconds.

"How's my best man doing?" Matthew asked as he punched Robert in the upper arm.

Robert grinned affectionately and gently slapped his brother's cheek like he was a baby.

"Not bad," he replied.

"Did you see how many people are outside?" Matthew asked without waiting for an answer. "It's crazy! How did Cara pull this off? Everyone Rosanna and I have ever known in Miami must be here."

"No, I haven't been out there yet. I just got here a few minutes ago," explained Robert. "Where's Rosanna?"

"Cara stole her, leaving me to check us in," he replied gesturing to the small suitcase he was pulling.

"Yeah, I haven't checked in either."

Matthew was only a couple of inches shorter than Robert's six feet two inches, so he was easily able to peer over Robert's shoulder at the woman standing behind them. There was a peculiar look of curiosity and mischief on his face. Robert looked back at him with a chastising frown. The two brothers had a wordless conversation for a couple of seconds.

"Robert," stated Matthew in a louder voice and with exaggerated politeness, "aren't you going to introduce us?"

Robert rolled his eyes at his brother's childishness and turned back to his replacement date that was definitely close enough to hear the question. As his eyes met hers, he remembered that she had not yet told him her name. Her eyes opened wider for a second as she realized his dilemma.

"Hi," she said as she reached out to shake Matthew's hand. "I'm Jay."

Matthew shoved Robert out of the way to step closer to Jasmine, gently enclosing her hand into both of his.

"Hi, Jay, I'm Matthew. It's nice to meet you. So, how do you know my surly brother?"

"Surly?" demanded Robert

Matthew ignored him and continued to smile at Jay.

"We've just met, actually," she finally responded.

"Really?" he replied as he gave Robert an exaggerated glance. "He picked you up in a hotel bar? How cliché, big bro. And so unlike you these days."

"If you must know, Jay is my guest for the party,"

Robert finally replied, practically through clenched teeth.

"A date? Robbie, that's even less like you," retorted Matthew.

Jay looked between them, her pretty mouth slightly open. Finally, she shook her head slightly and put a soft hand on Robert's shoulder.

"I'm sorry, I . . ."

"No," Robert interjected. "Matthew is sorry. His sense of humor isn't always appropriate. Right, Matt? Don't you need to check in? Isn't your fiancée waiting for you?"

His younger brother just chuckled. "Nice to meet you, Jay. See you at the party," he stated as he strolled away.

"Sorry about that," mumbled Robert.

"Oh, that's okay. I have an older sister, I get it," she replied with a wistful smile. "But you don't need to invite me to the party."

"You don't want to stay?"

"No, it's not that. I just didn't want you to think you had to. I mean, you were expecting Carole, and I've shown up instead. So, you know . . . I mean . . ."

Her voice trailed away. Robert found himself grinning. "Well, I'm sorry that Carole injured herself, but I'm okay with the back-up plan so far."

He laughed out loud as her eyes opened wide. Then he was rewarded with a twitch on her lips.

"So you'll stay?" he finally asked.

She let out at breath before responding. "Okay."

"Good," stated Robert with a charming smile.

"If you'll excuse me, I'm just going to check into the hotel before they give away my room."

"No problem. I'll just run to the bathroom and meet you back here?"

"Perfect."

They nodded to each other, and Robert turned to walk over to the front desk. It took him twice as long to get there because he could not resist watching Jay walk across the lobby toward the restrooms. She was easily one of the sexiest women he had met in a long, long time. Her face was very pretty, with soft features and a sweet, genuine smile. But her eyes hinted at a more serious, intense personality that Robert found intriguing. Then there was that sensuous, curvaceous body that seemed to be built from every man's fantasies. She was firm and healthy, but with just the right amount of soft fullness.

Robert found it hard to hide his delighted smile while providing the hotel staff his reservation details. Despite his happiness for his brother and future sister-in-law, his interest in the evening had now gone from an unwanted distraction to eager anticipation and a little excitement about the potential outcome.

Chapter 6

When Jasmine left her apartment that evening to meet Robert Rankin, her only goal was to tell him in person about Carole's unfortunate accident. She had refreshed her make-up and brushed her hair so it fell straight around her shoulders, but didn't bother to change her dress for the occasion. She did however put on high-heeled black peep-toe shoes that were more appropriate for the evening instead of the sandals worn earlier.

During the cab ride to the hotel, Jasmine tried again to reach Robert but there was still no answer. She then tried to figure out what she would say to him once she got there.

It was very unusual for her to be so nervous about meeting a client, or anyone really. Jasmine was usually steadfast and unflappable, comfortable managing almost any situation. It was that natural confidence that drove her to start her own business. Yet Robert Rankin frustrated and flustered her even though they had never even met. Now, as she stood beside him at his brother's party, it was hard to understand her reaction.

It was equally as hard for her to figure out how she ended up taking Carole's place, just as Madison had suggested. She had not planned on introducing herself as Jay—the casual nickname that her friends and family often used; it just slipped out. The moment Jasmine had realized that Robert did not know who she was and had misunderstood why she was there, she tried to correct him. She tried to turn down his invitation to stay for the party. But then he smiled at her, looked from her lips to her eyes and asked again. In that moment, Jasmine could not think of one reason not to stay.

Unfortunately, she was now trapped in a lie of omission and with no clue how to delicately get herself out of it.

By nine o'clock that night, the lavish outdoor party was in full swing with over two hundred guests mingling and nibbling on exquisite hors d'oeuvres. Some people danced by the edge of the pool to hit pop and hip-hop songs while others socialized, sitting on padded lounge chairs or in private cabanas. Cocktail drinks and expensive wine were served on demand.

Robert and Jasmine were standing at the far end of the pool with his sister, Cara, their future sister-in-law, Rosanna, and a couple of other people. She and Robert had spent most of the evening so far making the rounds, stopping as people called out to Robert and wanted to talk with him, find out how he was doing. Jasmine stood at an appropriate distance, listening to the discussions and watching his interactions. It was fascinating.

He was very polite, introducing her to everyone they met and including her in the conversation. He was charming and amicable, but with a dry sense of humor that was a little sarcastic. He was nothing like the cold, unreasonable jerk Jasmine had attempted to work with for weeks. Even more interesting was the occasional response people had to his presence. They acted like he was a rock star. The women flipped their hair and licked their lips, and men looked at him like they had a male crush. While Robert was a very attractive man, the reaction was a little much for a writer with two books on the shelf, even if they were best sellers.

Within the group they were with now, there was a sudden lull in the conversation, causing Jasmine to refocus her attention.

"So, Robert, why didn't you tell me you were bringing a date to the party?" his sister asked finally. "How did you two meet?"

Jasmine looked up at Robert, then back at his sister, curious to hear his answer. She wasn't going to try and attempt to explain this awkward and unforeseen chain of events.

"We were introduced by a friend," Robert replied smoothly.

"Really?" Cara asked back. "How long have you been seeing each other?"

Jasmine looked a little closer at Cara. There was a noticeable resemblance between the three siblings, including their long face, high cheekbones, and dark eyebrows. They were all taller than average with solid, thick frames. It was masculine and attractive on Robert and Matthew, but made Cara seem unfeminine. She wore white pants that were too tight for her heavy legs and a sparkly top that revealed more than necessary. Her stance was wide and aggressive, particularly as her face displayed her surprise at Robert's reply. She tilted her head, giving her brother a hard, quizzical stare. Jasmine could see silent communication exchanged between the two of them.

"This is our first date, actually," he told Cara, giving Jasmine an easy grin and a cheeky wink. "Maybe not the best venue to get to know someone, though."

"So what do you do, Jay?" she asked.

Jasmine drew a blank for a second, clearing her throat loudly to buy some time.

"Consulting," she finally replied in a lame attempt not to lie.

"*Hmmm*," Cara mumbled, barely hiding her disinterest.

"What kind of consulting?" asked Rosanna. "I work for a firm here in Miami that does human resources consulting."

Jasmine liked Rosanna from the moment they had met at the beginning of the party. She was a pretty girl, slightly taller than average, with a round figure, large brown eyes, and full pink lips. Her wavy black hair revealed her combination of black and Latin cultures. But her voice had a subtle Canadian accent.

"Really?" replied Jasmine, with a pleased smile. "What do you do with them? I used to be a corporate recruiter, up until very recently."

"I work in the finance department," Rosanna explained. "That's how I met Matthew, actually. He was working on a project for us in Toronto as a contractor. Then, once we were dating, he persuaded me to transfer to our Miami office."

"And the rest is history?" teased Jasmine.

Rosanna laughed, blushing slightly with obvious delight.

One of the hotel employees approached Cara and Rosanna at that moment, indicating that their attention was required. Both women excused themselves from the group to follow the staff member. The other couple there turned toward the music. Jasmine felt as though she needed to let out a deep sigh of relief.

"Would you like something else to drink?" Robert asked her.

Before she could reply, he took a glass of red wine from a tray as a server walked past them. It would be Jasmine's second for the night, but she took it anyway, feeling as though she needed something to occupy her hands.

"Thank you."

"Come, let's go for a walk," he said.

Robert placed a gentle hand at her lower back and guided her away from the crowd toward the private beach near the waterfront. They walked side by side silently until the music faded and the gentle lap of the ocean waves became more audible. The bright moon provided gentle light.

"So, you're probably wondering why I would choose an event like this for a first date," Robert stated.

Jasmine took a sip of her wine before she responded. Now that they were alone again, she was certain it would be more difficult to keep up the charade she had allowed to develop.

"It is a little unusual," she replied.

Robert laughed out loud, obviously amused by her simple answer.

"That was very polite," he finally stated.

He stopped walking and turned to face her. His back was to the moonlight, but a lamp post nearby provided enough light for her to see his smooth copper-tone skin and the strong line of his jaw. His light brown eyes looked down at her.

"Are you always so diplomatic?" he added.

Jasmine shrugged with one shoulder and raised her chin. The first glass of wine had worked its way through her body, loosening her tension and lowering her guard. The second glass was guaranteed to increase her bravado. She took another sip.

"I am, actually," she replied with a wide smile.

He laughed again. "Well, I appreciate it. But I'm thinking it wasn't a very good idea."

Robert turned again until he was beside her, looking out at the bay.

"Why did you?" asked Jasmine.

"It sounds pretty bad to say, but I couldn't find any other time in my schedule. That's probably not a good thing to admit to someone I'm trying to impress, is it?"

She was a little surprised by his honesty. And that he was trying to provide her with a good impression. She felt his gaze turn to her when she didn't reply right away.

"You're trying to impress me?" she asked.

"Isn't that what I'm supposed to do on a date? Get you to see that I'm worth more of your time?"

"I don't know. Maybe if we met under more conventional circumstances. But, you don't know anything about me. You didn't even have the benefit of reviewing my picture and profile, like you did Carole's. How do you know that I'm worth impressing?"

"I know," he immediately countered. "I've watched you over the last couple of hours in a fairly awkward situation, and I bet I know more about you than any dating service bio could say."

Jasmine was intrigued and the alcohol was slowly erasing her usual filters.

"Like what?" she asked, looking over at him.

Their eyes met and held longer than was considered a casual glance. The air between them became electric as they tried to decide what type of conversation would develop. Robert finally let out a deep breath, turning face forward again.

"I know you're poised, well-spoken, smart, lacking in obvious conceit. You're professional, and reserved, but probably have a rebellious streak when needed."

"Wow," whispered Jasmine. "That's quite a list. You've discovered all of that in two hours?"

"I'm very observant," Robert replied.

"Okay. What about my other statistics? The typical stuff that you can't observe?"

"Such as?"

"Like . . ." she replied, stretching out the word while she thought of examples. "Like my age, height, sign, do I have children? Am I into drugs or satanic rituals? Stuff like that."

His strong white teeth flashed in the diffused light.

"Your skin is too perfect for a drug user, and your aura doesn't suggest pure evil. The other things aren't important."

It was Jasmine's turn to laugh out loud. Her skin felt flushed by his indirect compliment.

"Touché," she mumbled. "So, it wouldn't matter if I have four kids at home right now?"

Robert moved in front of her again, and his eyes lowered to sweep down her body. Jasmine felt a slight chill, either from the gentle night breeze or the intensity of his gaze. Her breasts tingled, puckering in response.

"You're too young and too together to have

more than one, maybe two. But hey, life happens. I don't judge."

"Really? That's what you paid Croft Connections to find you? A twenty-seven-year-old with four kids?" Jasmine queried, her tone dripping with skepticism.

"No, I wouldn't be looking for that. But the right person sometimes comes in an unusual package, that's all," he replied, unfazed by her grilling.

"I thought the package you wanted was Business Barbie without the ability to speak?" she shot back, her filters failing again.

"What?"

He laughed again, clearly amused by her unruly tongue.

Jasmine shook her head, remembering that she shouldn't know the details of his confidential dating criteria.

"Isn't that what every man wants?" she replied lamely.

"Beautiful, smart, and a little jaded," mumbled Robert, as though updating his list of bullet points.

"I'm not jaded, just realistic. Be honest."

"Jay, every man has an unrealistic idea of what he thinks is the perfect woman. He can describe exactly what she would be like, the things she would say and be willing to do. But I guarantee it's never the woman he will want to spend time with, maybe commit to. You can't imagine or describe the *right* woman; you can only feel it when you meet her."

He said the words casually, almost flippantly, but the intensity they evoked lingered between them.

"You're trying to impress me again," Jasmine finally stated, choosing to lighten the mood with a joke rather than think more seriously about his statement.

"Perhaps," he grinned back.

She took another sip of her wine.

"So, tell me all about yourself, Jay, including your four kids if you have them."

Jasmine smiled up at him. She was feeling pretty good, and enjoying herself.

"Okay, let's see. I'm twenty-seven years old, five feet four inches, and a Cancer. And no kids," she added with a teasing smile. "Let's see, what else? . . . I'm from Fort Lauderdale originally, my mom is still there, but I live in South Beach. I have one older sister who is married with two kids, and lives in Jacksonville. I like action movies, trying new foods, traveling, and long walks on the beach."

Robert chuckled. It was a low, smooth sound that she was starting to really like.

"And," she added dramatically, "I love a good suspense novel."

He chuckled out loud.

"I'm just kidding. I haven't read anything in years," admitted Jasmine with a giggle. "No offense."

"None taken. But that wasn't a random comment, was it?"

"No, it wasn't."

"So, you know who I am," he stated. "Wow, that sounded pretty pompous, didn't it?"

They both laughed awkwardly.

"Come," he said softly, touching the back of her upper arm to urge her further. He guided her at a leisurely pace along the path until they reached a wooden bench. Jasmine took his cue, then Robert sat beside her.

"What else do you know about me?"

They smiled at each other.

"Well, let's see . . . You are thirty-two, you live in Key West, and you are a suspense writer. And you're a Leo, right?"

"That's it?" Robert demanded.

"Sorry, I didn't realize there was going to be a quiz."

"Beautiful, smart, jaded, and a little sarcastic."

Jasmine opened her mouth with exaggerated indignation, and he grinned harder with a twinkle in his eyes.

"Fine. Now it's your turn. Tell me everything there is to know," she demanded.

Robert spent a few minutes telling her a few facts about his life, including his own fondness for traveling. Jasmine probed for more information and they spent the next while talking about the places he had been to and where she planned to go. Eventually, Robert checked his watch and let out a deep sigh. She checked hers also. It was almost eleven o'clock.

"I should get back," he stated with regret.

"Of course. I should probably get going also. It's late."

They both stood up and walked back to the pool area of the hotel. The temperature outside had dropped a few degrees as the evening wore on. Jasmine shivered slightly, rubbing her hands up and down her arms. Robert immediately shrugged out of his suit jacket and draped it over her shoulders.

"Thank you," she said simply, and they continued to walk in silence.

The party was still going strong when they got there. They maneuvered through the crowd, then headed inside toward the front lobby.

"Is your car parked here? Are you sure you're okay to drive?" he asked when reached the main entrance of the hotel.

"No, I'm car-free at the moment. It's one of the reasons I love living in South Beach. Everything I need is right around the corner from my apartment, so it's just easier to take a cab if I need to go far. I'll just get one outside."

He nodded. They went through the front doors and Robert asked the valet to call a taxi for her. There was one on the way, so they stood beside each other in awkward silence, waiting.

"It was very nice to meet you, Robert," she finally stated, turning to face him.

"What are you doing tomorrow morning?"

Jasmine was completely unprepared for his question. She shook her head, meaning to tell him she had no plans, but forgot to use her words.

"Would you like to meet me for breakfast? We can go out on my boat for a little bit," suggested Robert.

"*Uhhh*, okay. Sure, why not," she stammered.

"Okay, good. Is ten o'clock too early?"

"No, that's fine."

"Good. We'll meet here at ten."

Jasmine nodded to confirm. Her cab arrived at that moment, and she started to take off his jacket, still hanging off her shoulders. Robert placed a hand on her arm, stopping her.

"Keep it until tomorrow," he instructed.

"Alright. Good night."

"Good night, Jay."

Robert stepped forward and pulled her into a deep hug. Even in her high heels, her head only reached the top of his shoulders, and it was briefly cushioned against the firmness of his chest. When he released her, his hands remained on her shoulders, his face hovering near hers. They both seemed frozen until Jasmine lifted her chin. Their lips met with the lightest brush, and the static charge caused them both to pull back. He looked down into her eyes, searching their depth for the answer he wanted. Then he kissed her with a gentle, soft brush of his lips.

"See you tomorrow," he whispered when he finally pulled away and let go of her.

Jasmine opened her eyes, blinking up at him. She could only nod, smiling wistfully as Robert opened the passenger door of the cab for her, then closing it firmly. He walked over to the driver's window and waited while Jasmine provided the address to her apartment building, then handed the driver two folded bills. As the car pulled away from the hotel, she turned in her seat to look back at him as he was still standing at the driveway, his fingers pressed against his lips.

Chapter 7

Sunday had clear, blue skies. The morning air was comfortably warm, and the ocean was brilliant and calm. Robert stood at the helm of his boat, high on the throttle as he cruised up the coast of Miami Beach at over one hundred miles per hour. Jasmine sat beside him looking out at the stunning scenery, wearing large dark sunglasses. Her hair whipped around in the high wind. She occasionally tried to tame it, wiping strands away from her eyes and tucking it behind her ears.

Jasmine had met him at the hotel lobby as planned, and returned his suit jacket draped nicely on a hanger. They then had breakfast at the hotel restaurant overlooking the pool and beach. Robert spent most of the meal telling her about the party after she had left, including a rundown of who got drunk and what they did. He had her laughing her head off by the time he asked for the check.

As much as he was enjoying himself since he

met her, Robert had no idea what he was doing or why. Instead of heading home early to work for the day, he was showboating around the ocean hoping to get a glimpse of her smile. Worse yet, at some point during their conversation on the beach the night before, Robert decided he wanted her to go to Matthew's wedding with him. It was an unreasonable idea considering that they had just met, and it was a three-day trip to Canada. But it was stubbornly fixed in his brain, and would not go away.

He just had to find the right opportunity to ask her.

Robert slowed down as they passed Bal Harbor just north of Miami Beach. He then turned into a channel that led back down to Biscayne Bay and the Miami waterways.

"Wow, that was fun," Jasmine stated once the engine was quiet enough to talk over.

Robert grinned back.

"I'm glad you enjoyed it," he replied.

They were moving through the shallow water close to land at a leisurely pace. He reached into the built-in cooler and took out a couple bottles of water, handing Jasmine one.

"Thank you," she stated.

They continued the boat ride for several more minutes.

"Jay, I think I mentioned last night that Matthew's wedding is next weekend. I know this is pretty short notice, but would you like to go with me?"

Robert looked over at her to gauge her reaction.

She was looking at him, but her expression was hidden by the sunglasses.

"Robert, I . . ." she began to reply.

"Before you decide, I should let you know that the wedding is in Canada. His fiancée, Rosanna, is from the Toronto area, so they're having the ceremony at a resort up there. So, it will be a weekend trip," he explained.

"Wait, Robert," stated Jasmine as she turned her head to look out at the passing coastline. "I have to tell you something first."

She sounded tense. The wide smile that lit up her face just moments ago was gone.

"Sure," he replied, curious but not really concerned.

Robert looked over at her, watched her take a deep breath, as though she were bracing herself for the task. He was now a little more alarmed.

"Before I explain, I want you to know that it wasn't intentional," she added.

"Okay," he replied, then gave her time to get to the point.

"My full name is Jasmine Croft," she stated softly. "Jay is my nickname, and Croft Connections is my company. I only went to the hotel to tell you the date with Carole was canceled. Honestly, I tried to tell you over the phone and called you repeatedly yesterday, but you're not the most reachable or responsive person. I had no choice but to tell you in person." Jasmine looked up at him. "Then you introduced me to your brother and asked me to stay . . . It seemed rude to tell you the truth at that point."

He continued driving the boat through the shallow waters, waiting until she was finished before responding.

"Anyway, I'm sorry," she added. "Of course, I will provide you with a full refund first thing tomorrow."

Robert smiled to himself, amused by how serious and dejected she sounded.

"Why would you refund my fees?" he asked. "Looks to me like you went out of your way to personally ensure your services were rendered."

"That's not funny," she whispered.

"Too soon?" he teased, chuckling softly.

She continued to look forward.

"Jasmine. That's a beautiful name," he stated.

"Thank you. My mom liked the flower but says it means *gift from God* in Persian," she explained.

"Do you go by Jasmine or Jay?" asked Robert.

"Both, but my friends mostly call me Jay," she answered after a few moments.

He nodded and they continued quietly for another few minutes.

Robert thought back to the interactions he had with her when she was just a persistent, sometimes annoying matchmaker trying to find him a meaningful relationship. He could not have been the easiest person to deal with. Then, there were some of the ridiculous attributes he had put on his wish list, more to amuse himself than anything else. It certainly explained Jasmine's reference to him wanting a Barbie doll for a date. Yet, the few times he actually replied to her e-mails or instant messages, she was polite and professional.

Regardless of how or why they met, her revelation didn't really change anything. For him anyway. She caught his attention the minute she walked into the hotel. It was impossible not to notice or physically react to those incredible eyes and that fantastic body. But that was not the only reason he could not stop thinking about her after her taxi drove away. Jay Croft, or Jasmine, made him want to make her laugh, to talk about himself and impress her with his fast boat. She made him feel excited for the first time in a very long time.

"I'm glad you told me" he finally stated. "Are you here now because I'm a client or because you want to be?"

"Robert, it would have been easier for me to turn down your invitation. But I had a good time last night. And your fee wasn't high enough to pay for me to be here. There's a big difference between matchmaking and escorting services, you know."

He chuckled at her sarcasm. "Nice to hear."

"But," she continued, "I do insist on the refund."

Robert shrugged, unconcerned.

"Now that we've settled that, what do you think about the wedding?" he asked. "The ceremony is on Saturday morning so I'm flying up on Friday, then back on Sunday."

He caught a glimpse of her smile as he waited in anticipation for her response.

"It sounds like fun," she finally replied.

"Great. I'll have my travel agent make the arrangements this afternoon."

They spent the rest of the boat ride talking about the upcoming weekend. About an hour later, Robert docked the boat at the hotel marina again, then walked Jasmine back to the front entrance to get a taxi.

"I will give you a call later," he told her as her ride arrived. "Should I use the same number you called me from yesterday?"

"Yes, that's fine. It's my cell phone number," confirmed Jasmine.

He nodded, and took both her hands into his as they faced each other. Their touch created a sharp charge of electricity that ran from the tips of his fingers straight up his arm. Jasmine's eyes widened and her lips parted with a gasp, confirming that she felt the same thing he did. Robert lowered his head to press his lips against hers. It was meant to be a quick good-bye kiss, but it stretched into a series of strokes and brushes against her lips that lasted longer than anticipated. The taxi driver eventually got tired of waiting and blew his horn. They leaped apart.

Jasmine quickly turned away to get into the car, but Robert stopped her with a hold on one of her hands. She looked up at him expectantly, her lips still moist, and pouted.

"I prefer Jasmine, by the way," he stated.

She flashed him a big smile before sliding into the car.

As Robert watched her departure, he could still taste the sweetness of her lips.

Back inside the hotel, he took out his phone and called Cara.

"Hello," she answered.

"Hey, where are you?"

"Hey Robbie, I'm still at the apartment. Why?"

"How long are you going to be there for? I'm about to head back home, so I can give you a ride," he offered.

"You're still here? It's after one o'clock. I thought you checked out this morning."

"Yeah, I did, but something came up. Do you want a ride back on the boat or not?"

"Sure," Cara stated. "Give me a little bit. I'll have to cancel my flight, then I'll grab a taxi."

"Okay. Meet me at the boat. The marina is behind the pool area. Just turn right on the path near the beach."

She arrived about thirty minutes later, pulling her expensive monogrammed suitcase. Robert was prepared for departure, and they pulled away from the dock right away.

"Wow, these are nice shades, Robbie," Cara stated. "But not really your style."

They were slowly moving through Biscayne Bay, just a few minutes away from the tail end of Miami Beach and the entrance to the Atlantic Ocean. Robert glanced over to see what his sister was talking about. She was holding up a pair of dark sunglasses, clearly belonging to a woman.

"Oh, those are Jay's," he explained. "Her full name is Jasmine, by the way. She must have forgotten them this morning."

"*Ahhhh,* that explains why you're heading home so late. A little someth'n, someth'n for breakfast, huh? Or was it a sleepover?" teased Cara.

Robert shook his head with displeasure. "We met for breakfast, that's all. Then I took her out on the water for a bit."

"Well, it's good to see you out, having fun for a change. You can't spend all your time shut away writing. It's not normal."

He didn't bother to respond. Cara knew exactly what his schedule was like and the deadline he was under, but somehow, she expected him to be out partying every weekend like she did.

"I still don't understand why you didn't tell me you were bringing someone to the party."

"There was nothing to tell. We met for the first time last night," he replied.

"Still, you could have said something. I've been trying to hook you up with a couple of my friends for months now, but you're never available. And Aisha was at the party last night. You know, the tall one? She was wearing a blue dress?" continued Cara. "She's had her eyes on you since that New Year's party last year. I was going to introduce you guys, but your friend never left your side."

"Her name is Jasmine, Cara. And she was my

date. I could not exactly leave her on her own to talk with another woman."

She twisted her mouth into an insolent pout. "Jay, Jasmine, whatever. Well, she was cute and everything, but not really your type, Robbie."

Robert shook his head again, trying to ignore her meddling.

He loved his sister to death, but was finding it harder and harder to put up with her need to control his life. Over the last three years, Cara had been there for him during the roughest times, helping him get back on his feet. She was there when the police knocked on his door to tell him about Lakeisha's accident, then went through all of the funeral arrangements with him.

Right around that time, Cara broke up with her boyfriend and decided she needed a change of scenery. She moved with Alex from Miami to Key West to live with Robert and offered to help him manage his schedule of book signings, charity appearances, and NHL obligations. It started out great. She took charge of everything including the grocery shopping and updating his Web site. Then, Cara started to take charge of every other part of his life.

He knew that his sister had his best interests at heart, and was doing what she thought was best for him. She was also stubborn and obstinate by nature. But her controlling attitude was starting to make him uncomfortable and claustrophobic. Robert didn't know how to discuss the issue with her, so he started to avoid involving her in certain aspects of his life.

"Why would Jasmine not be my type, Cara? Did you see her?" he finally responded, trying to make light of the conversation.

"I don't know. You're entitled to some fun, and all but, I'm just saying that she seems a little too straight, that's all."

"I don't know about that. But I've invited her to the wedding next weekend."

"No way. Why? You just met her! I was going to bring Aisha with me so you guys could get to know each other," Cara insisted.

Robert glanced down at his sister to see the big frown on her face, and her arms folded aggressively. He shook his head, but didn't bother replying.

"Well, at least Mom will be happy," she eventually admitted. "Every time I talk to her, all she wants to know is when you're going to meet a nice woman and settle down again."

Robert grinned at the comment because it was absolutely true. "Funny, Sis. She's always asking me the same thing about you, too."

"No thanks!" Cara snickered. "I'm too young and having way too much fun being single to tie myself up to a man."

The siblings smiled mockingly at each other. Robert then pushed the throttle forward until they were racing though the ocean down the coast of the Keys.

Chapter 8

"Good news! We have officially exceeded our target for May!"

The exciting announcement was made by Yvonne, Jasmine's very energetic and efficient assistant at Croft Connections. She was a tiny girl, just over five feet and no more than one hundred and ten pounds, with a slight figure and a full head of natural, kinky hair that was often twisted into corkscrew curls. When she smiled, it brightened her narrow face and revealed beautiful white teeth that were a stark contrast to her dark skin, about the same shade as Jasmine's.

It was Monday morning, and the women were sitting in Jasmine's apartment, reviewing last week's connections and new clients. For now, Croft Connections was run from her home, allowing her to save the operational costs of leasing an office. It had worked out great so far since it turned out her clients were more comfortable meeting for a coffee or a drink to talk about their dating needs. The money she saved allowed her to afford an assistant sooner than she had planned.

Yvonne started earlier that year, and her job was primarily to manage Jasmine's calendar of appointments and their basic database, and bill the clients. She was twenty-one and still idealistic about life and love, making her the perfect employee for a matchmaking service.

"That's fantastic, Yvonne," Jasmine replied.

"I know. And we have six new clients booked for this week already."

Jasmine nodded.

They were both sitting on club chairs in the living room, working separately on laptops. The television across from them was on, with the volume turned down, tuned to a Miami morning show. Jasmine had her balcony doors open to let in the cool morning breeze that blew in off the ocean.

"How did the weekend connections go?" asked Yvonne.

Connections was their term for first dates.

"Good so far," Jasmine replied. "Except the date for Robert Rankin. We're going to have to refund his fee."

"Oh no! What happened? Didn't he like Carole? She seems so nice."

Yvonne's shoulders drooped with disappointment and genuine concern, making Jasmine feel guilty about her plan to keep her dates with Robert a secret. She bit the inside of her cheek, trying to find the best way to explain the unusual turn of events.

"Carole had an accident on Saturday so she had to cancel."

"Oh. Okay, then shouldn't we just rebook? It took you so long to find someone he approved of."

"I know, Yvonne. But I already told him I would send him a check. Can you send it out today?" she instructed without looking up.

"If you say so, Boss. Well, at least you won't have to deal with him again, right? I know how much he annoyed you."

The phone rang for the business line at that moment, saving Jasmine from having to respond. Yvonne answered it, allowing Jasmine to go back to responding to e-mails from the weekend. They worked side by side for most of the morning, until Jasmine needed to get ready to meet a client. She headed upstairs to her bedroom, taking her BlackBerry with her. It beeped, advising her of a new text message, just as she reached the landing to the loft.

Good morning. How is your day going?

It was from Robert.

Jasmine smiled as she read it, still puzzled by the strange turn of events over the weekend. Less than forty-eight hours earlier, he had been impossible to reach and the thought of him made her annoyed and frustrated. Now, thinking about Robert conjured completely different feelings. And he seemed to be making a habit of communicating with her.

She took a breath and typed out a brief response.

Hi there. It's good so far. How is yours?

Yesterday afternoon, as Jasmine rode home in the taxi from Miami, she felt a little stunned by the direction things seemed to be taking in her life. As a matchmaker, she'd met more men than she could count, both socially and as clients. On occasion, she would meet someone attractive who piqued her interest, and even went out with a few. But inevitably, each of them would do something annoying or she would just lose interest. Almost all of the time, Jasmine knew how the relationship would end even before the first date was over, but went through the motions just in case she was wrong.

She never was.

I'm doing good, just taking a break from writing. I will call you later tonight about this weekend.

Jasmine read Robert's text and let out a deep breath before responding.

Okay, talk to you later.

She put down the phone on her dresser and went into the shower. Under the spray of water, Jasmine did what she usually did, and tried to identify the thing about Robert Rankin that would eventually put her off. She thought through their conversations, but couldn't find anything specific. He wasn't stupid or obnoxious. He didn't eat badly or tell vulgar jokes. He didn't stare at her boobs, or any others'. Or use the words *boobs*.

The only thing she really felt was excited.

When Jasmine returned downstairs again, Madison was there also. She was joining Yvonne and

Jasmine for lunch at a nearby salad bar. They headed out shortly after.

"Guess who called me Saturday night? At almost twelve-thirty in the morning?" Madison said once they were seated at the restaurant. "Calvin. Can you believe that?"

"Calvin?" Jasmine repeated dumbly, looking back and forth between Yvonne and Madison for clarification.

Yvonne shrugged.

"You know—Calvin? The one that I caught with his female roommate in his bedroom? Just before Christmas?" clarified Madie.

"Oh, yeah. Have you guys been talking again?" asked Jasmine.

"No! I haven't heard from him in over five months. Then he calls me out of the blue, like we're buddies or something. What's up with that?"

"Are you serious?" Jasmine demanded with disgust.

"Well, maybe he just misses you, Madie? This could be his way of reaching out," suggested Yvonne.

"Sweetheart, no offense, but you are so young," dismissed Madison. "He called me because he was horny, tipsy, and not far from my house."

Jasmine smiled, then chuckled, while Yvonne seemed deflated.

"You don't know that for sure," Yvonne insisted. "Maybe you should give him a chance to explain himself."

"What did you say to him?" asked Jasmine. "Did you cuss him out?"

Madison ate her salad quietly for a few seconds before she replied.

"He asked me if I wanted some company, so I let him come over. Just to talk, of course," she explained. "It started out innocent. We just watched television for a little bit."

"Then?" Jasmine probed, though with the look on Madie's face, she already knew the rest of the story.

"All right! We ended up in bed together. Well, technically we did it the living room first," she giggled.

"You slut!" teased Jasmine.

"What? It's been a few months for me. And he is still so fine!"

Yvonne listened with a confused frown on her face.

"So, what did he say," the younger woman finally asked. "Is he still in love with you?"

Jasmine and Madison both looked at her, then laughed harder.

"I don't know. I didn't ask," Madie explained.

"So, you had a good weekend, then?" Jasmine quipped.

"It was very satisfying," stated Madie with a sparkle in her eyes. "Hey, what happened with that client you had to cancel with?"

Jasmine looked at both women, trying to decide on the best way to answer. But her hesitation made Madison perk up, as though she sensed a good story coming.

"You went, didn't you?" Madie guessed. "You went as his date!"

"What date?" asked Yvonne.

"I couldn't get him on the phone," Jasmine explained defensively. "I only went to tell him his date was off."

"Who?" Yvonne insisted.

"You sly thing. What happened?" demanded Madison, leaning forward with anticipation.

Jasmine let out a long sigh, then told them the whole story, ending with his text message that morning.

"Oh, my God!" exclaimed Yvonne, each word punctuated sharply. "Robert Rankin?"

"I know," Jasmine admitted, covering her eyes with both hands and shaking her head. "I can't believe it either. But he's really nothing like I expected."

"Wait a minute. Robert Rankin?" Madison repeated. "I know that name."

Jasmine nodded. "Yeah, he's a writer. Suspense novels," she explained.

But Madison shook her head, her brows lowered in thought. "No, that's not what I mean. I think he was a football player or something. For a Florida team."

Jasmine shrugged. "I don't think so. He's a pretty big guy, but I don't know anything about that. Did we Google him at the beginning, Yvonne?"

"No, I didn't. I didn't bother since Maya referred him," her assistant replied.

"Well, I'm telling you there's something about that name," insisted Madison as she pulled her BlackBerry out of her purse. "Let's see . . ."

Jasmine leaned forward, intrigued.

"See, I told you. Robert Rankin played goalie for the Florida Panthers for eight years, then retired after a knee injury."

"What?" demanded Jasmine, leaning forward even more. "It must be someone else with the same name. My Robert is black, so I don't think he was a hockey player."

She and Yvonne giggled, but Madie continued scrolling through the Web page until she found some pictures.

"Yup, here you go," she finally stated, handing the phone to her friend.

Jasmine looked at the picture on the screen. It was a hockey player wearing an orange and blue jersey standing in front of the net, his goalie's mask pushed back to sit on top of his head. He was clean shaven, with a full head of curly, corkscrew hair, and definitely black.

"That's him," she stated as she handed the phone back to Madison. "I had no idea. I don't watch hockey."

"Neither do I, but I remember the story about his wife," Madie explain.

"Oh, yeah. Maya mentioned that he was a widower," Yvonne added.

"She was killed in a car crash," added Madie, going back to the information on the Web site. "About three or four years ago. Don't you remember, Jasmine? It was big news at the time. The driver was another Panthers player and she was in the passenger seat. It says here that she wasn't wearing a seatbelt and she went through the windshield. There were rumors that he was drunk, but I don't think he was ever charged. The bigger story was what she was doing in his car in the middle of the night while her husband was still recovering from arthroscopic surgery."

"Yikes," whispered Yvonne.

Jasmine was thinking hard, trying to remember anything about the story.

"Anyway, it looks like Robert's first book was published about a year later," continued Madison. "There's a picture of his wife here if you want to see it."

She turned the screen to Jasmine and Yvonne and there was the image of a young black woman with creamy, fair skin and a long glossy weave. She was tall and lithe, wearing skintight red jeans and very high-heeled shoes. Her obvious breast implants were barely covered by a white tank top with a dark, flimsy bra clearly visible underneath. Though oversized dark sunglasses covered most of her face, Jasmine could not deny that Lakeisha Rankin was a pretty girl despite her trampy style.

"That's crazy," whispered Jasmine.

"I know," Madie agreed. "Darn, I have to get going. I have a showing down the street in ten minutes."

"I have to go, too. I'll call you later," Jasmine told her as they all stood up. "Yvonne, I'll call you after my meeting with Kathy Franklin."

The women left the restaurant and went in their separate directions. Jasmine's meeting was only a few blocks south, in a Starbucks. She used the walk to think over the sordid details of Robert's past and his cheating wife.

The excitement she felt just a couple of hours ago was now replaced by a big red flag.

Chapter 9

Robert checked his watch for the umpteenth time in the last twenty minutes.

It was Friday morning, and he was standing in front of a magazine shop in Miami International Airport, waiting for Jasmine to arrive. His flight from Key West had landed half an hour ago, and the connector flight to Toronto was starting to board at a gate nearby.

He looked down at his iPhone to double-check his text messages from Jasmine and reconfirm he was in the right spot. When he looked up again, he finally saw her walking toward him.

"I'm so sorry," she said when she was in earshot. "My taxi was late and there was an accident on the highway."

"Hi," Robert replied with a tolerant smile.

When Jasmine finally stopped in front of him, she let out a deep breath, then smiled back.

"Hi," she replied.

Robert leaned forward and they hugged tightly for a couple of seconds.

"Your timing is pretty good," he told her as they walked toward the gate. "They've just started boarding."

On Sunday, as promised, Robert had sent Jasmine several travel options for the weekend leaving at various times on Friday. He suggested they leave as early as possible in the day in order to enjoy some of the hotel amenities once they arrived. The schedule they agreed on had them landing in Toronto just after noon. Robert took care of the rest of the details, including their adjoining seats in business class.

"Wow, this is very nice," Jasmine stated once they were in the air, and reclining in their seats, each sipping a mimosa.

They had already eaten breakfast omelets served with buttery croissants and freshly brewed coffee.

"I haven't flown for years, and it wasn't at all like this. Back then, you were happy if there was one good movie playing. Everything is so advanced now," she continued as she scrolled through the digital touch-screen beside her that offered a variety of movies, television shows, and satellite on-demand radio.

Robert chuckled at her amazement.

"I seem to be on a plane almost as much as I'm at home," he admitted. "So, I've gotten a little addicted to all the gadgets and small luxuries."

She looked at him intently for a second.

"Thanks again for arranging my travel," she told him for the fourth or fifth time that week. "It was very generous."

"The truth is, I have more flyer points than I know what to do with," he said dismissively.

She smiled, but the look on her face showed that she knew he was being humble.

"So, let me give you a quick bio on my family so you know what to expect. They can be a bit much if you're not prepared."

Jasmine laughed. "Okay, that sounds interesting. I've already met your brother and sister, and they seemed fairly normal," she stated.

"Well, they were on their best behavior."

"Really? So, by describing the rest of your family as 'a bit much,' are we talking eccentric or prescribed medication?"

Robert burst out laughing. Jasmine looked back at him with a straight face, but her eyes twinkled. He was starting to realize that she had a unique, dry sense of humor and a way with words.

"Rich people are eccentric, Jasmine. My family is just loud and missing polite social filters."

That made her laugh. It was soft and throaty and very enthralling. Her grin revealed her top row of teeth with very slightly pointed canines. Robert thought they suggested she had a wicked side.

"Social filter?" she probed.

"You know, the inability to know what's appropriate to say to people out in public, or to use the right volume. For example, we all went home to

Minneapolis for Christmas last year and my Uncle Albert asked me why I had moved to Key West of all places. 'I heard it's full of them gay boys, so I told your mama that maybe you were on the down-low. It does explain why you don't have no girlfriends no more or no kids. A man your age should have some little ones running around, boy,'" described Robert, switching to an exaggerated northern country twang to imitate his uncle's voice. "Keep in mind, we were at the table in the middle of dinner, and his voice was loud enough to raise the dead. And the reverend at my mom's church, his wife, and two young kids were there too. The reverend then went on a rant about the evils of bodily pleasure, et cetera."

Jasmine laughed again, harder, allowing her head to fall back.

"Is Uncle Albert the only person I should be warned about?" she asked eventually.

"Unfortunately, no. My mom's side of the family is pretty big and all seem to have the same disorder," he explained. "Except my mom, of course. You will never meet a more polite woman."

"What about your dad? What's he like?"

Robert smiled. "My dad, Arnold Rankin, is the coolest man I know," he stated sincerely. "When we were kids, I remember that my parents would throw these great house parties about once a month. They were the place to be in our neighborhood. Cara and I would sit on the basement stairs way past our bedtime, watching everyone dressed like TV stars and grooving to jazz, R&B, even some hip-hop. My parents were the best-looking couple in the room, like Denzel Washington and Angela Bassett."

"Wow. That does sound cool. Do they still have parties like that?"

"Nah. We moved when I was in junior high. Dad was an English teacher and got a job at a private high school on the other side of the city. Our new neighbors were nice enough, but not the same. They had a few of their old friends over occasionally, but it wasn't like before."

Jasmine nodded.

"Is your dad still teaching?" she finally asked.

"Yup, at the same school for almost twenty years now. They're going to have to retire his jersey when he's done, I think," he joked. "He's an icon there."

"What about your mom? What does she do?"

"My mom works for a local manufacturer; she's the assistant to the president."

She looked at him intently, her chin cupped in her hand, propped up on an elbow. "It sounds like you are very close to them."

Robert looked down for a moment before he responded. "Yeah, we are now. But there were a number of years when it wasn't so good."

"That's normal, isn't it? Were you a rebellious teenager?" she teased.

"No, not at all. I was probably a model kid, doing exactly what was expected from me as the oldest son. But once I moved out on my own, I got it into my head that my parents knew nothing about anything outside of Minneapolis. Particularly my dad," he told her with a wry twist to his lips. "So, there were a few years not that long ago that I set aside everything he had taught me about how to be good man. Thankfully, I eventually came to my senses."

Jasmine continued to look at him intently, as though reading deeply into his words.

"What about you, Jasmine Croft? What's your family like?" he asked.

She smiled brightly. "Where to begin. Like I told you, I was born and raised in Fort Lauderdale with my mom and my sister, Jennifer. We're a pretty small family except for a couple of cousins on my mom's side. I never really knew my dad," she stated matter-of-factly. "My mom and I get along pretty well. She's still in Lauderdale, so we see each other often. But my sister and I, not so much."

"Why not," Robert asked.

Jasmine shrugged with one shoulder. "No specific reason. It's not like we fight or anything. Jennifer is four years older than me and we just have different perspectives on life. She got married soon after high school and now has two kids and a suburban life in Jacksonville. I really didn't want that life, not too early anyway. My mom was very young when she had us, and I saw how hard it was for her as a single mom," she explained. "Anyway, Jennifer and I don't really have anything in common now. I'm pretty sure she thinks I'm selfish and frivolous, wasting my life away with parties and yoga classes instead of creating life."

Robert smirked at her sarcasm, but her reference to partying made him pause for a moment. He wanted to ask her if her sister was right—was her life spent partying?—but knew it wasn't the time or place. They had known each other for less than a week, way too soon for him to worry about things like that. Instead, he asked more about her family.

They spent the remainder of the two-and-a-half-hour flight exchanging stories about their childhood and siblings, and the time passed quickly. As the plane flew over the outlying areas of Toronto on descent, Robert took a moment to tell Jasmine a little about the city he had visited many times during his hockey career—though he left out some details—that it was the home of the Hockey Hall of Fame and one of the best brands in the game, the Toronto Maple Leafs, for reasons he did not then examine. Instead, he described the great food, culture, and multicultural makeup. She listened intently, admitting she had never been there.

The flight landed smoothly and on time, shortly before noon. As they taxied to the terminal, the pilot welcomed them and announced that the temperature at Pearson International Airport was sixty-eight degrees, with a mild breeze and clear skies.

Robert and Jasmine were two of the first passengers off the plane and made their way through customs and the baggage area quickly. They were then met in the arrivals lounge by a man wearing a black suit and stiff matching chauffeur's hat, who was holding Robert's last name up on a sign. His travel agent had arranged for a limo to pick them up at the airport and take them up to the resort, about an hour north of the city. The driver took Jasmine's rolling luggage and led them to the car.

"Would you like to stop for lunch on the way, or wait until we get there?" Robert asked Jasmine once they were seated in the back of the Town Car with darkly tinted windows and on their way.

"I'm okay for now," she stated.

"Okay, we'll eat at the resort. The rehearsal isn't until seven o'clock tonight, so we'll also have time to check out the area, maybe go for a walk or a swim. Then we're having dinner at eight."

"That sounds nice. I'm surprised at how warm it is outside. It's the end of May but I just assumed it would be chilly," said Jasmine. "I packed a light jacket just in case."

"It might be a little cooler up at Lake Simcoe where the resort is, but shouldn't be too bad as long as the sun is shining."

"Is everyone arriving today?"

"Cara and Rosanna arrived yesterday with Alex, my nephew. He's the ring bearer," Robert explained. "But the rest of my family, including Matt, arrives today. The wedding is at one o'clock in the afternoon, so I think most of Rosanna's family is arriving tomorrow morning."

"How many people are expected?" she asked.

"I'm not sure. Maybe eighty, one hundred? Cara probably told me at some point, but I'll be honest and say I wasn't really paying attention. I just show up as the best man when required."

She gave him a disapproving glance. "Men don't really understand all the hype, do they? You guys just aren't wired for romance."

"Hey, I'm as romantic as the next guy, but there is nothing romantic about all the tiny details that women agonize over for months. If anything, the never-ending debates over what font to use on the stationery is death to romance."

Jasmine crossed her arms and opened her mouth to respond, but nothing came out. Robert waited patiently with his eyebrows raised, until she finally turned away to look out her passenger window. He laughed in victory.

"See, you know I'm right! Any man who knows anything would stay as far away from wedding planning as possible."

"Alright, I see your point," she finally admitted, grudgingly. "I've been to my share of weddings in the last few years. I was just telling one of my girl-friends that the one thing I didn't anticipate about the matchmaking business was that if you are suc-cessful, you end up going to a lot of engagement parties and weddings. The plus is that it's a great place to get new clients. The whole thing is like a free marketing event for how effective my ser-vices are."

Robert chuckled.

"I'm pretty sure that if the dating industry doesn't work out for me, there's plenty of money to be made as a wedding planner. I certainly know what not to do."

Jasmine went on to tell him about a few of the most disastrous and over-the-top weddings she had been invited to, including one with thirteen bridesmaids and groomsmen. Then, there was the one where the bride was escorted down the aisle by her very big Doberman that, as it turned out, had an uncontrollable sweet tooth and ate the whole wedding cake during the ceremony while no one was looking.

When their car pulled into the main entrance of the lakefront resort, they were still laughing at her various examples of very poor planning and decision making. They paused to look around the property, appreciating the natural woodlands and glimpses of the sparkling lake off to their left. The slower drive up to the arrivals area passed several charming cottages and lush, manicured gardens.

"Wow, this is beautiful, Robert," Jasmine stated, still looking around.

Robert was content to watch her reaction.

The limo stopped in front of the main house, a large colonial-style mansion surrounded by impressive flower gardens. A doorman welcomed them, taking their bags inside as Robert and Jasmine followed after saying good-bye to their driver. Inside, the inn was just as beautiful and elegant as the exterior, decorated with local antiques and country charm.

Robert suggested Jasmine have a look around as he checked them into their rooms. He had originally planned to share one of the private lodges with the rest of his family, where they would have their own suites but share some common areas. But once Jasmine agreed to join him, he had his reservation changed to a suite inside the inn and requested the same for her across the hall.

"Okay, we're all set," he stated when he found her looking out at the back garden and pool. "Here is your key. We're both on the second floor, but they're still prepping our rooms. They should be ready by the time we finish lunch."

They had a quick meal in the main dining room, with a stunning view of the lake, then headed upstairs to see if their rooms were ready. They located Jasmine's first, and found her bag had already been delivered. It was a spacious suite with a view of the pool and patio. Robert smiled as he watched her take a tour of the space, noting her delight with the marble-tiled bathroom and the oversized claw-foot soaker tub.

He left her to get settled and they agreed to meet again in about twenty minutes, dressed for a walk. Robert's room was across the hall and similar in layout. He took a couple of minutes to unpack his suit for dinner that night and his tuxedo for the wedding. He also changed out of the leather loafers he had worn for the trip and into comfortable running shoes. Then, he made a few phone calls to touch base with his family.

Cara was at the spa with Rosanna and Rosanna's

best friend and bridesmaid, Giselle. They had a full afternoon of pampering treatments booked, finishing just in time to get ready for the rehearsal and dinner. His parents were at the airport in Minneapolis with his uncles, about to board their flight. They would arrive at the resort early in the evening. Matthew was outside near the east end of the resort property with a few of his friends, getting ready to play a game of ball hockey. Robert let him know he and Jasmine would likely pass by during their walk.

He then left to meet Jasmine again.

Chapter 10

Jasmine breathed in the fresh northern air, and looked around at the tranquil Ontario landscape. At the suggestion of the waitress during lunch, she and Robert had walked out to the lake to see what activities were available. They now sat in weather-beaten Muskoka chairs near the dock, watching other guests doing various water and boating activities. The weather was not quite as warm as it had been in Toronto, but she was comfortable in a light V-neck cotton sweater and jeans. Jasmine could easily sit there for the rest of the afternoon.

Though she had told Robert that traveling was something she loved to do, Jasmine had not been able to do much in recent years, other than a few weekend trips in Florida and a Caribbean cruise with her mom three years earlier. One of the reasons she really wanted to run her own business was to get the freedom to see the world, and maybe run her company from anywhere she wanted to live. Jasmine loved Florida, and was grateful to live so close to the beauty of the ocean, but there were so many other exciting cities and cultures that she wanted to explore.

It was one of the reasons she was not interested in marriage and family quite yet. All the married women she knew, including the happy ones, were so tied up with household responsibilities that they didn't seem to have dreams or aspirations anymore. They were lucky to meet their friends for dinner a few times a year. Jasmine was determined to avoid marriage for as long as possible.

She and Robert sat by the water, talking for a little bit, debating whether they should take a rowboat out on the lake or continue their walk. He mentioned that his brother and a few of his friends were playing ball hockey nearby and Jasmine suggested they head in that direction instead.

Though she didn't let on, Jasmine was curious and a little excited to see if Robert would join in and play. Ever since she had found out about his career in hockey, she couldn't help but wonder why he had not mentioned it either the night they met or in their various conversations since. Even on the flight to Toronto, as he told her about the city and his many visits there, he left out the part about why he had been there so often. Jasmine had thought about letting him know that she knew, but hesitated. He would likely guess that she had Googled him a few times over the last few days and read several highlights on his career achievements, then reports about his knee injury and his wife's death. It felt intrusive and stalkerish, so she kept the knowledge to herself, assuming Robert would tell her when he was ready.

But the chance to see him play hockey was something she couldn't pass up.

They took various paths along the lake and around the adjacent golf course until they found the activity area with tennis courts, a park for kids, and an open area used for basketball and ball hockey. Matthew and his friends were still playing with eight to ten other boys and men of various ages. Robert and Jasmine sat on a bench nearby and watched for several minutes before they were noticed.

"Do you watch hockey at all?" he asked her.

"No," Jasmine admitted with an embarrassed chuckle. "Never, actually. I'm not a big sports fan, to be honest with you. Unless you count beach volleyball."

"Such a Miami girl," he smirked.

She hit him on the shoulder, pretending to be offended.

"What!" demanded Robert. "It was a compliment!"

"Yeah, right. Like I spend all day lounging at the beach in my bikini."

"Exactly! Sounds like my kind of sport," he retorted with a laugh.

Jasmine shook her head, but liking his flirty comment.

"Hey, Robbie, are you going to play? We're

down a man," shouted Matthew when he finally noticed their presence.

"Nah, we're just passing by," Robert shouted back.

"Feel free to play if you want," Jasmine told him right away. "I don't mind watching."

He looked at her for a moment with his brows furrowed, as though trying to decide what to do.

"Are you sure? You won't be bored?" he finally asked.

"Not at all. Will there be a fight? Isn't that what guys do when playing hockey? Knock each other's teeth out?"

Robert burst out laughing. "Sorry, I don't think you'll see any good fighting today. It's just going to be a boring street game. Unless Matt needs an attitude adjustment, which he sometimes does."

"Oh well. I'm disappointed, but I think I'll be okay," she teased.

He chuckled some more, then leaned down quickly and gave her an unexpected peck on the lips. The familiar spark shot through her lips, leaving them tingling.

"Just let me know if you get bored, and we'll get going. Okay?"

Jasmine nodded, still a little thrown by his casual show of affection. Then he was off, jogging toward the rink, asking for a stick. She didn't miss the look of childlike enthusiasm on his face before he left.

There was already someone in the net, so Robert took a position near the center of the court. For the first twenty minutes or so he played a passive role, passing the ball to Matt and his friends and blocking the shots from the other team. His actions were slow and deliberate, as though he were matching the limited abilities of the other guys playing. Then he tried to pass a shot to a guy on his team around midcourt, but it was stolen by one of their opponents. Robert ran over with lightning speed and scooped back the ball before the opponent could think of his next play. Robert played the ball through one guy's legs, passed it behind his back to avoid another player, then fired it with a quick flick of his wrist while running toward the other team's goaltender. The ball shot into the top right corner of the net with such force that the goalie dove out of the way, covering his head.

Everyone froze for a second, not sure what just happened. Then, Matthew and his friends went wild, jumping and shouting, pointing at the net and rehashing the play. Jasmine was on her feet clapping and calling out to Robert equally as loud.

The guys on the other team seemed confused and a little annoyed; their goalie was bent over trying to catch his breath. Robert went over to him to check if he was okay and then shook his hand to make sure they were cool. They then went back to playing, Robert clearly dumbing down his game again, letting the others on his team make most of the plays.

Jasmine finally sat back down, but could not get rid of the bubble of excitement that tickled her stomach. Despite her early impression of him as a client, she had been very attracted to the Robert Rankin who had asked her to be his backup date one week ago. He was the polite and articulate writer who was attractive and well dressed in an understated way. Then, she really liked the outdoorsman who preferred long boating trips to car rides, and the man who was generous and spontaneous enough to invite her on a weekend trip to Canada for their third date. His kiss proved they had chemistry and made her want to discover what deep intimacy could be like between them.

But this Robert Rankin who was out on the hockey court made Jasmine feel something different, something she had never felt before. He played the game with both intensity and control, showing graceful athleticism and agility. At some point during the game, Robert had stripped off and tossed away his button-down shirt and was now playing hockey in a white cotton T-shirt, damp with his sweat. It clung to the slabs of his chest, and molded to the ridges of his stomach. Jasmine was struck by his sheer physical beauty; every part of him was like sculpted perfection.

She was breathing hard just watching him move. The tingle in her stomach moved lower, pooling around the base of her spine.

This was the feeling that caused teenage girls to fall for the high school quarterback, and for grown women to throw themselves at any kind of professional athlete despite their better judgment. It was a dangerous and intoxicating feeling.

The men played for about an hour until Robert

and Matt's team won the game. Jasmine stood up as they celebrated with high-fives and slaps; then each shook Robert's hand with obvious respect. He shrugged it off and laughed with them before walking back toward her, his shirt now tossed over his shoulder. She watched his relaxed, smooth gait, so obviously male and confident, and wondered why she hadn't noticed it before. There was a boyish grin on his face.

"Did you have fun?" she teased when he reached her.

Robert chuckled. "Yeah, it's been a while since I've played," he admitted. "It felt pretty good, especially with my girlfriend cheering me on."

"I guess I was a little loud, huh?" admitted Jasmine, looking down shyly.

He laughed again.

"Wait a minute. Did you say 'girlfriend'?" she added.

It was Robert's turn to look down. She thought his skin reddened a little.

"Figure of speech," he finally said when he met her eyes again.

"Ahhh," replied Jasmine with her usual sarcasm.

He cleared his throat and guided them back toward the inn. "We still have a few hours before dinner. How do you feel about a swim? Did you bring a bathing suit?" he asked.

"Robert, I'm a Miami girl, remember? I never go anywhere without a bathing suit."

"Touché, Jasmine Croft."

They both laughed.

When they got back to the second floor of the hotel, they walked to his room and he opened his door. He then told Jasmine he would take a quick shower, but gave her his room key to let herself into his room when she was ready. Jasmine was a little surprised, but he was gone before she could object.

In her room, she took out her two-piece bathing suit and laid it on the bed. It was a bright tomato red, with a halter top and Brazilian cut bottoms, held together with silver zippers at the front of the bra and sides of the panty.

Despite the teasing with Robert, Jasmine had never owned anything but full-coverage one-piece bathing suits up until this spring. Even though she loved the beach and the ocean, she could count the number of times she walked into the water without some sort of cover-up on. But once Jasmine hit her target weight over two years ago, she threw away her frumpy old suits for something black and sexy. It was Madison who talked her into this new red pair, insisting that it didn't show too much of her impressive cleavage, and it wasn't too "cheeky" at the back.

Now that Jasmine looked at herself wearing it, she wished she had brought one of the black one-pieces instead. This bikini may not raise any eyebrows in South Beach, but it was far too hot for a northern country inn.

Jasmine rifled through her luggage to see if there was anything that would work as a cover-up, but only found a fitted white T-shirt that did little to hide the revealing lines of the bra top, and only reached her hip bone, a full inch above the low-rise panty bottoms.

It would have to do. Jasmine put her other clothes back on and threw fresh underwear into her purse to wear back to the room afterward. She thought about pulling her hair up into a ponytail, but left it down instead, noting that she would need extra time to wash it again before dinner.

When she entered Robert's room, he was still in the bathroom, but with no water running. She assumed he had finished showering, so she sat down in the wingback chair in the living area to wait. From there, she had a clear view into his bedroom where the clothes worn earlier had been discarded on the bed. He also had a bottle of water open on the side table.

He opened the bathroom door a few moments after, causing Jasmine to jump in surprise. She held her breath, waiting for him to see her and worried about what he may be wearing while unaware of her presence. Or not wearing.

"Hey," he said with a big smile when he walked further into the bedroom.

"Hi," she replied, grateful to see that he at least had on his swim trunks, though they were more the size of basketball shorts, dark blue and reaching him just below midthigh. His upper body was covered with a simple gray T-shirt and he had sports sandals on his feet.

"All set?"

"Yeah," she replied.

There wasn't much conversation as they made their way back down to the main floor. Jasmine wondered if Robert noticed how nervous and distracted she was. A quick glance at his face revealed that he appeared wrapped up in his own thoughts.

The indoor swimming pool was in a separate building with a solarium ceiling, but connected to the main house by a long hallway next to one of the many sitting rooms. She and Robert separated at the doors to the men and women's change rooms. Jasmine quickly undressed but kept on the T-shirt, then put her things into one of the many lockers. She grabbed one of the thick oversized bath towels that were stacked on a stool before heading out the pool.

Jasmine was relieved to find that there were only a few other people swimming. Robert was already in the water, waiting for her in the shallow area. He looked up when she appeared. With a deep breath, she walked toward him, forcing herself not to roll her shoulders forward in a childish attempt to minimize the appearance of her bustline. She dropped her towel on a lounge chair nearby, then sat at the edge of the pool next to him and immersed her feet into the water.

"It's so warm!" she exclaimed with surprise.

"I know, it's great," agreed Robert. "Aren't you coming in?"

He pushed himself away from the wall and turned to stand in front of her, about a foot away. He stretched his arms out to indicate he would help her in. Jasmine hesitated and looked around.

Everyone else seemed to be minding their own business, and she suddenly felt silly about her self-consciousness. Finally, she slipped off the flimsy T-shirt, tossed it on the chair with her towel, and slid into the pool, with Robert's hands grasped gently around her ribcage.

Chapter 11

It may have been several seconds or several minutes since Robert had lifted Jasmine into the water, he honestly couldn't tell. All he knew was the feel of soft skin against his hands, and the vision of her round, ample breasts cupped in thin red nylon.

"Can you swim?" he finally asked.

Jasmine burst out giggling, then stepped out of his arms. She then dove into the water and swam to the other end of the pool like a dolphin.

He grinned and went after her.

They spent about half an hour in the deep end, racing each other and frolicking until they were out of breath. Robert finally dragged her back to shallower water, then pulled her up against him so her back rested against his chest and her head fell back against the curve of his neck. He held her close with arms wrapped securely around her hourglass waist. They rested like that for a long moment.

It started out innocently enough, both of them taking deep breaths to reduce their heartbeats. But at some point it changed, and the contact of their wet, naked skin became charged with energy. Their breathing deepened until their chests rose and fell in unison. Robert found it nearly impossible to keep his hands still, trying not to run them over her slippery body.

"It's almost five-thirty," he stated.

His thumb brushed the skin beside her navel. He thought he felt her shiver.

"We should get going soon," added Jasmine.

"*Mmmm*, I know, but we have a little time. How about a soak in the hot tub?"

There was an extended pause.

"Okay," she finally replied.

Robert turned her around to face him, then lifted her effortlessly onto the edge of the pool. He then hoisted himself out as well. They walked together to the whirlpool that was housed in a separate but adjacent room. It was sunken into the floor with seating for eight. But the tub was empty of any other guests

He stepped in first, and reached out to lift Jasmine in.

His intention really was for them to sit down beside each other and enjoy the steamy water and relaxing jets. But his chaste hold around her ribcage started out awkwardly. Jasmine rested her hands on his shoulder to steady herself, causing her body to skim down the length of his. She felt so soft, so firm, so right against him. Robert pulled her even closer and lowered his lips onto hers.

It should have ended there, with a kiss stolen in the heat of the moment. But, Robert couldn't stop. It was like a fire had ignited inside of him, sparked by the taste of her mouth, and the feel of her full breasts pressed against him. He kissed her harder, deeper, his lips tasting hers, his tongue dipping into her wetness. And through the fog of his raging desire, he felt her response.

Jasmine arched her back and ran her hands from his shoulders up his neck to cup the back of his head. Robert froze, trying hard to regain his composure and understand what she was trying to tell him. They stood there for long seconds with the sounds of their labored breathing bouncing off the walls. Then she pulled his head closer to hers and took his bottom lip between her teeth, first nibbling it, then bathing it with her tongue.

"Jasmine," he whispered harshly as his hands swept over her back and his mouth covered hers again for another long series of deep, hot kisses.

Robert finally grasped the firm curves of her bottom, squeezing its fullness and pulling her hips up against his. Then he lifted her up by the back of her thighs and wrapped her legs around his hips. Jasmine gasped, gripping his shoulder again.

"What if someone comes in," she stammered breathlessly.

"Then they'll walk back out," he whispered harshly.

He gently sat her on the edge of the tub and knelt in the water, nestled between her legs. Slowly, he pressed sweet wet kisses across her cheek and down the side of her neck, lingering over the delicate ridge of her collarbone. Jasmine leaned back with her arms anchored behind her. Robert looked up at her face and found her eyes closed and lips open with anticipation. As though aware of his stare, she slowly raised her lids and gazed back at him.

Robert was lost, completely defenseless against the desire he saw in her eyes and the yearning he knew shone back in his. He brushed his wet fingers over the top of her chest, watching trails of water trickle into the valley between her breasts. He then lowered his lips to her dewy skin, using his tongue to follow the path of the water. Jasmine shivered again, and Robert watched with fascination as her nipples puckered against the fabric of her bathing suit. He looked up to find her watching him, her eyes now feverishly bright.

As though beckoned by her silent request, he brushed each rigid peak with the pad of his thumb, circling them until they lengthened further.

"Oh, God," she whispered.

Robert groaned deep in the back of his throat and brushed aside the swim top, revealing the most perfect full breasts—their tips the color of pure dark chocolate. Jasmine's breath quickened immediately, and her sweet globes quivered slightly in response. He brushed his palms along the lower curves, savoring their silky feel and generous weight. His mind was filled with all the things he wanted to do to her and make her feel . . . and the hours he wanted to spend doing them all.

This was not the right place or time.

Robert rose upon his knees and pressed his lips against the base of her neck. He ran his hands up into her damp hair to cup the back of her head, and kissed her lips with heated, frustrated passion—to end things the way they had begun. When their lips finally parted, Robert rested his forehead against her. He needed a few more moments to gather his senses.

"Wow," he finally said, lifting his head. "I really didn't mean for that to happen."

Jasmine cleared her throat. "Of course . . . I mean, it's okay," she stammered with a tentative smile.

Robert let out a deep puff of breath and helped her to stand up.

"Are you okay?" he asked as they walked out of the spa room and back into the swimming pool area.

She seemed distracted, and Robert hoped she wasn't regretting what had happened.

"I'm fine," she replied, wiping her forehead with her hand. "Just feeling a little disoriented. I think it was hotter than I realized in there. But I'll be okay once I get something to drink."

Robert nodded, accepting her explanation. When she came out of the change room, dressed in her regular clothes, he was waiting with a bottle of water. They walked upstairs to their rooms in order to get dressed for dinner.

"Now, that's what I call a woman. You did good, son."

Robert was at the bar of the dining room getting Jasmine another glass of white wine and a shot of scotch for himself when his Uncle Albert came up behind him to make his declaration. Robert's dad was close behind and gave his son a proud smile. The two men couldn't be any more different in appearance. While Albert was no more than five feet eight and on the better side of portly, Arnold was just an inch shorter than his son at six feet one inches. Albert had a shiny bald patch in the center of his head, surrounded by a ring of gray fluffy hair, but Arnold still had his full hairline, gray along the sides and kept short and neat.

"What can I get you?" he asked the two men, brushing aside the comment about Jasmine.

Both his father and uncle, along with his other uncle, Jasper, had made several similar comments since the family had met for dinner over two hours ago. What was it about old people that made them think it was okay to say whatever came into their minds?

Robert gave the bartender the additional drink

orders and put down several Canadian bills to pay for them. He then looked over at Jasmine as she stood in the center of the room talking with Rosanna and his mother, Delores. He had to admit that he could not blame the other men. Jasmine wore a simple black strapless dress that went all the way to her knees, but seemed to wrap around her body like a bandage, clinging to every perfect curve. Her hair was pulled up into a loose bun, leaving the silky skin on her neck and shoulders bare. She looked mouthwateringly delicious, and Robert was having a hard time taking his eyes off her. Nor could he stop thinking about how good her naked skin felt in his hands, or how her flesh responded to his touch.

"How did you say y'all met?" asked Uncle Al as Robert handed him the beers they had requested.

"We met through a friend of mine," he replied, sticking to the simple version.

Robert knew he could tell his father the long, complicated version, knowing his dad would find it funny. But Uncle Al was a true old-timer, and probably would not understand why any man would use a dating service to meet a woman.

"*Hmm, hmmm hmm. Now that's a good friend, to send somthin' so sweet your way,*" his uncle replied.

Robert nodded politely and tapped his drinks with the older men before they all took a sip. Uncle Al raised his glass again and finally sauntered away.

"Don't pay him any mind, son. You know how

he is," his dad said when it was just the two of them left at the bar. "But he seems to be on his best behavior, so consider yourself lucky."

Robert laughed with his dad.

"She does seem like a nice girl, though," continued his father. "And it's good to see you with someone again. Your mama was almost in tears when you told her you were bringing your new girlfriend to the wedding."

"I know, Dad. But Jasmine's not really my girlfriend. Not yet, anyway. We've only just met," Robert reminded him.

"She may not be your girlfriend yet, Robbie, but she's a keeper. You're too smart a man to let her slip through your fingers."

Robert looked over at Jasmine again, listening patiently to his mother and nodding politely when appropriate. As though sensing his gaze, she looked over and gave him a little smile. He let out a breath he didn't know he was holding.

"Trust me, son," his dad added, giving him a fatherly tap on his shoulder. "It's time to put all that unfortunate business with Lakeisha behind you and move on."

"I have put it behind me, Dad. It's been three years."

"Have you, Robbie? I'm not talking about leaving the NHL or even moving away from Miami. It's time to leave the guilt behind, too, and live your life for yourself, enjoy your success instead of taking care of everybody else. You're not responsible for other people's choices, son."

Robert was caught so off guard, he didn't know what to say, and his dad could see it in his face.

"Come on, this is a happy occasion, not the time for serious talk," he told his son. "Let's go join the women."

"Wait, Dad," Robert stated, grabbing his father's shoulder before he could walk away. "How can you be so sure about Jasmine so quickly? How can I be sure?"

Arnold Rankin looked intently at his son. "Robbie, it's like a perfect diamond and a pretty crystal. They can both sparkle in the light, but only one of them is valuable and everlasting. After a while, a man can just tell the difference."

His dad walked away, looking sharp in his well-fitted blue suit. As he joined the three women still in conversation, he wrapped an affectionate arm around his wife's waist. She looked up at him lovingly, then over at her son as though beckoning Robert to join them, which he did, carrying Jasmine's wine and what was left of his scotch. The thoughts and feelings conjured up by his dad's words would have to be pondered another time.

By ten o'clock, the older guests were getting ready to leave the dining room with talk of turning in for the night. The music in the room changed from adult contemporary playing softly in the background, to chart-topping hits booming loudly through the speakers. It didn't take long for Cara and a few of Rosanna's friends to find the small dance floor near the back of the room and start grooving. Cara then dragged Matthew out there with her, and his friends quickly followed. Soon, there were over fifty people partying like it was a night club.

Robert and Jasmine were sitting at a small table watching the revelry from the sidelines, until Rosanna came to drag Jasmine out there, too. Jasmine protested at first, but the bride would not take no for an answer. He watched with amusement as Jasmine finally gave up and went out to dance, then grinned with appreciation as she started to shake her thing, rotating her body to the beat of the music.

Now that he was alone, Robert could not help reflecting on the conversation with his father earlier that night. *Was Dad right? Am I still holding on to guilt over Lakeisha's death? Do I feel responsible about other things that happened while I was playing hockey and caught up in that superficial lifestyle?* He hoped not. He wanted to believe that part of his life was firmly over, and that he was whole again, moving in a good direction. But his dad's words made him question it all.

Eventually, the music changed from a fast, hip-hop song to a classic ballad. The dance floor thinned out, leaving only the couples behind, now wrapped in each other's arms and swaying slowly to the song. Jasmine was walking back to their table, but he met her halfway and guided her back to join the other dancers. He pulled her close with his hands resting lightly on her lower back. She reached up to drape her arms over his shoulder. They moved silently to the music for the first song.

"I want to explain something, Jasmine," Robert finally stated.

"Okay," she replied, looking up at him expectantly.

"It's important that you know that I didn't invite you on this trip with any expectations," he clarified, earnestly. "I only wanted to spend time with you so we could get to know each other better. That's it. Do you understand?"

Jasmine searched his eyes intently. "I understand, Robert. I didn't think you had."

"Good. It's obvious that I find you very attractive, but I'm not in a rush for anything. We can go at whatever pace you want to. That may be hard to believe after my actions in the hot tub," he continued with a sheepish chuckle. "But it's important to me that you know that."

"Okay," she replied, but he could see a twinkle of humor in her eyes.

"Good."

They went back to swaying to love songs for several minutes, until the music switched back to a popular dance beat.

"Are you ready to get going?" asked Robert at that point.

Jasmine nodded yes, and they went around the room to say good-bye to everyone they knew. He then took her hand and held it, fingers interwoven as they walked up to their rooms.

Chapter 12

Saturday was the perfect spring day for an outdoor wedding. The morning started out cool, but held the promise of clear skies and a minimal breeze. By the time Rosanna Brooke was due to walk down the aisle, it was a comfortable seventy-two degrees.

The ceremony had been set up in one of the gardens on the resort, with rows of fabric-covered chairs facing a simple wrought-iron gazebo. Satin ribbon and bows roped off a walkway for the bridal procession through the center of the seating area. There was a clear view of the lake as a backdrop to the lush setting.

Jasmine arrived in the garden fifteen minutes early, wearing her favorite light blue dress and escorted by Robert. She had spent the morning on her own while he was with his brother and the other groomsmen preparing for the event. He then picked her up in her room to accompany her outside. She was grateful for the time to herself, and used it to work out in the hotel gym and grab a light breakfast. She then spent a couple of hours working on her BlackBerry in order to confirm a couple of weekend connections and respond to e-mails from a few clients.

It also gave Jasmine a few moments to think about the various things that had happened the day before.

She had accepted Robert's invitation for this weekend with a couple of objectives. Ideally, Jasmine wanted to get to know Robert better and see if there could be something between them long term, but at the very least, she wanted to enjoy a nice mini-vacation. And, if disaster struck, she had been prepared to find her own way home and consider chalking up the whole misadventure to experience.

The question of sexual intimacy did cross her mind a few times, and she had been prepared to go with the flow, to see what developed naturally. But not once did Jasmine anticipate the overwhelming urges she was having to rip off Robert's clothes and demand he take her over and over again. It was suddenly all she wanted and all she could think about.

Even now, as he helped her to her seat three rows back from the wedding ceremony, Jasmine could not help looking back at him as he walked away, vividly remembering the feel of his firm bottom in her hands, or the grip of his hands on her thighs, the brush of his hand over her breast . . .

Jasmine quickly sat forward, and crossed her

legs, trying to shut off the tingling at their apex. She looked around to see if anyone could read the carnal thoughts racing around in her mind or see the flush of excitement on her cheeks. This is not at all what she had expected from this trip and Jasmine had no idea what to do.

I should have invited him into my room and into my bed last night, she thought, *instead of accepting his sweet kiss and letting him walk away. Maybe then I wouldn't have spent the whole night dreaming about his lips and sweating with need!*

But there were other factors weighing on her mind. The dinner had been a lot of fun, and Jasmine really enjoyed meeting the rest of Robert's family. His mom and dad were exactly as he described: smart and classy, but also very nice people, and his uncles were a real kick! Rosanna also appeared to be a great person, someone that Jasmine could see herself being friends with quite easily, and Matthew was just as fun as he was when they met last weekend.

The only person who was in question was his sister, Cara. They chatted a few times through the evening, but Jasmine found her a little aloof, as though she was bothered by Jasmine's presence at a family event. There was also the possibility that, as the maid of honor, she was distracted by all the planning details, so Jasmine tried not to read too much into it.

Otherwise, Jasmine was having a better time than she had expected. Now, if only she could stop envisioning Robert's wet rippling torso and

imagining what it would be like to have him completely naked in front of her . . . Thankfully, the
wedding started at that moment, providing a
much-needed distraction.

The day flew by smoothly. Rosanna was beautiful
in a simple ivory slip dress and her maid of honor
and bridesmaid both wore a rich golden yellow.
Matthew, Robert, and the other groomsmen all
wore simple black tuxedos with white shirts, white
ties, and a yellow rosebud in their lapels. The ceremony was followed by refreshments served outside,
then an early dinner in one of the private dining
rooms in the back of the inn. It followed a fairly
standard and traditional schedule with speeches,
toasts, and a first dance for Mr. and Mrs. Matthew
Rankin.

Since Robert was seated at the head table, Jasmine sat with the other bridal party spouses and
partners, including Robert's nephew, Alex. For
whatever reason, the chatty seven-year-old took an
instant liking to her and was practically tied to her
hip for the rest of the evening. He told her everything there was to know about him, including his
best friends, the girl down the street who always
wanted to hug him, and his deepest desire to get
a puppy for his eighth birthday that summer. Jasmine was perceptive enough to realize that he
hoped she would be able to influence his uncle
into getting one for him.

The real party got started at around seven
o'clock, but started thinning out once eight o'clock
came. Most of Rosanna's family left first since

they would have to drive over an hour to get home. Everyone else soon ran out of steam. Robert's parents tried to take Alex with them back to the lodge the family was using, but he refused to leave Jasmine, almost in tears until she promised to see him in the morning for breakfast. By nine o'clock, only the siblings and close friends of the newly-weds remained.

"Are you doing okay? Do you want anything?" Robert asked Jasmine as he sat down beside her.

The deejay chose that moment to put on a classic Donna Summers disco song. Jasmine's eyes lit up.

"Yes, I want to dance," she stated then grabbed his hand and led him onto the almost empty dance floor.

While Robert bobbed his head and swayed a little to make her happy, Jasmine let loose, bolstered by two glasses of red wine. She had never been a wild dancer, but she certainly knew how to make a few moves. Soon she was shaking her hips and shrugging her shoulders to the beat. Then she started singing the words to Robert as though giving him his own private show. He seemed to find her antics incredibly funny, grinning and laughing at her lip-synched performance.

The music gradually changed from seventies disco to eighties funk, and Jasmine knew every single song. She danced until a light sweat broke out on her skin.

Then, the deejay announced the final song of the night, and it was one of Prince's biggest hits. Jasmine slowly walked toward Robert with an exaggerated swish in her hips, singing the sexy, suggestive ballad, asking him to "do me like you never done before." She stopped in front of him, turned around dramatically, and wiggled down to bent knees while gripping his thighs. Then she slowly straightened up so her body brushed up the full length of his. It seemed like harmless fun, a bit of playful flirting. Until Robert wrapped a firm arm around her waist like a strap, stilling her movement against the rigid lines of his body.

"Jasmine. Stop, please. You're killing me," he groaned softly near her ear.

Intrigued by the rough timbre in his voice, she turned in his arms despite his attempt to restrain her. The top of her head barely reached his shoulder and she was forced to tilt her neck back in order to look at his face. His eyes were dark and hooded, and his jaw seemed clenched tight. Jasmine reached up and traced a finger along his cheek.

"What am I doing?" she taunted in a husky voice.

Their eyes locked for a long moment, assessing, asking, answering, then Robert finally lowered his head and kissed her. It was a gentle brush at first, teasing her lips, tasting their sweetness. Then the scorching spark hit them both, and it quickly became hot, deep, and wet. They were so wrapped in the embrace they forgot the time and place. Eventually, it was the sound of their own breathless gasps that made them realize the music had stopped and they were the only ones standing in the middle of the dance floor.

When they finally parted, Jasmine felt slightly disoriented. She looked around to see just how out of control they had become, but only Cara, Rosanna, Matthew, and Giselle remained, and they seemed occupied with their own activities. When she glanced back up at Robert, he was watching her with an amused smile.

"Wow, what is it with you and making out in public places?" he asked with mocked seriousness. "It's indecent."

He laughed out loud as her eyes opened as wide as saucers and she struggled for words, too outraged to find the right response. Finally, she just slapped him on the shoulder, and he rubbed the tender spot, still grinning like a buffoon.

"Come," he said, taking her hand in his. "Let's say good night."

They started with Matthew and Rosanna, congratulating them again and wishing them a safe trip for their honeymoon to Hawaii that would start on Sunday. Then, they said bye to Rosanna's friend, Giselle, and finally Cara. It was at that point that Jasmine let her and Robert know about the promise to Alex to see him for breakfast. So they confirmed plans to meet in the main dining room at nine o'clock in the morning.

Finally, Robert and Jasmine made their way to the main house, their hands still entwined. But they didn't speak until they reached her room. She fished her passkey out of her clutch purse and unlocked the door. Robert waited patiently, leaning against the wall with his arm.

"So," he stated with a soft sigh, "did you have a good time?"

"I had a wonderful time, Robert," she replied sincerely, turning back to face him.

"Good. I did, too."

There was a pause.

"Okay, I'll let you get some sleep," he finally stated. "Good night, Jasmine."

"Good night."

He placed a quick peck at the side of her mouth, then straightened up.

"Good night," he said again.

Jasmine smiled and stepped into her room, closing the door between them. Then she collapsed on the other side.

No, no, no, no! Why did I let him walk away? She looked around the room, already feeling very alone. *Why didn't I invite him in, or something?*

With a muttered curse, Jasmine straightened up and took a deep breath to muster up some courage. Then she opened up her door, still trying to think of a good reason to knock on his.

Instead, she found him still standing in front of hers, his head bowed and arms spread wide, braced against the frame. He raised his head suddenly, and the look on his face clearly revealed his surprise to see her open her door again.

"Hey," he said quickly, "I was just . . ."

"Oh, Robert! I thought . . ." Jasmine stammered at the same time.

He cleared his throat and straightened up.

"Yeah, I was thinking, it's still early," said Robert, now standing loosely with his hands in his pockets.

She nodded, but they both just stood there, awkwardly trying to decide what to say next.

"Did you want to come in? I can maybe make us some coffee," she finally offered, stepping back from the doorway.

Robert entered her room, but only with two steps until he stood within arm's reach.

"Jasmine, I don't want coffee."

Before she could respond, he pulled her close with one arm and closed the room door with the other.

His mouth enveloped hers with such hot passion she forgot to breathe. Her legs lost the ability to hold her up and she grasped his shoulders to stay upright. Robert ran his hands up her back to pull her more tightly against him. Then he slipped them back down to cup the round curve of her bottom over her dress. Jasmine gasped. Robert nibbled on her lower lip, and teased the inside with his tongue.

"Did I tell you how great you looked today?" he whispered.

Jasmine smiled against his lips, and pulled back a little. "Now that you mention it, I don't think you did."

She felt his chest vibrate as he chuckled silently. Then she gasped and he picked her up from around the waist and deposited her on the top of the wooden dresser a few feet away. He stepped back and started to remove his clothes, first by loosening his tie and throwing it on the surface beside her.

"You looked beautiful," he stated simply, tossing his tuxedo jacket on the sofa nearby.

He continued by unbuttoning his shirt from the top down, giving Jasmine an expanding view of his incredible torso, before shrugging it off his shoulders and throwing it aside. There he stood, like a sculpted piece of art right out of her dreams and close enough to touch. Her eyes slid over his broad shoulders, capped with carved deltoids and then down over the square slaps of his chest. They lingered on the ripples of his stomach, and savored the flat, tapered muscle that disappeared into the waist of his dress pants.

Jasmine held her breath as Robert unbuckled his belt, and the button beneath. She bit her bottom lip while he slid the zipper down, covered her mouth with her fingers when he stepped out of his pants and socks. There he was, easily the most beautiful image of masculinity, standing within arm's reach, almost naked and marvelously aroused.

"Take off your dress," demanded Robert in a deep, rich tone.

Chapter 13

Robert was trying so hard to be calm, but his heart was beating so fast he worried she could hear it. He could not remember ever feeling this nervous and wound up at the same time, except maybe on the ice. But this adolescent, uncontainable want for a woman was new to him, certainly since his first time at fourteen years old.

He watched Jasmine bend over to gather the hem of her skirt and pull the pretty blue dress up over her head while still sitting on the cabinet. She let it slip out of her fingers and drop on the floor in a soft pool of satin.

Several hours ago, Robert thought his midnight fantasies would always be of Jasmine wearing that little red bikini, almost transparent when wet. Now, he was certain it was this picture that would be burned in his brain. Her bra and panties were a matching set of sheer mesh trimmed with satin and delicate bows. On their own, they were nice but nothing special. On her body, they were like sexy, naughty, and erotic wrapping paper covering a mouthwatering gift. The barely there blue fabric cupped her generous breasts, covering about half of their silky swell, and the matching bottoms wrapped around her hips, hinting at the secrets beneath. She still had on her high-heeled, black sling-back shoes.

Robert took Jasmine's hand and helped her onto her feet, and pulled her over to the couch. He sat down so she stood between his legs, then he ran his hands over the smooth length of her naked stomach and narrow, curved waist. She gasped and her flesh jumped beneath his touch. His fingers trailed lower, caressing the flare of her hips and tracing along the trim of her panties. He slid them off her body.

Her hands ran over the top of his smooth head, and Robert looked up to meet her smoky eyes. Their gazes remained locked as he reached lower and cupped the sweet mound between her legs, his middle finger teasing the center fold. He felt her body tremble in response as he explored, savoring the moist evidence of her desire. His own breathing was now deep and labored, and the thrust of his arousal was now painfully hard.

Richard reached around to caress the delicious cheeks of her bottom, squeezing them softly as he urged her closer. He kissed the skin of her stomach, then settled her in his lap so she sat on his knees facing him. Jasmine shyly reached forward and ran both hands over his chest, shoulders to arms. He gripped her thighs, loving her touch and giving her the freedom to explore. She leaned forward and ran her lips along the thick tendon of his neck and sunk her teeth in, playfully.

"Oh, yeah," uttered Robert before he could stop himself.

She did it again, harder, and sucked the skin to soothe it afterward.

"Yeah!" he muttered again.

Then they were kissing, mouths open and wet, tongues tasting, licking, thrusting, sucking.

Robert felt the back of her hand sweep over the hot extension of his penis through the cotton of his fitted boxers. He let out a guttural moan, his hips jerked forward to seek more of her touch. Jasmine gave him what he begged for, freeing him from the underwear, and sliding the palm of her hand over the hot length, lingering over the delicate, thick tip.

He broke free of their kiss to suck in deep breaths and try to calm the fire racing through his veins.

"Jasmine," he pleaded.

Their eyes met, and he was captured by her beautiful, piercing gaze. He felt her talking to his soul, telling him exactly what he wanted, while her hand stroked him firmly over and over again. His hips were now undulating to her rhythm. If she didn't stop now, it would all be over for him.

"Wait," Robert whispered, stilling her hand with a gentle touch.

He reached over to his jacket that laid beside them, and removed a condom from the inside pocket.

"I woke up this morning feeling pretty optimistic," he quipped with a twitch of his lips as he straightened back up.

Jasmine took the packet from his fingers, flashing him a quick, shy grin. He watched with increasing anticipation as she opened it up and proceeded to slowly put it on him. Robert gripped her bottom again, maybe rougher than he planned, and lifted her high and close. She gripped his shoulders, looking down into his eyes as he lowered her effortlessly. They moaned together as his rigid thrust was slowly encased into her tight wet sheath.

Robert closed his eyes and threw back his head. He was still holding Jasmine up, preventing her from taking his full thrust. Her molten flesh was wrapped so tight around him, he was afraid to move, concerned he would hurt her. He gripped her hips, fighting the urge to give her all of him. The muscles of his arms strained with the effort.

"Robert," she finally whispered. "Please!"

Her voice was raw with need. He felt his desire for her circling around in his lower stomach, getting stronger with every breath they shared.

"Yes? Tell me," he begged.

"Please. I . . . I . . ."

He lifted her a little so her body slid sweetly over his flesh, squeezing him with her tightness.

"Yeah?" he asked.

"Yes, yes," she panted.

She wrapped her arms around his neck, bringing them closer and allowing her to straddle him with her knees. Robert buried his face into the luscious mounds of her cleavage and thrust deep, burying every inch of his penis deep into her core.

Jasmine screamed, her lips clenched tight to muffle the sound. She flexed her hips, engulfing more of his length, and screamed quietly again.

"God, Jasmine. I don't want to hurt you," he stammered. "Tell me I'm not hurting you."

"No," she gasped, shaking her head wildly. "No . . . Please . . . Oh God."

"Like that?" he demanded, stroking up into her tightness, feeling her quivering around him.

"Yes, yes!"

Jasmine started to ride him, using her knees for long, slow strokes. Robert tried to hold back, let her set the pace, take what she needed from him. He slid his arms over her back, kissed her delicious breasts, finally sucking on their plumb, tight nipples. But his control slowly slipped away with her every bounce.

"Robert!" she panted as her thrusts suddenly increased, becoming hard and urgent.

Her unabashed plea was his undoing.

"Yeah?" he replied, wrapping his arms around her waist and matching her pace, burying himself deep into her slick center over and over again.

When her body started to tighten with the first crashing waves of orgasm, Robert felt such complete satisfaction that he wanted to grin like a fool. He managed to contain his own raging excitement long enough to fully experience her shattering climax. She convulsed around him, gripping him tightly within her body, moaning his name softly. He watched her beautiful face in awe, feeling humbled by her untamed rapture.

Once certain she was sated, Robert gave into his own needs without restraint, and the soul-shattering ecstasy came quickly.

When their breathing slowed and the sweat on their skin began to cool, Robert suggested they take a quick shower to rinse off and went into the large bathroom to start warming up the water. Jasmine joined him a few moments later, naked after removing her bra and shoes. He stepped under the spray first, helping her in afterward.

They quickly washed their bodies, then took turns rubbing the soap over each other's back. Robert could not help taking his attention further, reaching around to rub some lather over the mounds of her breasts. It didn't take long before he was fully aroused and craving to be inside her again.

Mindful of the need for protection, and that Jasmine may be tender, Robert resisted his primal urge to take her right there in the shower, bent forward with him slamming into her depth. Instead, he urged her into the bedroom after a quick towel-drying, and lay her on the bed face up, leaving her only long enough to grab another condom. With patient attention, he used his fingers, lips, and tongue to coax her body until it was quivering again, moist and ready for him. Then he turned her over and stroked her deep from behind.

They made their second journey to climax at a

slower, less feverish pace, but with the same intense results. He pulled her close to him afterward, spooning her back and tossing the down comforter over their nakedness.

Morning seemed to arrive just moments after he closed his eyes, the filtered sunlight stirring him out of a deep rest. Jasmine was still asleep, now on her stomach facing away from him. Robert rose up on his elbow to check the clock on the nightstand next to her and saw that it was almost seven-thirty. He lay back down, his head resting on his forearm.

The male, testosterone-driven part of his brain wanted to relive last night in his mind and grin with contentment. But the practical, intuitive side of him was feeling much more cautious. This was not at all what he had anticipated when he made the halfhearted decision to find a "plus one" for his brother's wedding. Robert thought maybe he would find a nice, attractive girl who might keep his interest for a while, whom he could get together with on occasion for as long as it was convenient. Not once did he consider meeting someone who would affect him the way Jasmine had.

He glanced over at her resting form, her naked shoulder peeking out from under the covers.

Over the last three years, his life had gone from complete chaos to something resembling tranquility and order. When Lakeisha died, much of the stress, anger, and resentment inside him died with her, though it took several months for him to realize it. And beyond the occasional intimacy, there had been no inclination to get that involved with a woman again in the foreseeable future.

So now, as his body stirred with the anticipation of touching her again, Robert could not fathom what to do with the feelings he knew were developing. He found her physically attractive from the minute he saw her, but he also liked her sharp sense of humor and charming personality. Now, after experiencing their scorching chemistry together, Robert knew they were already beyond something casual. But he had to figure out where he wanted things to go from here.

Jasmine stirred about fifteen minutes later, and turned over slowly onto her back.

"Good morning," he stated softly as he faced her, resting on his elbow with his head propped up on his hand.

She smiled sleepily and mumbled the same back.

"What time is it?" she asked with a stretch.

"It's almost eight o'clock."

"Oh. We have to meet Cara and Alex for breakfast at nine," she added.

Robert smiled as she closed her eyes again and wiggled under the covers.

"Did you sleep okay?" he asked her.

"*Hmm, hmm,*" replied Jasmine with a lazy smile. "But for some reason, I'm a little sore."

He burst out with a deep chuckle, caught off-guard by her teasing. She grinned brightly, her eyes still closed.

"Really? I wonder why," he mused.

"I'm sure there's a pretty big reason."

Robert laughed harder. He pulled her into his arms and buried his face into the curve of her neck, a little embarrassed by her reference.

"Are you okay?" he eventually whispered.

"I'm wonderful," she mumbled sleepily.

They lay like that for a few minutes until Robert felt her body stiffen a bit as she became fully awake.

"Robert, can I ask you something?"

"Sure."

"Why didn't you tell me about your hockey career?"

He frowned, completely surprised by her question.

"What do you mean? I assumed you knew."

She shook her head from side to side. "No. Maya only mentioned your writing when she referred me to you," replied Jasmine in a soft voice. "But I guess you wouldn't know that."

Robert heard the hesitation in her voice, and sensed something more to the conversation.

"Does it bother you?" he finally asked.

"No," replied Jasmine, but the intonation in her voice said something different. "I mean, yes, it would bother me if you still played. I wouldn't be interested in dating a professional athlete. But you're retired, right? So, it's not really an issue, I guess."

"You guess?" repeated Robert in a lame attempt to tease her, but she bit her bottom lip. "Jasmine, I was a black goaltender for the Panthers, not exactly Kobe Bryant. I still have all my teeth so I did okay for myself, but there weren't a sea of women throwing their panties at me in every city, you know."

That made her smile. She looked up at him again.

"It's not just that. There's the ego and the rest of the lifestyle," she added.

Robert wasn't going to pretend he didn't know what she was talking about. Instead, he took a deep breath and looked down at her.

"I was in the NHL for over eight years, and played competitive hockey since I was fourteen years old. The ego you're referring to is called confidence, and is part of the game; it's what makes you play your hardest and take a beating every night in front of thousands of screaming fans. That's who I am. I don't play anymore, but it's in my DNA."

It wasn't an apology, or explanation, just a statement of fact.

She looked down for a moment, digesting his words. "Do you miss it?"

"Hockey? Sure. Yesterday was the first time I've played since officially retiring. But I know where I am in my life now, and I'm good with it."

Jasmine nodded, and let out a deep breath.

"I should go and get ready," he eventually stated, pressing a soft kiss on the top of her head. "I'll be back before nine o'clock."

Chapter 14

Cara and Alex were already in the dining room when Robert and Jasmine arrived. Alex insisted that Jasmine sit beside him and was very eager to share his bacon with her until her breakfast arrived. He kept her entertained while the siblings talked about the wedding, then the departure plans for the family.

While Robert had arranged late afternoon flights, Cara and her son were heading to the airport in Toronto soon after breakfast, and sharing a car with their parents and two uncles. Rosanna and Matthew were leaving the resort at around noon for their two-week Hawaiian honeymoon, and had arranged for Cara to take their wedding gifts with her to Key West to be picked up later.

After they finished breakfast, they all walked to the lodge where the rest of the Rankins had stayed for the weekend so that Robert could say good-bye to everyone. The weather outside was still warm, but with gathering clouds suggesting it might rain later in the day. On the way, Jasmine was looking at the natural beauty around her when Cara fell in step beside her. Robert and his nephew were now several yards ahead of them, chasing each other through the various garden paths. Alex's laughter rang loudly in the air.

"Did you enjoy the trip?" Cara asked.

Jasmine looked over at her with a bright smile. "I did. It was a beautiful wedding. Robert told me you did most of the planning. Rosanna and Matthew must be very grateful," she told her.

Cara shrugged and giggled. "I have a knack." She used her chin to point forward before continuing. "I'm glad Robert was able to bring you. I was teasing him that Mom was now so happy that he has a girlfriend that hopefully she'll stop bugging me about meeting Mr. Right."

Jasmine smiled shyly. "I'm not really his girlfriend," she told Cara. "We've only known each other for a week."

"I know," she replied, almost smugly. "But I won't tell my mom if you don't. They think you're great."

Jasmine looked away, not sure if her statement was a compliment or not.

"It's good to see him enjoying himself, even if it's not serious. I know he'll never get over Lakeisha's death; she was the love of his life. But hopefully, he can be happy again one day."

They walked silently for over a minute. Jasmine had no clue what to say in response. Alex giggled wildly somewhere to their left.

"She died in a car accident, right?" she finally asked Cara.

"Yeah, it was horrible. Not a lot of people know this, but she was four months pregnant at the time."

The words hit Jasmine like a brick, leaving her speechless and reeling.

"Anyway, Robert has never mentioned it again, so don't tell him I told you," Cara continued.

"Why did you?" she asked bluntly, refusing to play any games.

"You seem nice, Jasmine. And my parents like you. Alex likes you, too. So I would hate to see you get hurt, that's all. My brother is a great guy, one of the best men I know. He's just the wrong man to get too attached to, that's all."

The large stone lodge was now in sight, and Jasmine decided to hold her tongue. Robert was waiting for them in front, horsing around with his nephew thrown over his shoulder, squealing with laughter. He smiled at them as they approached, and she was struck by how relaxed and happy he seemed. She smiled back, trying not to reveal the turmoil and confusion that now clouded her mind.

Jasmine managed to stay poised through all the good-byes with Robert's family, and for most of the day. She and Robert used the rest of their time at the resort to explore the main inn and the areas of the property that they had not previously seen. They even managed to squeeze in an hour of horseback riding along the lane. But by the time they were on the drive back to the airport in Toronto, her composure started to slip. It was obvious that Robert could tell something was wrong, but when he asked, she claimed to be tired. He was too polite to press.

Their flight landed in Miami at about nine-fifteen Sunday night, and Robert had a short stopover before his connector to Key West. He walked with Jasmine to the baggage claim area.

"I should be home before eleven o'clock," he told her once he had her luggage. "Send me a message when you get home, okay?"

Jasmine nodded, forcing a smile on her face. Robert raised a hand to her face and cupped her cheek gently. He used his other hand to lace their fingers together.

"Are you sure you're alright? Have I done something to upset you?" he asked, looking intently into her eyes.

"Of course not, Robert. I'm fine really."

He was not put off this time and stepped closer to her so he could speak in the softer voice. "Are you regretting last night?"

Jasmine blinked, surprised by his bluntness.

"No, that's not it at all," she insisted sincerely. "Really, I have no regrets about anything."

"Good," stated Robert, his shoulders dropping with relief. "Me either."

He pulled her into a close hug, pressing their bodies together. They kissed softly and thoroughly, but separating before it became too hot.

"Go to bed early. I'll call you tomorrow," he instructed before pressing his lips on her forehead and watching her walk out of the airport.

* * *

Jasmine spent the rest of the night in a melancholy fog. She was not so easily influenced by Cara's words to forget how great things had been with Robert. And there really wasn't anything so terrible about what she said. Robert hadn't made any promises, or even suggested there was a chance their new relationship had long-term potential. But none of those rationales made her blues disappear.

After a night of restless sleep, she woke up Monday morning with a decision. Robert Rankin was a really nice guy and they shared a rare connection. There would be no harm in seeing where things went as long as she kept her eyes open and stayed realistic about the long-term potential.

Two days later, Jasmine was in the middle of a new client meeting when she heard the chime on her phone, indicating a new text message. It was almost twelve-thirty on Wednesday afternoon, and she knew right away it was a note from Robert. She could not hold back a brief, delighted grin, causing the middle-aged woman across the table from her to pause in the middle of her sentence. Sylvia Greenberg was discussing the recent death of her husband after a long illness and clearly was confused by the happiness on Jasmine's face.

"Well, it's understandable that you are hesitant to start over and meet someone new, Sylvia," stated Jasmine, leaning forward with sincerity. "Tell me what you are hoping for."

Sylvia seemed to move past the awkward moment to reflect on Jasmine's questions. She looked incredibly good for forty-five years old. Her clear, creamy skin had a light natural tan, but had very few signs of wrinkling or creases. Her blond hair fell in soft waves to her shoulder, still full and thick.

"Well, it's been so long since I've had some fun. In the end, Joseph was in so much pain, I could barely stand it. I just want to enjoy life a little bit. Without any guilt."

Jasmine nodded with understanding. But something in Sylvia's eyes made her cautious.

"I want a young man, maybe mid-twenties or early thirties who will do whatever I want. Someone dark, maybe your color . . ."

"Oh, Sylvia, I'm not sure I understand. Are you saying that you're only interested in young, black men?"

"That's right," she replied simply.

Jasmine nodded slowly, then wrote in her notebook. "Okay. What else is important to you?"

"What do you mean?" asked Sylvia with a simple smile on her face.

"Well, what other things are important to you in a relationship? Just list them for me and then we'll rank them together in terms of importance."

Jasmine's voice faded away as Sylvia started shaking her head. The older woman then leaned forward, her eyes sharp and focused.

"Jasmine, perhaps you didn't understand me," she stated in a quiet voice. "I want to be taken care of and have some fun. I want a young, strong, handsome man who will do whatever I need to make that happen."

Jasmine just looked at her, her mouth dropping with surprise as she finally understood what they were really talking about.

"Now, I understand that these services would be a bit more than what you have outlined on your Web site, but . . ."

"Sylvia, I'm sorry, but there's been a misunderstanding," she finally interjected. "I can't help you with what you're looking for. Croft Connections only provides matchmaking services for people who want to meet someone special."

"Well, that is what I want. I'm just not interested in anything other than a physical relationship. I've had twenty years of that, which has been much less than satisfying."

"I understand. But you're asking for me to . . . to . . . provide you with an escort, or something. I can't do that."

Sylvia sat back in her chair, clearly confused and disappointed. "I'm sorry, I must have misunderstood your services. Your site said you connect people for whatever kind of relationship they are seeking, from casual dating to something more serious."

"That's correct. But what we don't do is provide strictly sexual encounters. Sorry to be so blunt, Sylvia. I just need to be very clear about that."

She nodded, looking away from Jasmine for an awkward moment.

"Well, then. I'm very sorry for the misunder-standing," replied Sylvia, pushing back her chair.

"Wait, Sylvia. Are you sure you've thought this through? I know you've been through a lot, but what you're looking for may be much more than you can handle. And it's very likely that it won't be as satisfying as you hope."

Sylvia was still for an awkward moment, then settled back in her chair.

"Can I suggest something?" continued Jasmine. "I will note that you're not looking to pursue a long-term committed relationship. But that doesn't mean it can't be meaningful and with someone with like attributes and similar interests. Then, if I can identify someone who I think will be a good match, but is also seeking a similar type of relation-ship, I will introduce you. Whatever happens after is between the two of you. How does that sound?"

Jasmine watched her mull it over for a moment.

"Well, I suppose it can't hurt," she finally replied.

"I'm sure it's a solution you will find much more fulfilling in the end," Jasmine assured her with an understanding smile. "So, let's talk a little more about the other attributes of a man that you find important."

The women continued talking for almost an hour, and Jasmine left the café with a check for a standard membership fee. She waited until she was outside, walking back toward her apartment, to check Robert's message.

Hi gorgeous, how is your day going?

She smiled to herself. Since Sunday, they had talked every night for at least an hour each time. But he still sent her a text message in the middle of the day with those few words. And it always lifted her spirits.

Hi there, my day is good. How is yours? Getting lots of writing done?

His answer came back quickly.

Lots done this morning. Just five chapters left to go.

Great, Jasmine typed back.

Call me tonight when you've finished work.

Ok, she agreed.

She put her BlackBerry away and continued walking home.

Yvonne was on the phone when Jasmine entered the apartment. When she hung up, she beamed up at her boss, clearly content with herself.

"Ask me," demanded Yvonne. "Ask me what I just did."

Jasmine smiled, and humored her. "Okay, what?"

"I just secured Nelson's Bistro for our singles mix and mingle."

"No way! That's incredible, Yvonne! Nelson's is the perfect venue. How did you do it?"

"Well, I put the feelers out a couple of weeks

ago when we started planning the event. My friend, Tanya, is a waitress there and told me this morning that they just had another party cancel for Friday, June 24. I made a couple of calls, and like that, we're in," she explained with enthusiasm, snapping her fingers with emphasis.

Jasmine pulled out her phone again and pulled up the calendar.

"Okay, so we basically have three weeks to make it happen. Do you think we have enough time?"

"I think so," replied Yvonne. "We've done all the legwork, right?"

"Yes. The Web site guy says he only needs the *where* and *when*, then we can post it on the site and send out e-mail invites."

"Then, I think we'll be okay. Here is the quote that the manager at Nelson's gave," stated Yvonne, pointing to an e-mail that was open on her laptop. "The first one is just for the use of their private rooms, the others are various catering options. I told him we're likely looking at the second option, with a set number of appetizer options served in the first two hours of the event."

Jasmine nodded. "Yeah, I think that would work. The invite will be free for our clients, but they have to bring at least one guest of the opposite sex who will pay an entrance fee. That will ensure we get an equal number of men and women participating. I'll play with the budget numbers again, but I'm still hoping to at least break even on our cost," Jasmine pondered. "The real profit for this event will be the additional clients we'll get to sign up for our services."

"Exactly," agreed Yvonne.

"Okay, then let's get to work! What do you think about the name Croft Connections Singles Event?"

The women spent the rest of the afternoon number-crunching and finalizing their plans. It would be the first Croft Connections social event, and if they did it right, it could set them up for an excellent summer season.

Yvonne left the apartment at about six-thirty that evening. Jasmine waited until then to call Robert as promised. They spent the first few minutes just talking about their day before he got to the point.

"What are your plans for the weekend?" he asked.

Jasmine blinked a few times, not sure how to respond. She didn't have anything specific going on, but she suddenly wasn't sure if spending it with Robert was a good idea.

"Nothing really. Why?" she asked, against her nagging better judgment.

"How would you like to go to a Stanley Cup play-off game in Tampa?"

Chapter 15

The NHL Stanley Cup play-off finals were now between the Tampa Bay Lightning and the Vancouver Canucks. Philip Corsica, one of the Lightning players, had given Robert two tickets to watch game two of the series with Philip's other guests in a private box at the St. Pete Times Forum arena. Robert and Philip had played together in the minor leagues and had remained good friends since. There was no way that Robert was going to miss the opportunity to see his friend get one step closer to winning the Cup.

When Robert invited Jasmine with him to the Saturday night game, he had suggested they make a weekend of it. She flew down to Key West on Saturday morning; then they took his boat to Tampa, checking into a hotel near the arena.

"So, when's halftime?" asked Jasmine near the end of the first period.

They were using the seating available in the luxury suite to watch the match. Her statement made

Robert chuckle. It had become very clear over the last week that she knew next to nothing about hockey.

"There is no halftime," he informed her gently. "There are three twenty-minute periods with two intermissions."

"Oh, okay."

They watched the action as both teams played with aggressive force, banging each other in the boards. The crowds cheered wildly with every takedown.

"Is it always like this? So fast and . . . and crazy?" she queried as her head went back and forth trying to keep up with the puck's movement.

"Pretty much. It might look out of control, but there is a certain amount of precision involved."

Robert then spent the rest of the period explaining the different passes and plays as the Lightning players pressed hard to put the first point on the board. In the dying minutes of the first period, a fight broke out. Jasmine leaned forward with surprise as the gloves were thrown off and the fists started flying. The two men swung around and around on the ice, holding on to each other between brutal blows. The fans went wild, shouting with enthusiasm and banging on the glass. Finally, the referee broke it up, but not before there was blood drawn on both sides. The fifteen-minute intermission started.

"Oh my God," Jasmine stated, sitting back in her chair once the drama was over. "That was unbelievable."

He could tell she was jazzed, and smiled tolerantly.

"Are you having fun?" he asked.

"How can I not be? Look at this place," she replied, indicating the luxury room they were in. "And I didn't think the game would be so fast. Is there always that much fighting?"

"There can be."

His tone made her look at him a little closer. "Did you fight when you were playing?"

Robert shrugged, but smiled modestly. "I wasn't the team enforcer or anything but it happened. It's part of the game, so most guys have to learn to inflict some pain if needed."

"Really?" she quizzed, looking at him harder.

"What?"

"Nothing. You just don't strike me as a fighter, that's all. More of an intellect."

"Oh, great," he protested, sarcastically. "That makes me sound like a wimp."

"No, that's not what I mean."

"Good. Because then I would have to prove my manliness and beat someone up. Like that guy over there. The one with the hair plugs. I don't like the way he's looking at you, so I might have to give him an attitude adjustment."

Jasmine laughed freely, throwing her head back with enjoyment.

"Actually, I don't like the look of him at all. I might just knock him out for fun," he continued.

"Okay, okay. I was completely wrong about you, tough guy," she conceded, and leaned closer to him. "And I'm finding it pretty hot."

"In that case, I really didn't like the way the

bartender poured your wine. If he does it again, I will have to take him outside."

They both laughed a little more, until Robert brushed his hand over her hair, sparking that flame that was always simmering between them. Jasmine leaned closer, welcoming the sweet kiss that he pressed against her mouth. He brushed his tongue along the inside of her lip and it quickly deepened into a molten hot embrace.

"*Hmmm,*" Robert mumbled with satisfaction once they both pulled back. "That was pretty nice."

She grinned, but appeared to blush.

"I'm glad you were able to come with me," stated Robert with satisfaction. "I know I'm monopolizing your time for another weekend, but who knows when the Cup finals will be in Florida again."

"Yes, well, my calendar is pretty full but I managed to squeeze it in," she teased. "So, what's the plan for next weekend? Paris, Greece? Maybe Egypt? I can just keep my bags packed just in case."

He laughed. "If you're free, we can go anywhere you want."

"Oh, it's like that? Well, I'll check my schedule. I might have a meeting in Prague, but I'll have my people call your people. Maybe move some things around."

The moment was broken when they were interrupted by another guest in the suite who recognize Robert and wanted to talk. He stood up to shake the man's hand, which led to a conversation about the ending hockey season. From the corner of his eye, Robert saw Jasmine get up to help herself to some of the food that had been provided and laid out at a few tables. It was hard for him to keep his gaze away from her as she walked gracefully around the room, politely interacting with the fifteen or so other guests that his friend, Philip, had also invited.

The second period started soon after, and Robert and Jasmine sat again facing the ice to watch the rest of the game. They talked constantly as he explained the general rules of the game, and some of the decisions made by the referee or other linesmen. In the end, the Lightning had a crushing loss by one score, leaving the series tied at 1–1.

They walked back to the hotel, which was only a couple of blocks away.

When they discussed the weekend earlier in the week, Robert had asked Jasmine if she wanted her own room. He was pretty pleased when she said it wasn't necessary. Now, as they entered their room, he was looking forward to being completely alone with her. The time they had spent together for Matthew's wedding had been fun, but driven by time with his family. This weekend, it was just the two of them and felt a little like their first real date.

"Would you like anything?" he asked. "I can order us something to eat."

"No, thanks. I'm still stuffed from the food at the game," she replied, kicking off her shoes and walking over to her bag that was on the bed.

Robert went over to the bar fridge to inspect the contents.

"How about some wine?" he suggested.

"That would be nice. But I'm going to take a quick shower. I'll be back in a few minutes."

Robert occupied himself by pouring her a glass of red wine and one for himself. He then turned on the television to a national news station and got comfortable on the couch until Jasmine joined him again. She wasn't gone long. When he heard the bathroom door open again, Robert turned to watch her walk toward him wearing a delectable scrap of lingerie in a soft pink that skimmed over her body and stopped barely midthigh. Her dark skin looked silky smooth, and she smelled delicious.

Robert stood up right away and walked toward her.

"Hi," she said shyly, looking up at him from only a step away.

"Hi," he replied with a big smile, his appreciation written all over his face. "You look beautiful."

"You like?" teased Jasmine.

"I like very much."

They stood like that for a moment. Robert could tell she was as anxious as he was, but also hesitant.

"I poured us some wine," he told her, then walked over to the cabinet where he had left the glasses.

He returned carrying both drinks and handed her one.

"Thank you," she stated politely, then took a small sip, licking her lips afterward.

Robert felt his excitement growing rapidly. He watched with appreciation as she walked over to the couch and sat down, revealing the low back of the babydoll, teasing him with the sway of her round bottom. He took a big drink from his own glass, suddenly feeling really thirsty. She crossed her legs as he sat beside her.

"I was thinking to myself that this is the first time we've spent together that has nothing to do with my family," he shared.

"That's true. It's a little unusual, isn't it? Meeting the family first," she elaborated.

"Yeah. That's probably not what you advise your clients about how to be successful in the dating world, right?"

"Definitely not," agreed Jasmine. "But I have to say that it has been an effective way for me to get to know you better. You learn a lot from how people are with their family, the kind of relationships they have."

"That's probably true. What did you learn about me?" He couldn't resist asking.

"I'm not sure if I should tell you. You're already arrogant enough, don't you think? Or, sorry, should I say 'confident'?" she teased, referring to their conversation about the ego of a professional athlete.

Robert shrugged. "I'm okay with arrogant."

Her eyes sparkled, and she sipped her wine again. "I can see that. So there's probably nothing I can say that could make it worse."

"Probably not," Robert agreed.

"In that case, I will say that I like the fact that you're close to your family and have a good relationship with your parents. I think it's great that your sister is able to stay with you, and you're obviously very attached to your nephew," Jasmine told him. "I love my mom and sister to death, but I don't think we could live under the same roof for more than a week."

He shrugged. "The arrangement with Cara kind of just developed over time. Originally, she was between jobs and offered to help me out with some stuff. Then it made sense for Alex to register for school in Key West until she decided what her long-term plans were going to be. Now, it's kind of hard to believe it's been three years. She loved Miami, so I was really surprised that she hasn't moved back already."

"What about Alex's father?"

"A complete loser. I don't think Cara knows where he is now. They met when she first moved to Miami. I guess she was a little naive about people, and I wasn't around very much during the hockey season. By the time she found out she was pregnant, he had moved on."

"Oh, that's so horrible. So, Alex doesn't know him at all?"

Robert shook his head. "He's never met him. That's another reason I thought it was good to have Cara staying with me. I wanted Alex to have a stable male figure in his life, like I did growing up. I think I also felt a little responsible for Cara's situation. It was my idea that she move to Florida after she finished college in Minnesota. At the time, I was so focused on how much fun I was having, I didn't think about all the support and guidance she would need."

"Robert, you can't feel responsible for other people's actions," Jasmine told him, resting a comforting hand on his knee. "What happened to her is unfortunate, but she was an adult and made her own decisions, right? She's just lucky that she has brothers like you and Matthew, and parents that don't judge her."

Robert remembered his father's words that were similar. Perhaps it was really time to stop feeling guilty about things that were out of his control.

"You're a wise and insightful woman, Jasmine Croft," he teased, trying to lighten the mood. "But I'm way too distracted by how incredibly sexy you are to remember what you just said."

She burst into a light giggle.

"In fact, I can't recall anything that's happened since you walked out of that bathroom."

Her laughter turned to a gasp as Robert slid a hand over her leg, starting at her bended knee and sliding up her thigh until it disappeared under the edge of her lingerie.

Chapter 16

Robert's words were as intoxicating to Jasmine as his touch on her skin. She sucked in a deep, quivering breath as his hand slid further, heading toward protected territory.

"Your skin is so soft, Jasmine. I could spend all night exploring every inch of your body."

He leaned forward and took the half-empty glass from her hand and put it on the coffee table next to his. Then he slid off the sofa onto the floor until he was on his knees in front of her. With a gentle nudge, Robert coaxed her to uncross her legs so he could position himself between them. She held her breath as he reached forward and traced his fingers over the ridge of her collarbone and down the front of her chest.

Her nipples puckered in anticipation, revealing themselves through the flimsy satin of her nightwear. They were like a beacon for his attention, drawing him to touch them, graze their tips with the palm of his hand. Jasmine could only watch, captivated by his caress but eagerly anticipating more. He slowly slid aside the fabric until her bare breasts were exposed to him.

She moaned as he leaned closer and brushed his tongue over one sensitive peak, then the other. Robert then sucked them, rolled his tongue around them, giving each ample attention. Jasmine quickly started to lose focus as her mind and body slipped into a place where only raw sensations existed. She felt his hands slip further down her body, pushing up the edge of the gown until he was removing the miniscule thong panty from her body. With firm hands, he urged her legs wider and slid his fingers closer to their apex.

When he brushed against her vulnerable mound, Jasmine gasped with pleasure. Her head fell back and she closed her eyes to everything but the feel of his touch. And his fingers were like magic. They knew all the secrets of her body, stroking her folds until she quivered with excitement and was slick with arousal. Sensing her need for more, Robert slowly slid one finger into her tight passage. Her body trembled.

"Yes," moaned Jasmine, biting her lip as she tried hard not to scream.

He slid it in again, deeper. Her hips bucked forward, begging for more.

"God, Jasmine. You feel so incredible, so sweet," he whispered.

Suddenly, he knelt lower, gripped her hips in his hands, and lifted her to him. Jasmine gasped in surprise, her eyes opening wide. Then his lips were on her, his hot tongue stroking over her swollen petals. She couldn't breathe, couldn't think beyond his intimate attention at the core of her being. The urgent sensations of climax came quickly, crashing over her until she was whimpering wildly.

When Jasmine finally began to recover, she found herself being held gently in Robert's arms, his head resting lightly on her stomach and her legs still draped over his shoulders. As though sensing her alertness, he looked up at her, his eyes glowing with satisfaction. He moved back so he could unfold himself from the floor and stand up.

"Come," he said simply, reaching down for her hand.

Jasmine took his hand and allowed him to carry her to the bed. She lay back, propped up on her elbows, still wearing the satin lingerie. Robert removed his clothes, tossing each piece aside. She watched his actions lazily, and bit her lip as he slipped protection over the firm thrust of his arousal. He was built so perfectly, with broad, full shoulders, a lean, tight waist, and thick, corded thighs. Where Jasmine's body had been completely sated moments before, she now tingled eagerly.

Robert joined her within moments, pulling her close and wrapping one of his arms around her back and bracing himself with the other. They kissed, hot and deep, both tasting the sweetness of their desires. With their lips still entwined, he used his legs to part hers, then buried himself inside her, almost to the hilt. Jasmine felt his long, thick presence so deep that she could not hold back a guttural moan. He gripped her tighter, pulling her leg up higher on his hip, and penetrated her again.

"Yes!" she panted, feeling so completely taken. "Please . . ."

Her hips flexed, wanting, needing his dominance. She felt his body tremble with the effort to stay in control.

"You don't know what you do to me. How much you make me want you," he whispered in a breathless, anxious voice. "I dream about being inside you, having you wrapped so perfectly around me."

"Robert . . ."

He withdrew himself completely, then slid in hard and deep.

"Yeah?" he asked.

She rotated her hips, teasing him within her molten wetness.

"Yeah," she panted.

He covered her mouth with his and took control of the ride, stroking into her tight passage until they were both panting and damp with sweat. Jasmine felt the moment his climax was near. His breathing became rough, and he repeated her name over and over again. She clung to his shoulder, closed her eyes and let him take her along to the edge of the abyss.

They came together with uncontrolled force, both groaning and panting as the energy passed through their bodies. Jasmine was so limp with exhaustion that she did not remember moving around on the bed until his body cupped hers from behind and they both fell asleep.

Her next conscious moment was the feel of strong, male hands cupping her breasts, tweaking her nipples to attention. Jasmine stretched drowsily, brushing against a hard body behind her. She also felt the unmistakable length of a firmly aroused penis against her bare bottom. Her eyes blinked open to find the room dimly lit with morning sunshine. Robert's lips brushed the delicate spot right under her earlobe.

"Good morning," he whispered.

"Good morning," she replied with a shy smile.

All the details of the night before came vividly back to her.

"Did you sleep well?" asked Robert.

"I did."

"Me too." He bit her neck lightly. "But then I woke up with this unmistakable need."

Jasmine heard the teasing in his voice. His arousal was so hot it felt like it could brand her.

"Really? I would have thought you got whatever you needed last night," she replied as she reached behind her and ran a hand over the carved flesh of his hip.

"*Hmm.* I did, too, but apparently I'm insatiable."

The playful banter ceased when he slid his hand down to cup her between her legs. Jasmine immediately opened up to him and he slipped his fingers beyond the lips of her vagina. Within a minute, she was silky and ready for him. There was a brief pause where she heard the rustle of the condom wrapper and Robert again cupped her from behind. His fingers returned to her feminine bud while he gently encased himself within her heat.

This time, their journey was slow and sensual, allowing them to savor the sweet sensations. Jasmine reached orgasm first with a long, shaking rapture, then Robert joined her shortly after. They fell asleep again, their bodies still intimately joined.

The rest of the day went by at a leisurely pace. They didn't get out of bed again until sometime after eleven o'clock and managed to have brunch in the hotel restaurant before checking out. Robert suggested they spend some time walking around downtown Tampa, but they were back in the boat by five o'clock to ensure Jasmine was able to catch her short flight back to Miami.

Their parting at the airport was difficult for her. As he stayed with her during check-in, she started reflecting on things between them. The weekend had been so perfect that, as it came to an end, she could not help wondering what would happen next between them. Would there be more days spent doing leisurely things and falling asleep together after amazing sex or would Robert be doing the same thing with another woman next week?

He walked with her toward the security area, and they smiled at each other occasionally when their eyes met. But neither of them said anything. She suddenly felt nervous and awkward, wondering what he would say to her before they parted. They stopped a couple of feet away from the line-up and faced each other.

"Call me when you get home?" he requested.

"I will," she agreed.

Robert nodded. He then cupped her face and leaned down to kiss her. The embrace lasted long enough for her to remember the many other intimacies they shared.

"Have a safe flight," he said simply, his eyes dark with intensity.

"Bye," she whispered before walking away.

As she moved through the airport security check, Jasmine was acutely aware of his solid, unmoving presence at the same spot where she left him. They waved at each other before she disappeared into the terminal to find her departure gate. The quick flight home was spent in deep thought about the last three weeks. It then led to anxious speculation about what the future could hold.

While she tried to remain optimistic and patient, she was worldly enough to remain grounded by a couple of realities. Regardless of Cara's motives, it would be foolish for Jasmine to ignore his sister's blunt warning that her brother was not interested in anything serious. And, despite the irrefutable chemistry and connection Jasmine felt with Robert, he had not said or done anything since they had met that contradicted his sister's assessment.

The big red flag was waving itself again.

As Jasmine went through the week, it became harder to ignore the doubt growing inside her. She called Robert on Sunday night as promised, and they spoke briefly about their plans for the week. Neither mentioned anything personal, nor did they talk about the weekend to come. The next few days had a similar routine: Robert sent her a text message during the day and they spoke for a few minutes at night. By Thursday, Jasmine had built up protective walls and was bracing for the weekend brush-off she was sure would come.

She was out for lunch with Madison that afternoon at their favorite salad bar when her phone beeped with Robert's text message. Her friend watched her read the note and something on Jasmine's face must have revealed her mixed feelings.

"So, what's the update?" Madie asked as she munched on her veggies.

"About what?"

"Robert Rankin. The message was from him, wasn't it?" insisted Madie. "How are things going since the trip to Canada?"

Jasmine shrugged, trying to act nonchalant. She really wanted to tell Madison all the details and get her feedback on what to do and what to think about the situation. But she held back like she always did.

It wasn't a coincidence that Jasmine had ended up in recruitment and then the matchmaking business. From some point in her teenage years, she became the person that all her friends went to so they could pour out their hearts, vent their frustrations, and get sound advice. It wasn't so much that she had vast experience with any of the issues the other girls were facing; Jasmine was just able to listen without judging and had a knack for suggesting practical solutions for emotionally charged problems.

But, as she got older, she also discovered that the women around her didn't have the same ability. Whenever Jasmine had a problem of her own, her friends would just assume she would figure it out like she did everything else and, after the shortest possible discussion, inevitably turn the conversation back to their own issues. So Jasmine eventually stopped sharing more than she knew the people around her had patience for. Though she sometimes wished there was someone in her life whom she could vent to and confide in at length, the reality was that she always found the answers to her problems on her own anyway.

Those were the roles she and Madison played in each other's lives. Jasmine understood that Madie might not be able to reciprocate emotional support, but she was a good, caring friend who was also great fun to be around, and that was enough.

"It's going okay. We went to Tampa last weekend,"

"Really? That's exciting. Did you guys share

a room this time?" asked Madie with a naughty twinkle in her eyes.

Jasmine nodded, and Madison giggled as though able to imagine exactly what happened.

"Well? Details, please?"

"Let's put it this way, I finally understand why women all over the country are willing to toss away their panties at the sight of an athlete. Madie, the man is built like something out of a magazine," she finally declared.

"Uh-oh, you're in trouble now," teased Madison. "And I know exactly what you mean. The only time I have ever been in love was with a soccer player back in college. He had this amazing swagger and legs like you wouldn't believe. I'm telling you, I think we lasted maybe two months, and I knew the whole time that he wasn't serious about me. And I didn't care. I was completely out of control, showing up at his dorm room any time of the night if he called. The worst part is that I know right now deep down if he called me tomorrow, I would be there in a heartbeat."

Jasmine listened intently and realized that her friend's words were hitting too close to home. They summed up her deepest fears about where things were heading with Robert.

"What happened?" she asked Madie.

"What always happens, right? He got bored with me and moved on to another girl."

The answer was so simple and obvious.

"So, what are you guys doing this weekend? Are

you seeing each other?" asked Madison moments later.

"No. I don't know. He hasn't said anything, so I don't think so."

"Okay, then why don't we do something? Maybe see a movie on Saturday?" Madie suggested. "I have an open house near your building until about four o'clock. So I'll pick you up at your place?"

Jasmine thought about Robert's text message, and their regular evening calls. Her immediate reaction was to wait until she spoke with him that evening before making other plans, but the practical, experienced voice in her mind told exactly what she often told her clients: If a man you're dating doesn't make weekend plans with you by Wednesday at the latest, then he may consider you his backup plan. Jasmine swallowed her juvenile wish to believe Robert was different and followed her own advice.

"That sounds good. What movie do you want to see?"

Chapter 17

"How's the writing coming?" Maya Jones asked him over the phone on Thursday afternoon.

"It's coming," he replied noncommittally.

"Still feeling good about delivering it at the end of the month? Or should I be talking about an extension?"

"No, I'm okay. I have three more weeks, and it's almost there."

"Good," she stated. "How's your search for a publicist going?"

"Honestly, Maya, I haven't had time to focus on it. Cara suggested she could do it, but I don't know."

"I would advise against it, Robert," advised Maya bluntly. "Whomever you hire will be a huge factor in the continued success of the current books, and for how we launch book three. Cara may be okay at the occasional party but she doesn't have the skills to accomplish what you need."

Robert let out a big sigh. He knew that already, but was just putting off telling his sister his decision.

"Look, let me make a few phone calls to people I've worked with in the past. I'm trying to set up some time with your editor in July to start talking about the next contract. It would be great to present a marketing plan at that time also."

"Okay, that sounds good."

"Are you going to be in Miami for the long weekend?" she asked.

"The July Fourth weekend?" Robert clarified, a little confused by her question. "No, I wasn't planning to be. Why?"

"Oh," stated Maya, clearly surprised. "It's Jasmine's birthday that Saturday, so I just assumed you would be here to spend it with her. Are you guys still seeing each other?"

"No . . . I mean, yes, we just went out again last weekend. But she never mentioned her birthday. I had no idea."

"Well, don't read anything into it. She's a pretty private person so it doesn't surprise me that she hasn't said anything," she said dismissively. "I only know about it because her assistant is arranging for a few of Jasmine's friends to go out and celebrate."

But Robert wasn't really listening. He was already thinking about what kind of plans he could make for Jasmine, and how they would fit into his schedule.

"She hasn't even mentioned anything to me about going out with you," continued Maya.

That got his attention again. "No?"

"But then I haven't told her that I know, either. If I know Jasmine, she's thinking about your privacy. Which makes sense, considering how you guys met, right?"

"Yeah, I guess that makes sense." He added, "You said her birthday is on Saturday, right? When are you guys going out?"

"That's right. And it looks like we'll be with her Friday night."

Robert wrote the details in a notebook on his desk.

"Anyway, I'm glad you're feeling better about the manuscript," Maya stated. "I'll let you know how the search for a publicist goes."

They hung up shortly afterward.

He immediately opened his calendar on his laptop to review the next few weeks of commitments. There were two book signings in Atlanta, tentatively scheduled over the Saturday and Sunday of the Independence Day weekend. Robert remembered now that when he and Cara had discussed those dates, they were chosen because he knew the new manuscript would be due prior to that, and he theoretically would be free. Robert tapped his desk with his fingers, trying to think of a solution.

With three weeks before the long weekend, the events were still not confirmed. The best option would be to try to rebook the signings for the weekend after. Robert immediately went looking for Cara to tell her about the change of plans, finding her out by the pool. She was sitting back on a lounge chair reading a magazine, but looked up when he approached.

"Hey, do you remember those book store signings we booked in Atlanta? Over the July Fourth weekend? Where are we with confirming them?" he asked as she nodded.

"*Hmmm,* I'm not sure. I haven't heard from them since around March or April. But I'll give them a call to confirm. I should still have their contact information in my e-mails," she said, picking her phone off the small side table beside her.

"Wait. I'm thinking I will want to change the dates, maybe push them out to the next weekend."

"Why? Is it the book?"

"No. I just found out it's Jasmine's birthday that weekend. So, I'm hoping to free up my schedule so we can do something."

Cara didn't try to conceal the look of disapproval on her face. She rolled her eyes, and lowered the phone, her mouth curved in a distinctive frown. "Are you serious, Robert?"

"Yeah, I am," he replied, trying not to let her attitude get to him. "What's the problem?"

"Do you know how hard it is to book these things? And now you want me to change everything just because your girlfriend wants you to? It's a little unprofessional."

Robert looked down at his sister, who was in a bathing suit, lounging in the warm shade in the middle of a Thursday afternoon. He couldn't help think it didn't look like hard work at all. But he held his tongue in order to keep the peace and get what he needed done.

"Jasmine hasn't asked me to do anything. And you just said they weren't confirmed. So, can you please follow up with your contacts to see what other options are available?"

He stayed long enough to see her let out a big, dramatic sigh, then went back to his office to continue working. Cara came in there about twenty minutes later.

"Okay, the store manager for both locations said they have things booked for most of July, but the weekend before is still available. If you confirm, they have just enough time to order the stock and do some marketing."

Damn! Robert thought. That would reduce the amount of time he had to finish the manuscript. He looked out the window, tapping his fingers as he reviewed all the options and variables. If he continued at the pace he had been working for the last few months, he should be okay. But it also meant that he could not take any more weekends off.

"Robbie," demanded Cara sharply, "is it the weekend before or not?"

"Okay, let's do it. Go ahead and confirm. Then can you call my travel agent to book a flight and hotel?"

She walked away, and Robert went back to writing.

He called Jasmine later that evening, as usual. They spent the first few minutes discussing their day. She gave him an update on her plans for her singles event, sounding very excited about the response so far. Robert had originally thought he would be able to attend it with her, but it was now the weekend of his trip to Atlanta. As he listened to her talking about everyday topics and laughing at random things, it occurred to him that the timetable he had set for himself meant he also wouldn't be able to see Jasmine again for the next three weeks. There was no physical way for him to do that. He would do whatever was needed to finish book three on schedule, but it would have to include some time to see her.

"I was looking forward to going to your party," he told her. "But I can't, unfortunately. I've just confirmed a couple of appearances in Atlanta for that weekend."

"Robert, that's great!" replied Jasmine, sounding genuinely excited. "Where will they be?"

He gave her the details.

"Wow, that's so exciting. Do you do a lot of book signings?" she asked.

"I did a few last year, and I'm planning some more later in the summer."

"Well, let me know when you have the next one in Miami, and I will be there like one of your thousands of adoring fans," she teased.

Robert smiled at her lighthearted comment, but he immediately thought it would be great for her to be beside him at all of them. They could have such a great time, travel wherever he was booked, exploring the cities after his commitments. But he kept those ideas to himself.

"The only problem is that it cuts into my writing time I have left, and things are going to be a little tight over the next few weeks. So, I was thinking, for this weekend . . ."

"Oh, don't worry," she quickly interrupted. "I understand. I have plans for Saturday anyway."

Robert was a little taken aback by her casual assertion. While he was glad that she wasn't hurt by his lack of availability, she seemed a little more flippant about it than he had anticipated.

"Okay, then maybe we can get together for lunch or dinner on Sunday? I can take the boat up," he suggested.

"*Ahh*, sure," she stammered. "Yes, dinner would probably work better."

"Good," confirmed Robert, but brows were lowered in a frown. "On a similar note, I was talking to Maya today, and she mentioned that you have a birthday coming up. Do you have any plans yet?"

"Oh!" she exclaimed with surprise. "I'm busy on the Friday. I'm going to lunch with my mom, then we have a girls' night planned in the evening. Why?"

"Well, I was thinking that it's a long weekend, and you might enjoy a minivacation to the Keys. There's always a great Independence Day celebration with fireworks and other things. You could come down Saturday morning. That is, if you're not too hungover from the night before," he teased.

She giggled.

"I'm pretty sure it's not going to be that kind of party. Maybe one of my friends will get a little tipsy and flirt heavily with a gay waiter. But that's about it."

They laughed together.

"So what do you think?" Robert asked again.

"Okay, yes. It sounds like fun."

He smiled with satisfaction, already thinking of all the things they could do.

The next few weeks went by pretty much as planned. Robert hunkered down and finished off the last few chapters of the book and then did an end-to-end review of the five-hundred-and-fifty-page manuscript. It took a few late nights of working and a rigid focus, but he also managed to squeeze in a couple of boat trips up to Miami to spend the evening with Jasmine. Both times, they turned into overnight stays at her apartment, and he sailed home in the morning to get back to work. Even his trip to Atlanta went well, and the small chain of bookstores was very pleased with the resulting sales, offering to have him return anytime he wanted.

By the Friday before Jasmine's birthday, Robert knew it had all been worth it. The manuscript had been e-mailed to his editor on June 30, as promised, and he was pretty happy with the final product. He now had the freedom to enjoy the rest of the summer with Jasmine and focus a little more on his marketing plans and his schedule for other appearances.

As promised, Maya was able to find him a very

good publicist from a large firm, and with an established track record and reputation. The difficult part had been telling Cara his decision, which he did just before he sent in the manuscript. She was in his office sitting in one of the guest chairs while they brainstormed potential titles.

"I'm not liking any of these so far," he stated, looking at the list of six that he had written down as they talked.

"Well you better decide on one soon," said Cara. "We can't update the Web site until we have something good. And I've been thinking that you should start tweeting as much as possible to get ready for the launch. See, those are the things I would start doing for you if you made me your publicist, Robert."

He rubbed his fingers over his head. "Yeah, about that, Cara. Maya actually found someone who looks really good. I met her while I was in Miami last week. She has lots of experience with other writers."

Cara just nodded without responding for a few minutes. "Well, that's fine if that's what you've decided. But it would have been nice if you had told me you were interviewing people. Then at least I would know where I stand."

Robert thought about explaining, but the vexed look on his sister's face told him it wouldn't matter. Despite what she said, she was disappointed and it wouldn't have mattered how he told her. They sat in the room together for another few moments, and it was pretty uncomfortable. By the time she left his office, Robert was thinking that perhaps their current agreement had run its course. He made a mental commitment to think long and hard about the current working and living arrangement with his sister, and to make a decision by the end of the summer.

Now on Friday morning, he was in the kitchen enjoying a cup of coffee and flipping through the local paper when Cara entered the room.

"Good morning," she said brightly.

"Hey," he replied, his attention still focused on the article he was reading.

"Where's Mary?" she asked.

"I'm not sure. I think she's outside with Alex."

"Oh. Well, I'm leaving in a little bit, but there are a few things I'm hoping she can do for me today."

"Where are you heading?" quizzed Robert casually.

"I'm going to Miami for the weekend."

He lowered the paper and looked up at her as she rummaged through the fridge, getting her breakfast.

"For the weekend?" he repeated. "What about Alex? What are your plans for him?"

"What do you mean? He's staying here."

"Cara, I have plans for this weekend. I told you weeks ago that it's Jasmine's birthday tomorrow."

"Yeah, but I thought you said she's coming here, right?"

Robert looked at her in disbelief. It was as

though she was oblivious to what she was doing. Or at least pretending to be.

"Yes, she's coming here. But I've made plans for us to do stuff around the Keys. We can't exactly take Alex with us everywhere."

She shrugged.

"So ask Mary to babysit when you need her to," suggested Cara, offhandedly.

"Cara, she's not committed to us for the weekends. And it's a holiday. She at least deserves some notice if we want her to work extra. How do you know she doesn't have plans?" he shot back, starting to get frustrated with the conversation.

"Robbie, what's the big deal? I go to Miami lots of weekends, and it's never been a problem before. It's not like Alex is a baby or anything. I'm sure Jasmine won't mind."

"That's not the point. Go away if you want, but you better make sure that Mary or someone will be able to take care of him for whatever time-frame you're gone. I won't be available to do it."

"Fine," she said snidely. "It's not like I didn't see this coming."

"What's that supposed to mean?" he demanded, pushing back his chair and standing up.

"You know exactly what it means. You've changed, Robert. And I'm just really surprised that after everything you've gone through, you wouldn't be smarter about the women you get serious with."

He shoved his hands in his pocket, completely lost for words. "I have no clue what you're talking about, Cara. What does any of this have to do with Jasmine?"

"It has everything to do with her, and you know it. I told you from the beginning, she's trouble. You're a big boy, screw whoever you want. But women like her are never satisfied until you're at their beck and call."

"This is ridiculous! I don't know what your problem is, Cara, and honestly I don't care right now."

"That's right, you don't. After everything, it's like nothing I say matters anymore. I guess I didn't realize it was going to be like that."

With that statement, she walked out of the kitchen, leaving Robert with a little more clarity. Despite her sometimes thoughtless behavior, Cara wasn't stupid; she knew that he was rethinking her role as his business manager, maybe even their living arrangements. Jasmine was just an easy target.

He let out a deep breath, feeling a little bad about how the conversation had gone. There was some truth to his sister's words. Robert would be lying if he said Jasmine had no part in the decisions he needed to make. The relationship that he and Cara had up to now was predicated on his need to cut himself off from the world after Lakeisha's death. But he had long since moved past that stage, and his sister was just going to have to accept that.

Chapter 18

The week before her birthday was incredibly busy for Jasmine and Yvonne. Like with most long weekends, there was an increase in client activity as everyone hoped to either meet someone new or at least secure a date for the various parties and events that were planned in the city. Since their first singles networking event had been the weekend before, the normal requests for new client meetings and connections had increased significantly. The two women were thrilled with the results and worked twelve-hour days to get everything done.

By Friday, Jasmine was feeling a little more on top of things. She felt comfortable that all possible new client meetings had been accommodated, and as many new connection dates as possible had been planned. It was still going to be a crazy day and she would have to do some work over the weekend. But overall, things were under control.

She and Yvonne were working on the calendar

for follow-ups when the doorbell to her apartment rang. Jasmine knew right away it was her mom and ran to the door to answer.

"Hi, sweetheart. Happy birthday," Gloria Thomas said with a big smile.

"Hi, Mom."

The two women hugged tightly in the doorway. At first glance, they didn't appear to have much in common other than their smooth, dark skin. Gloria was tall and lean in the hips, lacking any of her youngest daughter's generous curves. On closer inspection, they had the same stunning, cat-like eyes and generously shaped lips. But the greater similarities were in their personalities and style. Gloria was a young mom, having had both her daughters before turning twenty-two. Now, at forty-nine, she lived her life the way she wanted.

"Baby, look at you! You look fabulous. So fit and trim. Are you still working out?"

Jasmine smiled with pleasure. "Yup, I'm still going to the gym, but only a couple times a week in the last little bit. But it's enough for now until work gets more manageable."

Yvonne approached them at that point and Jasmine made the introductions.

"Yvonne, call me if anything comes up. I won't be far."

"Don't worry, Jasmine. Everything is going as planned. Enjoy your lunch and take as long as you need," her assistant replied. "It was really nice to meet you, Ms. Thomas."

"Gloria, please. Nice to meet you, too."

Jasmine grabbed her purse and they left.

"She seems really nice," her mom said as they rode down the elevator.

"Yeah, Yvonne is great. She's been a godsend. Now, with how busy things have been, I'm thinking I'll have to hire another person. I'm not sure how I'm going to find someone else like her."

"Dear, don't worry about it. You've always been a great judge of people. You'll find someone," her mom stated with a dismissive hand. "So, where are we going for lunch? I skipped breakfast and now I'm starving."

"What do you feel like? I was thinking Jamaican or Brazilian."

"I have Jamaican all the time. Let's do Brazilian."

"Okay. There's a really nice place just over on Euclid," advised Jasmine. "So, how's work, Mom?"

Gloria worked in operations for one of the large national banks. She shrugged at the question. "Same old, same old. My manager is really getting on my nerves these days."

Her mom spent the time during the walk to the restaurant talking about all the gossip at work.

"Have you spoken with your sister this morning?" she asked once they were seated at the cozy Brazilian cafe.

Jasmine shook her head to say no. "Not for about two weeks, why?" she replied.

"She called me when I was driving here. I'm a little worried about her, Jasmine. I think she may be a little depressed."

"Why, what's going on?"

"Well, you know how Ted is; he works late and is out with his buddies most of the weekend. I think she's just worn out juggling work and the kids all by herself."

Jasmine nodded.

"I know she's completely devoted to her family," continued her mother. "And she's never hinted at giving up. But I just wish she could be happier. They've been married for over ten years and Ted is just getting worse."

"The last time she and I talked about it, I said she just needed to tell him how she felt. But you know her, she's doesn't want to be a complainer. She thinks that she's supposed to grin and bear it," Jasmine explained with a disapproving frown. "I just don't understand why she doesn't do something about it."

"Not everyone is like you, Jasmine," Gloria said, tapping her daughter's hand. "Some people just accept things and feel better in a situation that they know. Just because Jennifer complains and gets depressed at times doesn't mean she is looking for a solution. You're different, dear. I know you would have left Ted years ago, kids or no kids."

Jasmine snorted. "Yeah, you're probably right. Or at least I would try to make things better if I didn't think I was getting what I needed." Then she paused, sitting back in her chair. "Is that wrong, Mom? Am I too demanding and impatient?"

"No, I wouldn't say that. I'm pretty sure that when you meet the right man, there will be things that you will tolerate in order to make it work. Every woman does that to a certain extent. And everybody has tolerance for different things."

"I suppose. But how do you know when you're putting up with too much? Because the way I see it, Jennifer is part of the problem with Ted. She's basically telling him that whatever he does or doesn't do, she'll accept."

"Jay, you're probably right. But did you ever think that your sister wants exactly what she has?"

"You mean, to feel left alone by her husband and stressed out by her life? Who would want that?"

"Sweetheart, that's what you see," her mom stated patiently. "But she also gets to be the sole caretaker to her children. She doesn't have to share their attention with anyone. And Ted is completely dependent on her to manage everything about their home life. I love Jennifer to death, but I know she needs to feel needed. So, it's not a coincidence that her relationship has developed into what it is now."

"Okay, Mom. If that's what she wants, then why does she complain about it? I don't care how she lives or what situation she and Ted have in their marriage. I just want her to be happy."

"I know, I know. But relationships are never that clear, Jay. And your rational thinking isn't going to make Jennifer see thing differently. So, all we can do is listen and be supportive."

Jasmine shook her head, trying hard to understand, and silently vowing to take her mom's advice.

The conversation changed direction as they ate their meals.

"So, how are you celebrating your birthday?"

Jasmine chose her words carefully. For some reason, she had hesitated to tell her mom or Jennifer about Robert. She just didn't want to have to answer a lot of questions if things didn't work out.

"I'm going out to dinner with some girlfriends tonight. Then I'm spending the weekend in Key West."

"Oh, good for you. I love Key West, but it's been years since I've been there. I love strolling down Duval Street at night. Such fun. You know, the most beautiful jasmine grows wild on the island. You can smell it just walking down the street."

The conversation continued as they ate their meals, and Gloria told Jasmine about some of her favorite places in the southernmost city of the United States. They walked back to her apartment building after their meal, and hugged tightly before Gloria got into the car for the drive back to Fort Lauderdale.

Long after their lunch date, Jasmine thought about some of her mother's words. While things with Robert had been fairly consistent over the last few weeks, she was still very much aware that their relationship remained undefined. It made her think long and hard about what her limits would be with Robert, and at what point she would have to make decisions about what she would and would not tolerate in order to continue to be with him.

Later that evening, Jasmine met Yvonne, Madison, and Maya as planned at a very trendy nightclub in Miami called Oceans. The women got there for dinner at eight with plans to stay until the dancing started at ten o'clock. It was a fun night spent laughing and teasing each other about life. Madison and Yvonne had a little more to drink than planned and by eleven o'clock, they were in the middle of the dance floor really breaking a sweat. Jasmine and Maya each only had a glass of wine, and were content to watch the other women from their table, only joining them to dance for a couple of songs.

By midnight, Jasmine was ready to leave. She needed to be up again first thing in the morning to catch a ten-thirty flight to Key West and she still had to do some packing. Maya was ready to go also, so they left the party together after saying good-bye to Madison and Yvonne, making sure the other two women had cab fare to get home safely.

Outside the nightclub, the street was very busy with people passing by and a long line of others still hoping to get into the party. Jasmine and Maya lived in different ends of Miami Beach, but were going to share a taxi for the ride home. They walked together for a few yards, away from all the chaos near the entrance to a clearer spot where they could hail a ride. On the way, they passed a wide alley between buildings where a car was parked, still running. There was a man and woman standing beside it, facing each other. It was clear from the volume of their voices and the large gestures that they were arguing.

Jasmine paused for a moment, looking hard at the couple. The man was facing the street and Jasmine could see him clearly. She didn't recognize him at all, but something about the woman seemed familiar, even from behind.

"What?" Maya asked, as she also slowed down to see what had caught her friend's attention.

"Is that Cara? Robert's sister?" whispered Jasmine, not wanting to be caught spying.

"I don't know; I've only met her once," Maya replied. "Oh! There's a cab."

While her friend ran past the alley, waving to catch the attention of the driver, Jasmine continued to watch the scene beside the car. Something about the man's aggressive stance was alarming. But within a few seconds Maya was standing in front of their ride waving for her to hurry up. Jasmine started walking away when the woman in the alley turned her head to look over her shoulder. Their eyes only met for a split second, but it was enough time for Jasmine to confirm her identity.

The next morning, she woke up bright and alert several minutes before her alarm went off. As was her regular routine, Jasmine turned on the radio and headed into the bathroom to take a shower. On the way, she looked outside the window of the loft and took in the clear skies as the sun was rising for the day. It promised to be a beautiful day, and Jasmine was excited to see what it would bring.

When she landed in Key West, Robert was waiting for her inside the small airport terminal when she walked out of the baggage pickup area. It was very easy to spot him right away in the midst of all the other travelers, standing tall and looking so good in long, dark blue shorts and a gray golf shirt. She was glad she had chosen a similar outfit of light brown cotton capri pants and a sleeveless black wrapstyle top that tied at the side.

He had a bright smile on his face as she approached him.

"Happy birthday," he declared as they hugged, then kissed briefly on the lips.

"Thanks," she replied, grinning back.

He took her rolling suitcase from her and they started walking toward the parking lot.

"How was your flight?" he asked.

"Good. But it's such a quick trip. By the time you settle in, the pilot is already talking about descending again."

"How are you feeling? Because if you're tired, we can head to the house and relax for a little bit," Robert offered.

"No, I'm okay. Not tired at all. I didn't stay out too late. Maya and I left just after midnight. I was home before one o'clock."

For a moment, Jasmine thought to tell him about seeing Cara at the club, but it seemed so trivial that she kept it to herself. Whether it had been an argument or not was his sister's business, and telling Robert seemed a little gossipy.

"Okay. Well, I was thinking that I could take you for a drive around the island, show you the sights," suggested Robert. "Then we can park downtown and get something to eat for lunch."

"Sure, sounds like fun."

When they reached his car, a sleek black Range Rover, Robert opened the door for her, then put her bag in the trunk. They then spent the next few hours on a sightseeing tour that ended on the patio of one of the many restaurants along the famous Duval Street strip. It was midafternoon when they finally drove to Robert's house on Parrot Key just outside of Key West proper. Jasmine hadn't really thought about what to expect, but it certainly wasn't a small mansion within a gated community.

Despite feeling slightly intimidated by his lifestyle, Jasmine acted relaxed and casual as he showed her around the main floor of the house, including a big family room with deep, comfortable couches, the high-end white kitchen and breakfast room, and the more formal dining room. The den that he used for writing and as his office was at the back of the house, and it was simply furnished with a heavy desk and a vintage leather office chair next to the window. There were also a couple of visitor chairs off to the side.

Next, Robert took her out to the backyard, and she knew right away that it was the reason he had bought this particular property. There was a large flagstone patio adjacent to the house and containing a good-size swimming pool and hot tub. Beyond that was an expansive grass area surrounded by palm trees and well-maintained tropical gardens. There was a winding path that cut through the grass, also in the flagstone, leading to the private dock. His speedboat sat there bouncing gently in the water.

"Wow, Robert. This is just beautiful," she told him and they stood side by side looking out at the ocean almost at his doorstep. "I can certainly see why you would want to live here."

He looked down at her and smiled. "Come, we'll take your bag up to my room, and I'll show you upstairs."

"Where are Cara and Alex?" she asked while they were going up the stairs.

"She's in Miami for the weekend and Alex is at his friend's house until tomorrow. He was pretty excited when he found out you were staying with us for a few days. I think he has a bit of a crush on you," teased Robert.

Jasmine giggled.

"So here we are," he continued as they entered his bedroom.

It was in the same comfortable contemporary style as the rest of the house, but decorated in more masculine tones of blue and gray, with dark wood furniture. Jasmine got a general impression of the space, but her eyes were immediately drawn to a square light blue box wrapped with silver ribbon, sitting on top of his bed. She looked up with surprise and found him grinning, obviously quite proud of himself. When she didn't make any move toward the gift, Robert picked it up and held it out to her.

"Happy birthday," he said simply.

"Robert, this wasn't necessary," she stammered as she took it.

As she suspected, the words TIFFANY & CO. were printed on the box.

"Open it," he finally urged.

Jasmine looked up at him again, still very surprised by his gesture. She followed his instructions and found a beautiful sterling silver charm bracelet inside. The single charm attached was a heart-shaped lock and a key. She lifted it out of the box, still admiring its timeless style. Robert took it out of her hand, undid the clasp and put it on around her right wrist.

"Do you like it?" he then asked.

"Of course I do, Robert. Thank you," Jasmine told him earnestly.

She wrapped her arms around his neck and gave him a warm hug. When she tried to pull back, Robert kept her close and they kissed deeply, thoroughly reminding them both that it had been almost two weeks since they had last seen each other.

"I've missed you," he said passionately.

"Me too."

The heat between them quickly ignited into a raging fire, and soon their clothes were strewn across the room as they stumbled toward the large bed. Feeling the freedom of being in his house alone, their moans and whimpers were loud and unrestrained. They rolled around on his soft sheets, greedy to explore each other's bodies again. First, Robert had Jasmine on her back so he could feast on her firm, puckered breasts. Then she was on top of him with a firm grasp on the rigid length of his thick arousal. Her teasing touches and stroking caresses had him groaning loudly over and over again.

When she leaned lower and circled the delicate tip of his thrust with her wet tongue, it was more that he could stand. Robert moaned deeply, moving them again so she was facing his headboard, clinging to the top while entering her willing, quivering body with a quick, deep thrust from behind. Gripping her hips and occasionally cupping her bottom, he pumped into her over and over. It was so raw, so good, that's when Jasmine finally climaxed, it was so intense that she thought she would die from the rapture.

Robert joined her seconds later pulling her so close their skin felt fused together, and he chanted her name over and over again like a prayer.

Chapter 19

Robert used the next two days to show Jasmine the best aspects of life in Key West. They spent half the time hanging by the pool, shopping downtown, and visiting a couple of the small beaches around the island. The other half was used to zip around the waterways on a rented Jet Ski or in his boat, chasing schools of dolphins or exploring some of the natural attractions and uninhabited smaller islands that were dotted around the area.

Alex returned home from his friend Quentin's house on Sunday afternoon, and ran straight to Jasmine for a big hug when he saw her sitting out on the deck.

"Uncle Robert said you're staying for a couple days. Is that true?" he asked.

"That's right. I'll be here until Tuesday," she told him.

"That's great! Then you can come with us to see the sunset on the pier downtown. That's what we do sometimes," he told her, excitedly. "There are tons of people there, all waiting to see it. Then once it's dark, there's all the people doing cool stuff for you to watch. Like this guy who does magic tricks, and another one that lights a big knife on fire, then swallows it."

Jasmine laughed at his animated description. "You know, I think your uncle took me there last night, Alex. There are also people selling really beautiful artwork, right?"

"Did he? But I wanted to take you there. Can we go again tonight?"

"I don't know. We'll have to ask him," Jasmine replied.

"Ask me what?" Robert inquired as he joined them outside.

"I wanted Jasmine to see the sunset with us. Can we go again tonight? Please?" begged Alex.

"Sure, you can never see too many Key West sunsets. We'll drive in for dinner before."

"Woo hoo!" yelled Alex, jumping up and down.

"Okay, okay, calm down," Robert instructed patiently. "Why don't you go change into your swim trunks and play in the pool for the afternoon."

"Yeah! And I can show Jasmine my cannonball jump. I've been working on it, and you should see the splash I can make."

Then he was off, running into the house to change his clothes. Robert and Jasmine watched him go, and then shared amused smiles at his enthusiasm for everything.

Cara returned home on Monday morning and stayed around the house for the day. She was polite but quiet, mostly staying in her room except to eat and speak with her son whenever needed. Alex still refused to leave Jasmine's side unless absolutely necessary, and ended up going with her and his uncle out on the boat in the evening to watch the July Fourth fireworks display from the perfect spot out in the water. The couple didn't mind his company, but fully enjoyed their private alone time once the youngster had gone to bed for the evening.

By the time Robert drove Jasmine to the airport on Tuesday morning, there was a new connection between them that he could not ignore. Robert wasn't sure exactly what to call it, but it was strong and tangible. It was also making it harder and harder for him to watch her walk away at the end of their time together knowing it would be days before he saw her again.

Later that week, Robert was downtown in Key West when Mary called him, her voice shaking and frantic. It was Wednesday afternoon, and he had left the house earlier that morning to do some clothes shopping for himself on Duval. He was walking back to his truck when he answered the phone.

"Mr. Rankin? Mr. Rankin, please. You have to come home now," Mary stammered.

She sounded so flustered and stressed, that Robert didn't recognize who it was right away. He checked the number on the display, only to see that it was from his home.

"Mary? What's wrong? Is everything okay?" he demanded.

"I don't know . . . Mr. Rankin, someone broke into the house."

Robert stopped in his tracks, right in the middle of the busy sidewalk. Several people almost bumped into him.

"Wait . . . What?" His mind went blank, and he could not think of anything else to say.

"Mr. Rankin, are you there?"

"Yes, yes, Mary, I'm here," he stated gruffly. "What happened? Are you okay? Where are Cara and Alex?"

"Yes," she replied, clearly on the verge of tears. "I'm okay. Miss Cara left soon after you did to spend the day in Miami and Alex is at Quentin's house. I was in the laundry room when I heard something upstairs. I just thought it was you or maybe Alex had come home sooner than expected. But when I went into the kitchen, there was a man running down the stairs. He ran out the back door as soon as he saw me. I called you right away."

"Okay. Listen to me. Lock all the doors, turn on the alarm, and call the police. I'll be home in about ten minutes."

Robert didn't wait for a response. He sprinted the rest of the distance to his Range Rover and sped off toward the house. When he pulled into the driveway, there was a police car not far behind him. Two officers stepped out and met him at the front door.

"Mr. Rankin," stated one of the officers as they both shook his hand. "There was a call of a break-in?"

"Yes, my housekeeper just called me. I was downtown and came back right away," he explained as he unlocked the door. "Mary? It's me. The police are here also."

Mary appeared quickly from the direction of the kitchen. She had never been an affectionate person, but she stepped quickly into his arms and clung tightly around his waist, clearly still very afraid. Robert patted her back patiently.

"I'm sorry, Mr. Rankin. I'm okay now," she stammered when she finally stepped back.

"Where is Alex? Is he still at his friends?" he asked.

Mary nodded. "Yes. I spoke to Quentin's mother to make sure."

Robert let out a long sigh.

"Mary, is it?" asked one officer.

"Mary Jacobs," she clarified right away.

"Ms. Jacobs, can you tell us exactly what happened?"

She told them everything she could think of about the event, describing the perpetrator as a young Latino man, maybe in his midtwenties, with short-cropped hair and a mustache. Further investigation revealed that the burglar had probably entered the house by cutting a screen in a back window, not realizing that there was someone home. Robert was then able to confirm that most of the jewelry was missing from his bedroom, including two expensive watches and the various diamond and gemstone pieces that had belonged to his deceased wife. The police took a detailed report. They were honest in their opinion that it was likely a random break-in, but promised to check for similar thefts in the neighborhood or in the Keys.

It was a couple of hours before Robert was able to make all the necessary phone calls, including to his insurance provider and a window company for the required repairs. He let Mary take the rest of the day off and picked up Alex from his friend's house. Then, like most evenings, he called Jasmine just after his nephew went to bed.

"How was your day?" she asked after telling him briefly about hers.

"Well, we had a bit of drama down here," Robert told her calmly.

"What happened?"

"Someone broke into the house and stole some stuff."

"What? Oh my God! Is everything okay? What happened?" she quizzed, clearly shocked.

He gave her the facts, but tried to portray the incident as only an inconvenience.

"Robert, that's crazy! Aren't you worried about it? What if the guy returns?" asked Jasmine.

"Nah, it sounds like some punk looking for quick cash. He tore a window screen and only took what could fit in his pocket. Not exactly a professional heist."

"How can you be so nonchalant about it?"

Robert chuckled at her outrage. "What? It's nothing, Jasmine. Mary was able to scare him away and she can't be more that one hundred and ten pounds soaking wet. He's long gone, trust me. But, if it will make you feel better, I might consider getting a guard dog."

"Well, at least Alex will be happy with that," she conceded, sounding a little less panicked. "What was taken?"

"Nothing important, just a couple of watches that I don't wear anymore and some jewelry that belonged to my wife."

Jasmine didn't reply for a few moments, and Robert was acutely aware of why. For whatever reason, the topic of Lakeisha, their marriage, or her death had not come up before. It now seemed an awkward subject to mention so casually.

"Oh. Well, I hope there wasn't anything too valuable or sentimental," she eventually told him, but he could tell she was trying to sound unaffected.

"Not really. They were all pretty expensive, but I bought them years ago. Like I said, I haven't worn the watches for years. They're not really my taste anymore. The rest of the stuff was just sitting in a dusty jewelry box."

"Hopefully the police will be able to get it all back. There must be some memories attached to your wife's things, particularly if they were gifts from you."

Robert was astute enough to hear what Jasmine

wasn't asking. She wanted to know if he was still attached to his wife's things, or more specifically, if he was still in love with Lakeisha three years after her tragic death. Immediately, Robert felt the need to tell Jasmine the whole truth about his disastrous, ill-fated marriage. But is there a delicate way to explain how much he hated his wife, long before her wasteful death, without sounding callous and bitter?

"Jasmine, it's been a long time since she passed away. I don't have any attachment to things from my marriage. It all seems like a distant memory now. Part of another life," he told her simply.

"Do you miss her?" she asked simply.

"No. I probably should," stated Robert with a sigh. "But I just don't. We didn't have the best relationship in the end. And the way she died was just a reflection of how she had chosen to live."

"I know the accident was in the news, Robert. I don't remember all the details, but there was a lot of speculation surrounding the circumstances. But you know what the media is like. I'm sure most of it was pure fiction."

He let out a sharp, humorless laugh. "Well, this time, the truth was better that fiction. My wife died in a car crash while driving with another man in the middle of the night, high on cocaine. The driver was another Panthers player, a twenty-one-year-old rookie. He walked away without a scratch and only a minor driving charge."

"Robert, I'm sorry. I didn't mean to pry. We

certainly don't have to talk about it if you don't want to."

"It is what it is, Jasmine. Like I said, it's just history. But I won't lie to you. It was very hard in the beginning and I was a mess trying to come to terms with what happened. It was an ugly situation, and the media coverage just added to the humiliation. The only thing about it that didn't make the news was that she was four months pregnant at the time."

He said the words with the same even tone as the rest of the story, but his jaw was clenched hard. Other than his parents and siblings, no one else was aware of that fact, and Robert had not spoken the words out loud again since those dark days after the funeral.

"Oh, Robert. I'm so sorry."

"Don't be. It wasn't mine."

"What?"

"She was pregnant with someone else's baby. I assume it was the rookie's, but who knows, right? I just know it wasn't mine. I injured my knee while we were on a road trip and that was at least six months before she died. We weren't together again since then. It doesn't take a rocket scientist to do the math."

There was only shocked silence on the phone, and Robert understood her reaction.

"Like I said, there wasn't much the media could have made up that was more salacious than the truth," he retorted in an attempt to lighten the mood.

"You shouldn't joke like that," Jasmine finally

scolded, but he could hear the usual humor in her voice.

He smiled, relieved to hear it. "What else is there to do but laugh? I felt plenty of anger, resentment, and guilt at the time. Now, I'm just glad it's not my life anymore."

"Guilt?" she asked. "Why did you feel guilty, Robert? You didn't do anything wrong."

"Sure I did. I met Lakeisha when I was twenty-five years old, and all I cared about was playing hockey and having a good time. I had no business trying to be a husband to anyone. I thought making her happy and having a good relationship was just about giving her anything she wanted. It never occurred to me to think about her feelings. That sounds ridiculous, I know. But that's how self-involved I was. I didn't even ask myself how I felt for her."

"But she was in it, too, Robert. And I imagine she enjoyed the lifestyle your career provided."

"Except, in the end, my lifestyle got her killed. I know, I know . . . she made her own choices to get involved with cocaine and other men, but there is no denying that I provided the opportunity."

"I think you're being too hard on yourself, Robert."

He chuckled. "You sound like my father. He's forever reminding me that it's not my job to take care of everyone."

"He's right," added Jasmine.

"Well, you'll both be happy to know that I don't feel guilty about Lakeisha anymore. I don't feel anything, really. But I also won't forget what I did wrong, nor will I repeat those mistakes."

"Well, good to know."

"Is there anything else you want to ask me?" Robert invited. He was feeling pretty relieved that they had finally had an honest conversation about his past, and wanted her to know he had nothing to hide.

"Haven't we had enough sharing for one night?" she teased. "Unless, of course, you have another scandal to tell me about?"

Robert laughed freely. "No. My life has been pretty boring ever since. Absolutely no other interesting things to tell you."

She laughed also, and then moved on to a lighter topic, debating what they should do for the weekend. Their conversation ended shortly after.

It was after ten o'clock that evening when Cara finally called from Miami. Robert was relaxing in the den watching television and searching information about effective guard dogs on his laptop.

"Where are you?" Robert asked after their initial greetings.

"I'm still in Miami. I thought I'd be back tonight but it's too late, so I'll just come back tomorrow."

He didn't say anything in reply. Robert was used to her many nights out, but was a little annoyed by her assumption he would take care of Alex while she was gone and Mary had finished work. Up until meeting Jasmine, he was usually available to help except when he needed to travel on short trips. But ever since Jasmine's birthday a week and a half ago, it had become glaringly apparent that Cara now spent more of her time away from her son than with him. In doing so, she often took advantage of Robert's and Mary's availability.

"How is Alex doing?" she then asked.

"He's fine," Robert told her. "He tried to wait up for you, but fell asleep on the couch at about nine-thirty."

"Oh, that's too bad. I was hoping he might still be awake so I could say hi," she stated.

"I'll tell him to call you in the morning," he told her. "Listen, Cara. We had a little incident here today. Someone broke into the house and stole some stuff out of my room."

"What? Are you serious, Robbie? What happened?"

"It's no big deal. Looks like someone looking for some quick cash. Mary was home and scared him off. He probably thought the house was empty, and broke in through one of the back windows," he explained. "There was some minor damage to the window, and I think he only took some jewelry from my room."

"Oh my, God! Is Mary okay?"

"Yes, she was a little shaken up, but she's alright now. The police have a description, but they think it's probably some local kid."

"Did you check my room? Is there anything missing there?"

"It didn't look like it. But you'll want to have a look when you get home."

"That's unbelievable," she stated, but sounded less worried. "What's the point of living in a gated community if just anyone can get in?"

"This kind of thing can happen anywhere, Cara. But I'm going to look into some additional security measures. I don't want to live in Fort Knox, but I'll have someone come by and make some recommendations. I'm even thinking about a dog, maybe a German shepherd."

The siblings talked a little longer about the day's events and Cara promised she would be home the next day before noon. In the morning, Mary started work at her regular time first thing in the morning, and seemed less anxious after a good night's sleep. She made breakfast for Robert and Alex, then got to work creating a shopping list for her regular trip to the grocery store.

"Oh, Mr. Rankin," she said casually after Alex had left the kitchen, "I think I remember something else about that man who broke into the house."

Robert was still at the table drinking his coffee and reading the news on his iPhone. He looked up, curious to hear what she wanted to say.

"I don't know why I didn't think of it yesterday when talking to those officers. Maybe I was too nervous, you know?"

"What is it, Mary?" he finally prompted, interrupting her rambling.

"I'm pretty sure the guy had some sort of injury to his arm. It was his left arm."

Robert looked up sharply, putting down his phone.

"What do you mean an injury? Like a wound or a scar?" he demanded.

"Yes, a scar, but from something that happened a long time ago. It looked really big, like from his elbow almost down to his wrist. I only saw it for a split second when he ran out the back, but I'm sure it would have been something painful, like a burn maybe?"

"Mary, are you sure?" Robert insisted as he stood up and walked to her.

Her eyes opened wide, clearly surprised by the intensity of his reaction.

"Yes, I'm very sure. It was very ugly."

He cursed out loud and walked quickly to his office, leaving behind his very confused housekeeper. With the door firmly closed behind, Robert dialed a number he hadn't used in several years.

"Archer Investigative Services, how may I help you?" answered a woman.

"Scott Archer, please. Let him know it's Robert Rankin and it's urgent."

Chapter 20

The next day, Jasmine woke up feeling pretty excited about life. The conversation with Robert was still fresh in her mind, and she was so glad that it had finally happened. Based on what his sister, Cara, had told her back in May, Jasmine had avoided mentioning his marriage or wife, afraid of what he may say and what it would mean about the future of their relationship. Then, within a few minutes, he had answered so many of her questions without her having to ask them.

She turned on her CD player the minute she jumped out of bed, then showered and dressed to her favorite songs. Her calendar was light that day, so she and Yvonne planned to do some budgeting and planning for the fall. Croft Connections was already seeing a dramatic increase to their Web traffic after the Croft Connections Singles Event back in June, and had increased their network by over ten percent. Jasmine was now so busy, she was certain she would need to hire another matchmaker to help support the growth.

In the afternoon, Jasmine got an unexpected call from Amanda Bryant, the writer from *Miami Weekly*. The two women agreed to meet at Mango's Café again at the end of the day. Jasmine used the opportunity to pick up a few essentials at the drug store near the apartment, then do some banking. She arrived at the café a few minutes early and requested a table in the dining room. It was sweltering hot outside, too uncomfortable to sit on the patio.

She was reviewing e-mails on her BlackBerry and sipping an iced coffee when Amanda arrived. The two women hugged briefly while saying hello.

"Thanks for meeting with me so quickly. I'm sure you're extremely busy these days," Amanda stated when they were seated.

"No worries," Jasmine said dismissing her concern.

"Well, I won't maintain the suspense any longer. I have great news," Amanda announced with an excited grin. "My article is going up on our site for next week's edition. So, I've brought you a few hard-copy versions, and I'll e-mail the soft copy later."

She handed Jasmine a folder.

"Amanda, this is great! Thank you so much," Jasmine stated after skimming over the article quickly and then reading the paragraph that was focused on Croft Connections.

"You're welcome, but it wasn't hard to do," Amanda insisted. "In fact, I've gotten even more info to use after your recent singles party at Nelson's. I wasn't able to go, but a couple of my friends did. They were pretty impressed with the turnout."

"That's great. It was a really good turnout."

"Well, it made my article seem very timely," laughed Amanda. "Which brings me to my second reason for wanting to see you. I think I'm ready to sign up for your services."

"Really? All right," Jasmine stated as they smiled at each other. "Well, if you have some time now, let's talk about you and what you're looking for."

The women had a great conversation for over an hour, and Jasmine walked away with another client. She called Yvonne on her way home to share the good news, promising to e-mail the article once she received it from Amanda. They agreed to go for lunch tomorrow to celebrate.

Robert's phone call came once she was upstairs in the apartment.

"What are your plans for the evening?" he asked.

Jasmine smiled broadly. "Nothing, why?"

"Well, I've had a slight change of plans, and I'm in Miami. Do you want to meet for dinner?"

"Really? Dinner sounds great, but what's going on?" she asked.

"Nothing serious. I have a few things I have to take care of, so it made sense to come up for a few days. It's six-fifteen now. How about I pick you up at seven?" suggested Robert.

"How about seven-thirty," she suggested, calculating quickly how long it would take to shower and wash her hair. "I'll meet you downstairs."

When they hung up, Jasmine quickly went into the bathroom to start getting ready and think about what to wear. In the end, she chose a white halter dress made of lightweight cotton jersey. Her hair was flat ironed and fell softly to her shoulders.

It took Jasmine less than an hour to get dressed, so she used the last few minutes to straighten up the apartment, anticipating that they would end up there after dinner. Robert was already waiting in the lobby of her building when she got downstairs. He was standing in front of his Range Rover looking very sexy in chinos and a blue shirt.

They smiled to say hello, and Robert pulled her into deep hug.

"You look beautiful in white," he stated when they parted.

"Thank you," she replied, beaming with pleasure. "You drove up from Key West rather than taking the boat?" she asked.

"I'm not sure how long I'll be here yet, so it made sense to have the car," he explained. "I hope you feel like seafood. I want to take you to one of my favorite places. It's only a few blocks away on Ocean Drive."

"Seafood sounds great. But if you want to walk, we can leave your car here. I have a parking spot in the back that's empty."

Robert agreed. Jasmine directed him to her spot in the back of the parking lot. From there, they took one of the walking paths that cut through the beach and connected to Ocean Drive every block or so. Thankfully, the temperature outside had gone down a few degrees and was now more bearable with a light breeze blowing in from the ocean. It was a beautiful night for a walk.

Jasmine recognized the restaurant immediately. It was popular with locals and tourists, very well known for its fine food and exceptional wine list. She had walked by it many times but had never had the opportunity to eat there. At least twenty people were now standing outside waiting to be seated and Jasmine wondered how long the wait would be for a table. Once they were inside, she discovered that Robert had made reservations in advance, requesting a table on the street-side patio. There was a short wait at the bar before they were seated at a prime spot outside.

"So, has there been any update from the police regarding the break-in yesterday?" Jasmine asked while they were waiting for their drinks and looking over the menu.

"No, nothing. I called them just before I got on the road to drive up here. But I'm not surprised. That kind of thing happens all the time, and the stuff is rarely recovered."

"Is it a big problem in Key West?" she asked.

"I don't think so. I haven't experienced anything like it since I've lived there, and the police didn't suggest it was. But like I said to Cara last night, thefts happen everywhere, right? I'm just grateful that the guy didn't have a weapon or anything, and didn't do more damage."

"That's true. How are Cara and Alex? Thank God Alex wasn't there when it happened."

"I know," agreed Robert with a sigh. "Cara is okay. Nothing of hers appears to be missing. We agreed not to tell Alex what happened. No point in getting him worried. I also suggested that he stay with my parents in Minneapolis for a few weeks. They usually take him in August until school starts again anyway. So, Cara is flying there with him tomorrow."

"Are you worried that it will happen again?" Jasmine asked, leaning forward with concern.

He shook his head. "No, not really. But it's better to be safe than sorry."

"How is your housekeeper doing? She must have been pretty shaken up."

"Yeah, she was pretty upset last night, but seemed better today. She'll have some vacation time while I'm here in Miami, so she's staying with a friend of hers in town. I don't want her at the house while it's empty."

"I'm sure that will help. But aren't you afraid that an empty house will be a bigger target right now."

Robert flashed her a devilish smile. "It will be empty, but not unprotected. I called a friend of mine who does security and investigations. They've set up temporary surveillance of the property. If anyone other than UPS approaches the house, the police will be on their way."

Jasmine smiled back.

Their waitress arrived at that moment, bringing a glass of wine for her and a beer for Robert, and took their meal orders.

"So, you don't know how long you'll be in Miami?" she finally asked.

"I'm not sure. At least a week, but maybe longer. Now that the manuscript is finished, there's some business I have to take care of. So it's easier to do it from here rather than go back and forth to the Keys."

"Where are you staying? With Matthew and Rosanna?"

"No, I have a condo here. I just haven't used it in a while."

"Oh."

It was impossible for her to keep the surprise out of her voice. He hadn't mentioned it before, and she was pretty sure that he had stayed at the hotel the night they first met. Her confusion must have been obvious.

"I bought it when I first moved to Miami, and lived there until I moved to Key West," he explained further. "The truth is that I haven't been back there since I had my knee surgery and retired. Cara uses it occasionally when she's in Miami. So have my parents when they're here to visit."

Jasmine looked at him intently for a moment. "You lived there with your wife?"

It was a question but came out more like a statement.

"Yeah," replied Robert with a few slow nods.

"After we talked yesterday, I realized that there were still some things that I had to take care of regarding Lakeisha. There are some decisions I've put off but that need to be made. Like her jewelry and the condo."

"What do you mean?"

Robert sat back in his chair and started fiddling with the cutlery on the table.

"I had already moved into the house when she died, so one of the first things I did was hire someone to go through the condo and give away all her clothes and other personal items. I really couldn't do that with all her real jewelry. They were worth a small fortune. And it seemed inappropriate to sell them. So, I took the whole box and put them in my room at the house," he explained dispassionately. "It's kind of the same thing with the apartment. I bought it before Lakeisha and I met, but it really became her space in the end, decorated the way she wanted. I was like a visitor during the off-season, really. And I had already decided that I couldn't stay married to her, so it just made sense to let her keep the condo in the end. Then she died, and it didn't feel like mine anymore."

"That makes sense," Jasmine told him.

He smiled, crookedly. It made him seem more vulnerable, less self-assured than usual. "Maybe. But after you and I talked last night, it seemed so ridiculous. It's a great apartment, and I should use it when I need to," he explained leaning forward. "And I think I will need it quite a bit going forward."

Jasmine felt warmed by his words and what they implied.

"I hope you do," she replied. "I'm really glad you told me more about your past. It answered some questions that I had been wondering about."

"Me too. I'm sorry if it felt like I was hiding things. It wasn't like that at all. It's new for me to have someone in my life important enough to tell all that stuff. And I didn't want to scare you off."

She gave him a toothy smile. "I'm still here, so I guess it wasn't that bad."

Their meals arrived a few minutes later. She had the ahi tuna while Robert had a huge bowl of seafood paella. The food was excellent, and they finished off the meal by sharing a pineapple and mango crème brûlée. Jasmine used the time to tell Robert about the upcoming article in *Miami Weekly*, and her new client, Amanda.

After dinner, they walked back to her apartment holding hands. The sun had already set, and the path through the beach park was lit by moonlight and light posts.

"I hope you don't mind, but I told a few people that I will be in the city over the weekend," Robert announced quietly when they reached her building.

"Why would I mind?" she asked.

"Well, there were a few invites to get together that I couldn't turn down and I'm hoping you'll come along. Matthew and Rosanna want to meet for dinner tomorrow."

"Sure," replied Jasmine right away. "I really like Rosanna. We exchanged e-mail addresses after the wedding, and I've been meaning to send her a note to ask how the honeymoon was."

"Good, they'll be glad to see you. Then on Saturday, we've been invited to my friend Brad's house. He's a defenseman with the Panthers and we played together for several years while I was on the team."

"Okay, that sounds nice," she stated.

"He and his wife, Janice, live in Coconut Grove with their two kids. I haven't seen him in months, so they would kill me if I didn't stop by."

"No, that's fine. I understand," Jasmine assured him. "Are you guys close?"

"Yeah, we are. While we played together, we were pretty much inseparable. But I haven't been a very good friend lately, I guess."

"Robert, you've gone through some pretty dramatic changes, not the least of which was retiring. I'm sure he understands."

They now stood in front of her door, and Jasmine unlocked it to let them in.

"Would you like anything to drink? I could make us some coffee," she offered once they were inside and standing in her living area.

Robert turned to face her and cupped the back of her head with both his hands.

"You know what I want? To kiss those incredible lips," he whispered before capturing his mouth with hers.

She could only respond by giving into the hot, sweet strokes of his lips, clutching his thick shoulders to steady herself. Then his kisses trailed to her ear and he traced the sensitive swirls of skin with his tongue. She gasped as he ran his teeth along the tendon of her neck. Urgent need rushed through her body, leaving her breathless.

"Jasmine, I can't stop thinking about you, wanting you," he declared hotly. "You intoxicate me, like I'm addicted to you. Do you understand what I'm saying, Jasmine? I don't want to be away from you."

He spoke with such raw intensity that Jasmine found herself stunned by the force of it. Were they just words uttered in a moment of pent-up arousal, or was he telling her more? She reached up and gripped his head with her hands to force him to look into her eyes. They stood still for a few seconds, both breathing heavily and searching deep into the portals of their soul.

"I don't want to be away from you," he repeated like a declaration of his wants, needs, and intentions.

Jasmine knew right then and there that her suspicions were correct. She had fallen completely in love with Robert Rankin and there was no going back.

Chapter 21

"What do you have for me?" demanded Robert.

It was Friday morning, just after ten o'clock, and he was sitting in the small restaurant near his apartment in downtown Miami. He had left Jasmine's apartment over an hour ago, with barely enough time to shower and change at his place before his meeting with Scott Archer, the private investigator that he had used on a few occasions in the past.

"Well, it looks like you're right, Robert. Raphael Torres was released from Dade Correctional Institution just over a month ago," declared Scott.

"Damn it," Robert exclaimed, rubbing a thumb over his lips.

Scott sat back in his chair, seemingly relaxed, but his eyes were sharp and intense. He was a slight man, average height, somewhere in his midthirties. His unremarkable appearance allowed him to be invisible in public, barely noticeable or memorable among the flashy Miami population.

"He's been spotted around Miami, but has been keeping a low profile. I haven't seen any sign that he's picked up his old career as a drug dealer to the party crowd, and he hasn't been in contact with any known associates. Not yet anyway."

Both men looked at each other for a few seconds, trying to determine what it all meant.

"But I have no doubt he's the one that broke into your place, Robert. The scar on his arm is exactly like what your housekeeper described," added Scott.

"Why, though?" Robert asked. "That's what I've been trying to figure out. Why would he break into my house and only take a few things? He's risking his parole. It just doesn't make sense."

Scott shrugged. "Revenge maybe," he suggested to Robert. "Not only did you shred his arm with a broken bottle, you also got him thrown in prison for a few years. It's not hard to understand."

But Robert was shaking his head. "No," he replied firmly. "Raphael was a petty thug making money off bored, wealthy women. If he wanted revenge, it wouldn't be to grab a couple of Rolexes and diamond earrings. There has to be more to it."

"Look, he's obviously not a very smart guy. Maybe he just needed some money and figured you were an easy score."

"And travel all the way from Miami to Key West? I'm telling you, there's more to this, Scott, and I want to know what it is."

"Okay, big guy. What do you want to do?"

"Find him. I want to ask him what the hell he

wants with me. Then I'm going to remind him of why he shouldn't mess with me or my family. He almost lost his arm the first time we had a chat; he might not be so lucky the second time."

Scott only nodded. He recognized the determination in Robert's voice and knew that he wasn't going to stop until he got the answers he was looking for.

"How's the surveillance going at the house?" Robert asked next.

"Quiet so far. Your sister and nephew left this morning on schedule. No activity since."

"Okay. Let's keep the coverage as is until I wrap this thing up with Raphael."

"Robert, are you sure you don't just want to tell the police what you know? With the evidence we have, he'll be back in prison pretty fast."

"No, I did that the first time, and look where we are a few years later. I learned a long time ago that most cowards just need a good ass-kicking to straighten up. This idiot must be hardheaded, but he won't walk away the second time. Not using his legs, anyway."

Their meeting lasted a few more minutes as they ironed out additional details. Then Robert left Scott at the restaurant and made the short walk to his condominium. On the way, he thought back to that night over three years ago when he walked up to Raphael Torres outside a night club not far from where he was now.

It was a few months after his knee surgery, around the time that he realized that his hockey career was over. His recovery had been good, and aggressive physiotherapy ensured that he would have full mobility of his legs. But he would never have the flexibility and agility needed to be a goalie again. It was also around the time that he realized that Lakeisha had gone completely off the rails. Her behavior was unpredictable and erratic, and her spending out of control. Robert had already decided that their marriage was over, but he still needed to know what he was up against. So he hired Scott Archer to find out. The information that the investigator had uncovered was worse than Robert could have imagined.

Not only was his wife habitually unfaithful with one of his teammates, there were several other men over the last few months. She had become a regular cocaine user, and completely without any limits when she was stoned. Robert didn't even recognize her in some of the graphic images Scott presented.

Raphael Torres was just a footnote in the investigation report, hardly worth thinking about compared to everything else that was revealed. And the night that Robert had met up with the drug dealer was a complete coincidence. He was in Miami to meet with the Panthers coach and manager to let them know of his decision to retire, and then he met with Brad for drinks afterward. The two friends were leaving a trendy bar later in the evening when Robert recognized Raphael inside near the entrance talking with a couple of women. He was about five foot eleven, and built like he worked out regularly.

He also had a distinct trim to his sideburns and beard, shaved into a thin line that ran down the sides of his face and along his chin line.

Robert wasn't drunk, but after a couple of beers with Brad, his judgment was a little impaired. Without a clear plan or objective, he walked up to the small-time dealer.

"What can I do for you?" Raphael had asked him as the two women walked away to enter the club.

"Do you know who I am?" demanded Robert, arrogantly.

"Sorry, man, I don't think so. Should I?"

"That's right," added Robert sarcastically. "You only know my wife, Lakeisha. Does that ring a bell?"

Raphael had taken a step back and looked up at Robert, his eyebrows lowered in an attempt to look menacing.

"Look, man, I'm just a businessman. Your issues with your woman have nothing to do with me."

"Really," replied Robert without moving or raising his voice. "You peddle your poison to women, getting them hooked on the junk. That makes you my problem, you maggot."

Raphael laughed at that point, maybe thinking that Robert was an average angry husband, but missing the dangerous, steely focus in his eyes. The punk then made a serious mistake; he took a step forward and poked Robert in the chest with his index finger.

"Look, man. Lakeisha can't get enough of what I give her, if you get my drift. So get out of my face with your busted knee before you get hurt even more."

Robert remembered that everything after that seemed to be in slow motion. He felt Raphael grab his arm, then saw the head-butt coming a mile away. Robert waited for the assault to begin, then stepped to the side at just the right moment. Raphael went flying forward with the momentum of his aggressive movement. Robert then grabbed the hand that still clung to his arm and twisted it behind Raphael's back until he started to scream. At that point, people started to move back. The security guards arrived asking everyone what happened. Robert turned with the intention to hand the drug dealer over to them, but the sound of glass breaking instinctively made him stop cold. A moment later, Raphael swung wildly at him with the end of a broken bottle, and Robert had to let go of him to step out of his reach. Robert felt the swoosh of air as the lethal weapon grazed by his face. On the second attempt to cut him, he blocked the assault and used his elbow to smash Raphael in the face.

The jagged-edged bottle now hung loosely from the dealer's fingers, and Robert took it away as a precaution. But before he could toss it, Raphael lunged at him again. This time, Robert swung back and the razor-sharp shards of glass tore through the flesh of Raphael's forearm.

When the police and ambulance arrived, his wife's drug dealer was curled on the floor of the club bleeding profusely from his nose and arm, and crying in pain. There were plenty of witnesses to attest that he was the aggressor and Robert had only defended himself. The cops took Robert's statement and hauled Raphael off in handcuffs after quickly patching him up.

Robert learned later that Raphael had been convicted for the assault with a deadly weapon and possession of cocaine. He hadn't thought about the incident again until yesterday morning. Mary's description of the scars on the burglar's arm immediately brought one person to mind, and it seemed like an unlikely coincidence. Within a couple of hours of Robert's phone call, Scott had a security consultant at the house to set up surveillance.

Cara arrived home from Miami in the middle of the implementation, and it was pretty easy for Robert to convince her that she and Alex would be safer out of the house for the next few days while he put in additional security, and until they knew for sure that the thief wouldn't return. He suggested that she take Alex to see their parents a couple of weeks early. She agreed without much fuss, making it unnecessary for him to tell her about the background with Raphael.

By one o'clock in the afternoon on Thursday, Robert had a bag packed and was on the highway to Miami. His plan was to stay there until the situation was resolved.

When he got back to the apartment after meeting Scott, Robert spent a few minutes in the master bedroom putting away his clothes and toiletries still in his suitcase from the drive yesterday. As he had told Jasmine last night, it was a great apartment, with views of Miami River and Biscayne Bay, and in the heart of downtown Miami. Looking around at the space, trying to see it with fresh, unattached eyes, Robert couldn't find very much fault with it. The three-bedroom corner unit was spacious and finished with the best materials. The furniture was a little over the top for his tastes, but easily changed. If he was going to spend more time in Miami, it was more than adequate.

Robert let out a deep breath and got ready to leave again. He had several errands to get done and a meeting with his new publicist before he was to pick up Jasmine that evening. He was doing some shopping when Cara called his cell phone after four o'clock to say she and Alex had reached their parents' house in Minneapolis.

"How was your flight?" he asked while walking through the aisles at the grocery store.

"Long, but not bad," she replied. "Alex watched movies for a bit and then slept the rest of the way."

"Good. Was Dad able to pick you up at the airport?"

"Yeah. We're at the house now. He says Mom will be home from work in a couple of hours. Did you know they had renovated most of the house in the spring? It looks great."

"Mom had mentioned it a few months ago. But I didn't think it would be done that quickly," he stated.

"It's pretty much done except for some minor stuff in the bathrooms."

"Good for them," he replied while picking out bananas in the produce section.

"Wait," Cara suddenly said. "Alex wants to say hi."

"Hi, Uncle Rob," his nephew stated as soon as he got on the phone. "Where are you?"

"Hey, Alex. I'm still in Miami. How's Grandpa doing? He must have been happy to see you."

"Grandpa's good. He's on the couch now taking a nap. Can't you hear him snoring?" Alex asked in an exaggerated whisper.

Robert burst out laughing, knowing exactly how loud his dad's snoring could get when he was really tired. They talked for a few more minutes until Alex handed the phone back to his mother.

"How long are you planning to stay?" he asked Cara.

"I'm going to leave Alex here for the rest of the summer, but I've booked a return flight for next weekend. Is that long enough?" she asked, referring to the break-in.

"Yeah, that should be fine. I'll be staying at the Brickell Avenue apartment until then, too," stated Robert. "Listen, Cara, I've been thinking about you and Alex staying with me in Key West, and it doesn't really make sense anymore."

It took her so long to respond that Robert began to wonder if the call had been disconnected.

"What does that mean?" she asked, and he could hear the tension in her voice.

"Well, I haven't really been fair to you, expecting you to give up your life to help me out. Now that I've finished the book, I'm thinking I can manage my calendar myself. Especially since my publicist will be doing most of research and event planning. Plus, you've been spending most of your time in Miami anyway, right? So, you won't have to feel guilty about moving back."

"I see. Well, it sounds like you've made up your mind, Robert. Just like that, you don't want Alex and me to live with you anymore," she stated coldly.

He pinched his nose to prevent his blood pressure from rising. Robert had known it was going to be a difficult conversation, but he still wasn't prepared for the bitterness in his sister's voice.

"Cara, that's not what I'm saying, and you know it. It's been great having you guys stay with me. And you know how much I love Alex, but it's not fair to you."

"Right," she stated sarcastically. "Where are we supposed to go?"

"Anywhere you want, Cara. Maybe you should stay with mom and dad for a bit, decide what you want to do next. Or we can find you guys a nice place in Miami," he suggested calmly.

"It's because of Jasmine, isn't it? Don't bother denying it again because now you're putting her before your family," she spat bitterly.

"Okay, that's enough. I'm not going to keep

having this conversation," Robert finally insisted in a firm voice. "Just think about what I've said. We'll talk about this another time."

Her only response was a click of the phone and then a dial tone.

Chapter 22

A week later, Robert was still in Miami. He and Jasmine were spending almost every evening together and he stayed overnight at her apartment on the weekends.

It was Saturday morning, and when Jasmine woke up, she was alone. Robert had left her about an hour earlier in order to get ready for a book signing in Aventura later on. Her plan was to get to the gym, then meet him at the signing. It was already too late to catch her regular Pilates class, but she decided to take another class later that morning. She freshened up quickly in the bathroom and slipped on a yoga top, comfortable jeans shorts, and flip-flops for the walk to the gym. In her gym bag, she carried additional workout clothes, toiletries, and an outfit to wear afterward.

She was halfway to the fitness center when Robert called her on her cell phone.

"Hi there. I barely heard you leave this morning," she stated with a big smile.

"Sorry about that. You looked so peaceful; it seemed like a shame to wake you up. Did you sleep well?" asked Robert.

"I did, and now I'm on my way to the gym."

"Darn, I was hoping to catch you before you left. Are you coming to Aventura right after your workout or are you going back home?"

"I brought everything with me, so I was going to go straight there. Why?"

"I was thinking that you should just bring enough stuff to stay at my place for the weekend. I'll just drive you home on Monday morning."

"Oh, okay. The gym is just a few blocks from my building, so it's no big deal. It'll just take me a little longer to run home after my workout, that's all."

"Why don't we meet at the apartment instead of the bookstore? I should be done at about one o'clock," he suggested.

"But then I'll miss the book signing," she objected with a frown. "I really wanted to be there."

"Don't worry about it. I would much rather spend the whole weekend together than have you stand around at a boring appearance. And there will be plenty of others over the next few months."

"Okay, if you're sure," she said, relenting.

"Good. So, I'll meet you at my place at around one-thirty. I'll text you the address, and call you a little later in case I'm running late. But Cara is flying in from Minneapolis this morning, so she should be at the apartment by then anyway."

"Alright," she agreed and they hung up.

At the gym, George was at the front desk when she arrived.

"Hey, gorgeous, you missed Mark's class this morning," he stated with a big smile as he swiped her membership card.

"I know; I just couldn't get out of bed," explained Jasmine. "I'm going to take Raven's instead."

"Okay, I'll sign you up.

"Thanks, George."

"Anytime," he replied with a casual wink.

Raven's class was much more focused on toning and core training than the class that Jasmine usually took with Mark. It didn't provide the same intense workout, but left her feeling relaxed and pretty good. It also gave her the opportunity for calm reflection about the ways in which her life was changing.

Jasmine had started the summer fully committed to growing her business and hoping that she would steadily increase her clients enough to have a stable monthly revenue and profits. So far, with the successful networking event and the article in *Miami Weekly*, July was turning into her strongest month yet and there was every indication that August would be even stronger. The volume of new client meetings in the last week made Jasmine wish she already had another matchmaker on staff to manage it. Yvonne was going to post the job on Monday.

Two months ago, the success of Croft Connections was the only priority in her life. Everything else was fairly low on the list, except the well-being of her family. A meaningful relationship wasn't even on the radar, except maybe as something to avoid as a destructive distraction. Now, just weeks later, she was completely overwhelmed by her feelings for Robert. She woke up each day looking forward to his quick notes and phone calls. Their evenings together over the last few days felt natural, and her weekends were now about spending time together with him, instead of just more work.

Jasmine was feeling excited about their future and Robert was giving her signs that he felt the same. For the first time, she felt absolutely ready for what a long-term relationship would bring to her life.

After the gym, Jasmine went back to her apartment as planned and packed an overnight bag along with her laptop, then she took a taxi into downtown Miami. During the ride, she got a text message from Robert.

Sorry Jasmine, it looks like I will be about a couple of minutes late.

No worries. I'll just wait in the lobby for you, she replied.

Cara is at the apartment so she'll let you in, he texted.

Okay.

Jasmine bit the side of her lip trying to decide what to do. It had been several weeks since she had seen Robert's sister. When Cara had returned to Key West from Miami on Independence Day, they had passed each other in the house a couple of times, exchanging only a few polite words. But there was no denying the persistent tension that was between them. It was very obvious that Cara didn't like her, and didn't think Jasmine had a chance for a real relationship with her brother. For weeks after Matthew's wedding, Jasmine had taken the warning seriously, trying to stay as unattached to Robert as possible so she wouldn't get hurt. But it didn't work. He only had to smile at her, make her laugh, or touch her in the slightest way and she would forget everything but the way he made her feel.

Then, as Jasmine and Robert got closer and he shared some of the devastating details of his ill-fated marriage, Cara's warning no longer rang true. Jasmine was not thinking that Cara had deliberately misled her from the beginning, but had no understanding of why she had said what she did.

The taxi ride into Miami was about fifteen minutes long, and dropped Jasmine off on Brickell Avenue in front of the exclusive high-rise building where Robert owned a unit. Looking up at the luxurious complex that advertised a five-star restaurant and full-service spa, she straightened her shoulders and made up her mind to try and talk to Cara again. She used the ride up in the elevator to think about the best approach.

Cara opened the door after the second ring of the doorbell, and she didn't look happy.

"Oh, it's you," she said when her eyes met Jasmine's.

"Hi, Cara," Jasmine replied in a friendly tone even though the other woman had already walked into the apartment. "Did Robert mention that I was coming over?"

"Yeah, he called a little while ago," she replied with a glance over her shoulder, and her eyes landed on the large overnight bag Jasmine carried. "But he didn't say you were moving in."

The comment was laced with heavy sarcasm, but Jasmine chuckled lightly.

"I'm just staying for the weekend. How was your trip to Minnesota?" Jasmine asked.

She followed Cara through the center hallway of the apartment, past the galley kitchen and into the open living and dining area. There was a heavy, marble-top console table against the wall, and Jasmine put her purse on it.

"It was alright. Boring as usual. There is just nothing going on in Minneapolis."

"And your parents? How are they doing?"

"They're doing pretty good."

"Great."

Jasmine watched Cara sit down on the couch in front of the television.

"Well, maybe I'll just put my stuff in Robert's room. Do you mind pointing it out?"

"It's the door to your right," Cara stated, indicating the direction with a tilt of her head.

With a slowly exhaled breath, Jasmine walked away carrying her travel bag. The master bedroom was bigger than she had anticipated, with a full wall of floor-to-ceiling windows and French doors opening out onto the large veranda. There was a king-size bed in the center of the room and a lounge chair by the window, both in an ultra modern, sleek design. The only other furniture was a long media cabinet with a flat-panel television on top.

Jasmine looked around the room and was surprised by the sleek, sparse décor in there and the rest of the apartment, thinking it was the opposite of the furniture at the house in Key West. But then she remembered Robert telling her that the space really reflected his wife's tastes. She put her bag on the chair and walked over to the television. The remote was on top of the cabinet and she used it to turn the TV on.

As she walked away, intending to find the bathroom and explore the rest of the space, Jasmine's attention was caught by a folder on the console. The outside had the words ARCHER INVESTIGATIVE SERVICES, but it was the photo peaking out that made her stop. It only revealed the top of the man's head, but something about the hairline made her slide it out further with her index finger. She recognized him immediately as the guy Cara had been arguing with in Miami the night before Jasmine's birthday.

She stared hard at the picture, trying to understand the relevance of it in that folder. Thinking back to that evening outside of the club again, she was still very certain that this man was trouble. His body language said he was pissed about something, and his anger was clearly directed at Cara.

Now Robert had a picture of the guy as part of some kind of private investigation. Why?

It was an act that was completely against her nature, and Jasmine knew she was crossing the line, but she could not resist opening up the folder to look what was inside. There were several other pictures of the same man, and a couple of documents. Holding her breath, she glanced at the door then back at the contents, reading the details as quickly as possible. What she discovered made her very concerned, particularly for Cara, who could be in some serious trouble.

As carefully as possible, Jasmine put all of the photos and papers back into the investigation folder exactly the way she found them. She then took a deep breath and went back into the living room.

Cara was in the kitchen getting something out of the fridge when Jasmine approached her.

"Cara, can I ask you something?" Jasmine stated in a calm voice.

"*Hmm,*" was the ambiguous response while Cara munched on a handful of green grapes.

"Who was the guy you were arguing with outside of Oceans, a few weekends ago?"

Cara looked at her sharply. Her chewing slowed as she became quite tense.

"What?" she demanded.

"The Friday before Independence Day, outside that club, Oceans, off Biscayne Boulevard," insisted

Jasmine. "I saw you outside and it looked like a pretty heated discussion."

Cara rolled her eyes before responding.

"I don't know what you're talking about, Jasmine," she said dismissively.

Jasmine blinked for a few seconds, completely unprepared for her denial.

"Cara, I know you saw me, too. You looked right at me," she stated evenly.

"And what of it, Jasmine? It's none of your business where I am or who I'm talking to," snapped Cara, her voice heavy with resentment.

"Look, I'm not trying to be nosey, really."

"Yeah, you are. What are you doing anyway? Spying on me?"

"What? Why would I do that?"

"I don't know, Jasmine. You tell me?" demanded Cara, the volume of her voice slowly rising.

Jasmine took a step back, completely confused by the direction the discussion was taking. "Cara, I really don't know what you're insinuating."

"You're trying to cause trouble, aren't you? You act all sweet and polite, but you don't fool me, bitch!" she spat.

"Excuse me?" stammered Jasmine as she moved farther away from the ranting woman in front of her. "What is your problem? I saw that guy yelling at you and he looked like trouble, that's all. Now, Robert thinks he's the one that broke into the house in Key West . . ."

"What?"

Cara looked genuinely surprised, so Jasmine tried again to explain things.

"Robert has a picture of the same guy, Cara, in an investigation report. He thinks it's the person that broke into the house last week."

"You're lying!" Cara snapped back.

"Why would I lie? I'm just trying to help."

"No, it doesn't make any sense. Robert said it was just a random break-in . . ."

"Cara, he hired a private investigator to look into it. It definitely was not random."

"No! No . . . It's a mistake, okay?" she shouted back, now pacing in the kitchen with a hand pressed against her forehead.

Jasmine now had a very bad feeling, but needed to know what was going on.

"His name is Raphael Torres, isn't it? Did you know he robbed your brother?"

"Shut up, you don't know what you're talking about. Okay? You don't know anything!"

"Cara, what's going on? Are you in some kind of trouble? Just tell Robert what . . ."

"No!" she screamed lunging at Jasmine, pushing her back with a hard push to her shoulders. "Just shut your mouth. Don't you dare say a word to Robert. Do you hear me?"

Jasmine was completely unprepared for the physical force of the attack and stumbled backward. Cara seemed fueled by irrational fear and desperation; her eyes looked wild, like a caged animal's.

"Cara, stop it!" begged Jasmine. "Listen to me . . ."

"No! Shut up, just shut your damn mouth!"

Her final shove sent Jasmine flying against the wall across from the kitchen, the back of her head slamming against the hard surface. Dazed from the blow, she tried to catch her footing again, but fell to the side. There was a sickening crack as she fell on the marble top hall table, the side of her head cut open on the sharp edge.

Chapter 23

Robert checked his watch discreetly for the third time in as many minutes. The book signing had been over for almost half an hour, yet people were still waiting to meet him and get his signature in the novels they had purchased. It had been a strong turnout, with each of his current novels selling one hundred copies within two hours. Despite similar success at the event in Atlanta, Robert was surprised by the response.

Finally, the last person in line stepped up to the table holding both novels, and Robert wrote a few words on the front flap of each. There were another few minutes spent wrapping things up as he thanked the bookstore staff for their help. By the time he got to his car, Robert knew he was going to be about forty minutes late to meet Jasmine. He sent her another text message with an update before getting on the road for the drive back to his apartment.

Aventura, a suburb of Miami, was about thirty

minutes to the north. Robert was more than halfway from home when he got a call on his cell phone. He answered using the Bluetooth speakers inside the Range Rover.

"Robert, it's Scott Archer here. Looks like we've located the subject."

"Where?" demanded Robert.

"We haven't found where he's staying. But it looks like he's back in the business of selling party drugs, just changed his territory. He's supposed to be at a party tonight in Fort Lauderdale."

Robert was silent for a few minutes. His first instinct was to confront the punk and make sure he knew he had messed with the wrong man for the second time. But Robert also couldn't ignore the risks. What if something went wrong? How would he explain it all to Jasmine? Maybe it was better to let the police handle it like Scott had advised from the beginning.

"Robert, he's definitely our man, and not very smart," continued Scott. "He's been seen wearing what looks like a gold Rolex."

"Okay, Scott. Thanks for the heads-up. Stay ready, but I'll call you later with how I want to manage it."

They hung up and Robert spent the rest of the drive trying to decide what to do. By the time he got out of the elevator in his building, his mind was made up to call the police and let them deal with the whole mess. Since Raphael obviously still had some of the stolen property, it was likely he would be back in prison pretty quickly like Scott had commented. But there was one small piece of the puzzle that was stopping Robert from calling the Key West detectives right away: Why would this petty dealer risk going all the way to the Keys to break into his house and steal some stuff?

Robert's instincts told him there was more to the story, and it didn't sit well with him not to get the answers. When he finally entered the condo, he was distracted with his thoughts, but then stopped in the foyer as he heard what sounded like moaning. He paused at the front door, which was still slightly open, and listened for a second.

"Oh God, oh God! Please, Jasmine. Wake up . . ."

It was Cara's voice, low and desperate.

"Cara? Jasmine? Is everything okay?" Robert asked with concern as he walked further into the apartment. What he found there made his heart stop.

"Jasmine!" he shouted, running forward.

All he could see was her crumpled form and a pool of bright red blood slowly expanding from somewhere near her head. Cara had been crouched over her, but now straightened as he approached. Her eyes looked terrified.

"Jasmine," he repeated when he was close enough to touch her.

She was lying on her right side and he gently brushed her cheek, hoping that she would hear his voice and open her eyes. But she remained deathly still.

"Robert, it's not my fault," sobbed Cara. "It was an accident, I swear!"

He looked over his shoulder at his sister.

"Cara, what the hell happened?"

"I . . . I . . ."

"Did you call 911?" Robert demanded cutting her off. He was dialing the numbers before she could respond.

"911 emergency. My name is Olivia, how can I assist you?"

"I need an ambulance right away. My girlfriend has fallen and it looks like she hit her head. There's blood and she's not responding to me."

"Okay, sir. Can you give me your address please?"

Robert gave the woman the details.

"Thank you, sir. We will send emergency paramedics right away. They should be there in about five minutes."

"Thank you."

"Sir, what's your girlfriend name?"

"It's Jasmine Croft."

"Okay. Now, can you tell if she is still breathing?" asked the dispatcher.

He froze in that second, and felt panic start to take over. *Is she breathing? Please God, she has to be breathing!*

"Sir, is she breathing?" the voice over the phone repeated.

"Ah, I'm not sure," he whispered, then pressed a shaking hand lightly on Jasmine's back. "Yes, yes! She's breathing."

"Okay. Don't move her, and the medics will be there shortly."

The woman kept him on the phone, advising

Robert of when the emergency response unit had arrived at the building. The uniformed EMTs entered the apartment a few moments later, pulling a narrow gurney. They immediately took charge of the situation while Robert could only stand back and watch. Finally, when he couldn't stand the sight of Jasmine's blood any longer, he turned away as her head was being wrapped with thick gauze to protect the nasty gash on her temple.

He found Cara sitting on the couch in the living room, biting her nails with obvious anxiety.

"Cara, tell me exactly what happened," demanded Robert as he stepped in front of her, his legs spread wide and arms crossed firmly.

"I don't know, Robert. It's not my fault. She attacked me for no reason so I pushed her to try and get away. Then she slipped or something and hit her head. It was an accident, I swear!"

"Wait, wait . . . What do you mean she attacked you? Why? It doesn't make any sense, Cara."

She looked forward avoiding his eyes and rubbing her forehead with the back of her hand.

"Cara! What the hell is going on?" he yelled.

"Alright! Alright," she finally replied, jumping to her feet. "I didn't want to tell you this, Robert, but she's not who you think she is, okay? I think she's involved in something shady, and when I confronted her about it, she attacked me. That's what happened."

Robert could only look at his sister with complete disbelief. Nothing she said made any sense to him.

"What are you talking about?" he finally asked in a voice that was so calm it was chilling.

"I know I should have told you all this a few weeks ago, but I didn't want to hurt you, Robert. After everything you went through with Lakeisha, I wanted to protect you."

"Cara! Tell me everything, now!"

"Okay!" she yelled back, now pacing. "She's been seeing someone else, Robert. And I think it's the same guy that broke into the house."

He had no idea what to expect, but never in his wildest imagination did Robert anticipate those words.

"No," he said simply. "Cara, that's ridiculous."

"Robert, it's true. I saw her with another man with my own eyes, the Friday before the July Fourth weekend. That's what we were fighting about earlier. I told her that I was going to tell you as soon as you got home. And she threatened me, told me that if I didn't keep my mouth shut she would make sure that Alex was home the next time we were robbed."

For several moments after she finished speaking, all Robert could hear was the echo of her words in his head. He stood staring out the window at the beautiful view of the bay, completely frozen with disbelief, breathing with short, sharp puffs of air.

"Robert, I'm sorry. But I knew from the beginning that she was nothing but trouble. I told you that she wasn't right for you."

He raised a hand, silently demanding that she stop talking. Then he walked into his bedroom, grabbed a picture from inside the folder on the TV console and went back into the living room.

"Is this the man you saw her with?" he asked, showing Cara the photo of Raphael Torres.

She looked at the image a long moment before finally nodding. "That's him."

Robert dropped his arm, and the picture slipped out of his fingers, falling silently to the floor. The faint twinge of apprehension at the base of his stomach quickly flared into an intense, crippling pain centered on his heart and radiated through his body in waves. He heard voices, saw Cara's mouth moving but couldn't make out what she was saying. Then someone tapped him on his shoulder. Robert turned around to find one of the EMTs talking to him. They had Jasmine loaded on the gurney and were starting to move her from the apartment.

"Sir, will you be riding with us to the hospital?" the medic repeated.

Everything rushed back to him in that second, snapping him out of his shock.

"No, I'll follow you in my car," he stated, his mind now crystal clear and thinking several steps ahead. "How is she?"

"She's stable, but still unconscious. We've stopped the bleeding, but she'll need stitches."

Robert nodded and started to follow them out.

"Where are you going, Robert?" demanded Cara grabbing his arm to stop him.

"I'm going to the hospital," he told her quietly
"Why? Hasn't she caused enough trouble?"

"Cara, I can't let her go there alone. I have to make sure she's okay. Then, when she's awake, I have some questions for her."

"Robbie, don't even bother. She's just going to lie to you. You can't believe anything she says."

"Look, I'm sorry that you've been dragged into whatever mess is going on here," he told his sister. "I'll call you later."

The minute Robert got into the Range Rover, he called Scott Archer back. "I'm going to Fort Lauderdale," he stated without any preamble. "What time is our friend expected at the party?"

If Scott was surprised by the decision, he didn't say. "Looks like it's going to get started at around nine o'clock tonight. But Raphael probably won't show up until after ten, maybe eleven o'clock. If he's providing the blow, then he'll want to make sure it's in full swing so he has as many customers as possible."

"Right," Robert agreed. "Then we'll meet at ten o'clock. Send me the address by text message."

A few minutes later, he was at the hospital and watching the medics push Jasmine into the building before he parked in the visitor's lot. He found her in an exam room being checked by a doctor. The white bandage around her head was stained with red, but it seemed to have staunched the bleeding. Robert stayed in the back of the room as the emergency staff cleaned the wound and closed up the gash with a string of fine stitches.

"Mr. Rankin?" asked the doctor when they were finished.

"Yes," replied Robert, pushing himself off the wall.

"I'm Dr. Kemp."

"How is she?"

"Well, it was a pretty nasty cut, but she seems stable now. We put in twelve stitches to close up the cut along her temple. She might have a faint scar, but nothing too bad."

Robert let out a deep breath, nodding at the details. "Thank you, doctor. But she's been unconscious for a long time. What does that mean?"

"She's actually sleeping right now. She came to in the ambulance on the way here, but she was in a lot of pain so we gave a sedative. Her vitals are good so we'll just keep an eye on her for a few more hours, maybe overnight."

When the doctor left, Robert moved to stand over Jasmine. She seemed so vulnerable, so fragile that he had to resist the urge to wrap his arms around her. Looking at her face, still so beautiful despite the raw wound, it was impossible to imagine she was capable of the deceit Cara described. The whole thing was so unthinkable and confusing to Robert. How the hell had Jasmine become associated with Raphael? Was it a scheme from the beginning? Or did she meet him afterwards? It just didn't make logical sense.

But the evidence was overwhelming. She had admitted her duplicity to Cara. Now he was left to accept it and walk away. The problem was that Robert had no clue how to do that. It was one thing for him to end his marriage to a woman he never loved and no longer respected. It was another to leave a woman that fulfilled him in ways he never thought possible.

Right now, the idea of cutting Jasmine out of his life felt like cutting off his arm. And if this was to be the last time he saw her, touch her skin, Robert knew deep down that the ache he had for her would never go away.

He sat down by her bed for the next couple of hours, stepping out of the room only to get some water. By six o'clock that evening, Robert realized she may not wake up before he had to leave. Despite the circumstances, it seemed cruel for Jasmine to not have someone beside her when she woke up in the emergency room. He didn't know how to contact her family, so he made the decision to call Maya.

"Robert, this is a surprise," she stated enthusiastically when she answered the phone. "How did our signing go today?"

"Maya, I'm calling about Jasmine," he replied bluntly.

"Jasmine? Why? Is everything okay?" demanded Maya, clearly concerned.

"She's had an accident. I'm with her at the hospital now,"

"What? Oh my God, Robert. What happened?"

Robert gave her the basic facts, leaving out the fight with Cara and other incriminating details.

"I'll be there as soon as I can," Maya promised. "But it might not be for a couple of hours."

"Okay, thanks. I'll be here," Robert promised.

He sat back and waited, using the time to think about how he would get through the night. About an hour later, he felt Jasmine stir. He sat forward as she moved her head slightly and then moaned. Finally, she opened her eyes, blinking as though adjusting to the light.

"Robert?" she whispered in a raspy voice.

He didn't know what to say, couldn't trust his voice.

"Robert, where am I?" she asked as she turned to look at him.

"You're at the hospital," Robert stated simply.

"The hospital? What? Ugh . . ." She tried to move, then froze in obvious pain. "My head hurts . . ."

"Jasmine, you fell and hit your head really hard. They've had to put some stitches in. Do you remember what happened?" he asked in a calm, even tone.

"I don't know. Cara . . . Cara . . ."

She suddenly stopped and looked over at Robert, guilt and shame written all over her face. "Robert, I'm sorry! I should have talked to you first, told you what I knew," whispered Jasmine, her eyes pleading with him.

Robert clenched his fist tight, unable to process what he was hearing. Up until that second, he thought maybe, *maybe* there was some other explanation. He had the hope that he would talk to her, look her in the eyes, and know the whole thing was a big misunderstanding. Now, he felt light-headed from the certainty that she was a lying, cheating bitch.

"Cara was . . ." she tried to continue.

"Don't say another damn word," he spat, standing up. "Why, Jasmine? What did you want from me?"

"What? Robert, what . . . What do you mean?" she asked, closing her eyes and swallowing in obvious pain.

He leaned close to her, fueled by a growing rage that was threatening to overwhelm him.

"Listen to me, and listen to me well. If you ever come near me or my family again, you will regret it. Do you hear me? And I will be delivering that message to Raphael in person."

Jasmine opened her eyes wide, looking up at him with a mix of shock, fear, and confusion. Her mouth was open as she sucked in gulps of air.

"Robert, I said I'm sorry I invaded your privacy, but I was trying to help. I was worried about Cara, that's all," she stammered quickly.

"Shut up! Invaded my privacy?" Robert snickered through clenched teeth. "You got my house robbed, put my family in danger. You made me love you . . ."

The last few words were uttered in a raw whisper as they stared at each other for several intense seconds. Finally, Robert straightened, stepping back from her bed as though needing distance between them.

"Stay away from me," he demanded, then walked away.

"Robert, wait. I don't understand," whimpered Jasmine, but he ignored her words, blocking out the sound of her voice.

Outside her room, Robert didn't know where to go. He walked around in circles, pacing, breathing hard, and trying to hold himself together. Finally, he collapsed in a chair near the waiting area, his head hung low in defeat.

"Robert? Robert?"

It took a few moments for him to register that someone was calling him. When he looked up, Maya stood in front of him, her brows pinched in obvious concern.

"Are you okay? How is Jasmine?" she asked.

Robert stood up. "She's in the room next to the nurses' station," he stated coldly, then walked away.

Chapter 24

After leaving the hospital, Robert went back to the apartment.

"Cara," he shouted after closing the door.

There was no response. He continued down the front hall until he reached the kitchen. His eyes were immediately drawn to the marble console table along the wall, then the tile floor beneath it. The small puddle of Jasmine's blood was now gone. Robert sent a silent thank-you to his sister for taking care of it.

"Cara?" he called out again, but there was still no answer.

He went further into the living area, then the bedroom she used whenever she stayed there. They were both empty, and there was no sign of her luggage or other items. Robert walked back out to the living area and stood in front of the windows, looking out at the view. Finally, he took out his cell phone and called his sister.

There was no answer, so he left a message. "Hey

Cara, it's Robert. I'm back home from the hospital, but you've already left. Did you head back to Key West? Anyway, give me a call. It looks like Jasmine is going to be fine. She's regained consciousness, but needed stitches," he explained smooth, then paused. "Listen, I'm sorry to drag you into this mess. We'll talk later."

He hung up his phone and went back to looking out the window. His mind was filled with so many details, images, memories of Jasmine, all of which just made him more confused and frustrated. After several long minutes, he checked his watch and realized he needed to get in the shower if he was going to meet Scott in Fort Lauderdale as planned.

The party where Raphael was expected was being held in a hotel in Harbor Isles. He and Scott met at the bar in the lobby with a good view of the main entrance. One of Scott's associates was watching the back door from the parking lot.

"Are you sure you want to do this?" asked Scott once they were settled in for about twenty minutes.

"I don't see much choice," Robert told him simply. "This guy is like a cockroach. I want some answers and then I want him gone for good."

Scott smirked a little. "Are we talking gone, *gone*? Or . . ."

Robert chuckled a little.

"Because I may have brought the wrong team for the job," the PI continued.

"Relax, I don't plan on hurting him. I'll just make it worth his while to take his drug enterprise to another part of the state."

At around eleven-fifteen that night, they spotted Raphael walking through the lobby alone. Scott fell in step behind him and followed him into the party as planned. He was going to approach Raphael in the party, and ask to do some business with him. Several minutes later, Robert received a text message.

I'm taking him into the washroom at the back of the club, Scott advised.

Robert immediately made his way into the party and went straight to the men's room. When he entered, there were two other men there beside Raphael and Scott. Raphael was busy looking at himself in the mirror and didn't notice Robert's entrance. Wordlessly, Scott nodded to Robert and then left the room to prevent anyone else from entering. The two other men left as soon as they finished using the facilities.

"Funny running into you here, Raphael," stated Robert as he walked forward to stand behind the other man in front of the sinks.

Raphael froze for a second as their eyes met in the mirror. It took a few seconds but the ex-con's eyes finally widened with recognition. He swung around, looking around the room, presumably for the man he had come in there to sell to.

"Don't worry. This conversation won't take long. You'll have plenty of time to sell your dope when we're done," Robert told him.

"Look, man. I don't know what you want," replied Raphael as he took a step back.

He was wearing a short-sleeved shirt, and the twisted skin of his scarred forearm was clearly visible. So was the gold band wrapped around his wrist.

"Oh, I think you do, Raphael," he replied with a smile. "Nice watch, by the way. Business must be good. How much did the Rolex set you back? Twenty, twenty-five thousand?"

Raphael moved further away from him, throwing his hands up defensively.

"Hey, man. It's just business," the dealer told him, licking his lips nervously.

"Business, eh? See, that's the thing, Raphael. Whatever business you and I had together was finished the last time we talked. So what am I missing?"

"It's not you, bro. I have no beef with you."

Robert laughed out loud this time and took two fast steps toward Raphael until they were practically nose to nose.

"You broke into my house and stole my property. How is this not about me, Raphael?" he demanded in a low whisper. "Or is this about Jasmine?"

"Who?" Raphael shot back, looking confused. "Look, I told you. It was strictly . . ."

"Let's get to the point! I want answers, and I want them now! Why did you steal from me, and what the hell does Jasmine Croft have to do with any of this?" snarled Robert.

"It was a debt, alright? That's all."

"Who's debt? Jasmine's? For what?"

"I told you, I don't know anyone named Jasmine."

"Then who's debt, Raphael? And what does it have to do with me?"

Raphael looked down and took a deep breath. He was obviously nervous at Robert's aggressive presence, but equally apprehensive about whatever information he was hiding.

"I just wanted my money, that's all," he explained when he finally looked up again. "I got out of the pen, and just wanted what was owed to me. I kept my mouth shut for three years, waiting until I was free. That money was my ticket to starting over. I told her that, and she promised me she still had it. But she lied, man. She had spent it all."

"Who?" demanded Robert. "Who, Raphael?"

"Cara."

Robert blinked rapidly, trying to understand. "What? My sister, Cara? What are you talking about?" When Raphael hesitated, Robert lost his patience. "What the hell are you talking about? I want to know everything right now, or that scar on your arm will look like artwork compared to what I'll do to your face. Do you understand?"

Scott stepped inside at that moment. "Ahh, we're starting to get a line out here. We'll need to wrap this up," he advised.

Robert and Raphael eyed each other.

"You're coming with me," Robert explained with a menacing snarl.

As casually as possible, he escorted Raphael out

of the bathroom and then through the party, with Scott bringing up the rear. They stopped at a dimly lit spot outside the hotel near the parking lot.

"Okay, now start talking," demanded Robert. "How the hell do you know my sister?"

The other man swallowed and finally let out a deep breath.

"We go back, alright? We even went out a few times. When she found out I was selling blow on the side, she hooked me up with some people," he explained. "So we had a good thing going for a while. She would make the arrangements and I would provide the goods."

Robert listened intently, pinching the bridge of his nose in an attempted to stay calm. "Then what happened? Why does she owe you money?"

"You happened, that's what. That night when you cut up my arm, we had our biggest deal ever. I had already delivered to the party, and Cara was supposed to collect the money at the end."

Robert grimaced, understanding what Raphael was not saying.

"So she still had your money when you were arrested?"

Raphael nodded.

Robert turned away and looked up at the dark Florida sky.

"What did Lakeisha have to do with all of this?" he finally asked.

"Nothing, she was just a regular customer. Cara introduced us, but then she started coming to me directly for whatever she needed."

When Robert turned back, his eyes met Scott's in the dark. They communicated an understanding.

"And Jasmine?"

"I told you already, I don't know anyone named Jasmine," insisted Raphael. "Look, I told you everything. So, are we square or what?"

"No, no we are not square!" bellowed Robert. "Where's the rest of my stuff that you stole?"

"I pawned it, man. It's gone."

"Good. Consider Cara's debt repaid. But now you owe me, do you understand? You owe me your freedom. Take it and stay clear of me or anyone else I know, including my sister. In fact, I don't want to find out that you're anywhere south of Fort Lauderdale or I guarantee you'll be back in prison before you can blink. Are we clear?"

Raphael nodded vigorously, his Adam's apple bobbing up and down.

"My good friend here will be watching you," Robert added with a head nod toward Scott. "Just in case you forget what's at stake."

He and Scott walked away, leaving Raphael standing in the shadow, contemplating his future.

The full force of everything revealed that night did not hit Robert until he was driving back to Miami. It was almost one o'clock in the morning, and he had no clue what to do. About anything. He felt completely helpless and frustrated. It was as though there was a world that existed around him that he didn't even know about. How the hell had he not seen what Cara was into back then? How could she hide this all from him, living with him since Lakeisha died?

Then came the anger. Robert ran through all the details from Raphael, looping together these new details with what he thought he knew. The story it painted was so ugly it made him nauseous. It was even worse than Lakeisha's betrayal. His sister, the person that he had relied on the most during the worst time of his life, had played an active part in the destruction of his life.

If it was only about Lakeisha's drug abuse, Robert could maybe rationalize Cara's role in it. It happened several years ago, and his wife was an adult and made her own choices. But when he thought about the robbery to his house and threat she brought into Alex's life, her behavior was unforgivable.

Then there was Jasmine, lying in a hospital bed with twelve stitches to her beautiful face and Robert had no idea what had happened in the apartment. But he was now certain that his sister had spun a web of vicious lies to blame Jasmine and ensure he cut her out of his life.

More details about the events of the day flooded his mind, including the way he had treated Jasmine and the things he'd said to her in the hospital. Robert was then filled with gut-wrenching remorse and a fear so strong he could taste it. How was he going to be able to apologize to Jasmine for Cara's behavior? What could he possibly say to justify the way he behaved? And what if the damage he had done was so severe it was irreparable?

It was the middle of the night, but he could not stop himself from taking the exit off the highway toward the hospital. He parked in the visitors' section for the emergency department. But even as he walked into the quiet building and headed toward the examining room where they had put Jasmine, he had no idea what he was going to say to her. He only wanted to make sure she was okay, and be close to her in case she needed anything. Hopefully, once she was clearly on the mend, they could talk.

He passed the nurses' station and walked into Jasmine's room, only to find it empty. Robert stood there for a few seconds, and looked around, trying to understand where she may have gone. Finally, he went back out into the hallway and waited until he found a nurse.

"Can I help you, sir?"

He turned around to see an older woman walking toward him. Her pale skin accentuated the dark circles under her eyes, the obvious result of working through the night.

"Yes, please. I'm trying to locate a patient that was brought in at about three o'clock this afternoon. Her name is Jasmine Croft. She had a head injury."

"Let me check the computer," the nurse stated. "I didn't start my shift until midnight."

Robert watched her actions, trying hard to hide his anxiety.

"Here you go . . . It looks like she was admitted into a hospital room for observation through the night."

"Thank you," he stated. "Can you tell me what room?"

"Sir, it's the middle of the night. Visiting hours are from nine AM to eight PM. Come back in the morning, and the information desk in the main lobby will be able to help you." She dismissed him by walking away.

Robert took a deep breath, reluctantly accepting that he had no choice but to do as she suggested. He walked back to his car and drove home to the apartment. His plan was to return to the hospital in the morning with a clearer mind, and bring Jasmine a change of clothes and whatever else she may need. Until then, he could only try and get some sleep.

Chapter 25

Jasmine read the message on her phone and then tossed it on the coffee table of her apartment.

"You know you can't just ignore him forever," Maya stated as she stood across from her in the living room.

"Sure I can," whispered Jasmine as she lay down on the sofa next to where Yvonne sat.

It was Monday morning, sometime after ten o'clock, and Jasmine had just made her way downstairs after a sleepless night. The hospital had discharged her on Sunday afternoon with prescription painkillers and instructions on how to care for her wound until the stitches were removed a week later. Maya and Gloria, Jasmine's mom, were with her at the time and helped her get back home. Gloria stayed the night, sleeping on her daughter's couch, and Maya returned the next morning. Yvonne and Madison arrived soon after and they were all in Jasmine's living room when she finally woke up.

Her mom was in the kitchen getting her a glass of water so she could take another dose of pills to dull the pain in her head. Madison was perched on the arm of a chair next to the sofa.

"Jasmine, you should have seen him yesterday. He's in pretty bad shape," continued Maya. "I'm not saying you have to forgive him, but at least hear what he has to say."

Jasmine closed her eyes, not bothering to respond to Maya, and hoping her friend would take the hint to stop talking about it. She only lifted her head to take the medication her mom brought.

"Maya, I know he's your client and you think he's a good guy, but he has no right to expect Jasmine to talk to him ever again," stated Madie, her arms folded aggressively. "Look what his sister did to her. If I were you, Jasmine, I would block his number from my phone. After the things he said to you, he doesn't deserve the time of day."

"Don't you think that's a little harsh, Madison?" Yvonne replied. "His sister is obviously crazy, and he made a mistake in believing her. But he knows that now. It can't hurt to at least talk to him."

Jasmine covered her closed eyes with her arm, wishing they would all just stop talking about it.

"I'm sorry, I think the way he treated Jasmine was unforgivable," Madison insisted. "What happened to trust and respect? The minute someone said something bad about Jasmine, he believed it and turned on her. And while she was in the emergency room!"

"It's not that black and white, Madison," replied

Maya. "There's a lot more to it than that. Robert has been through a lot over the last few years. It's obviously made it hard for him to trust someone new."

"Well, that's his problem, not Jasmine's."

"Okay, ladies, let's give it a rest," Jasmine heard her mom finally say. "Jay doesn't need to make any decision right now. She needs to get better first, then she can decide what she wants to do. Okay?"

The doorbell to the apartment rang before the other women could respond. Jasmine opened her eyes again when she heard her sister's voice. She tried to sit up, but it only made her head start pounding again.

"Hey, sis," Jennifer stated softly a few moments later as she crouched down on the floor in front of the sofa so she could give Jasmine a gentle hug. "How are you feeling?"

"Not great," whispered Jasmine. "You didn't have to come all the way down here, Jennifer."

"Of course I did, silly."

Jasmine smiled. "Where are the kids?"

"I left them in Jacksonville. They're at summer camp in the day anyway, and I just told Ted that I was taking a week off to be with you. So, he's going to have to take care of the kids for a change."

"Wow. What did he say?" Jasmine asked.

Her sister shrugged and grinned a little. "He said 'no problem'."

Jasmine could not help smiling, even though it looked more like a grimace. Then she closed her eyes again and tried to block out the constant chatter. Eventually, the codeine in the pills did it for her, and she fell into a deep sleep. Three and a half hours later, she woke up, still lying on the couch, and with a blanket thrown over her.

It was blessedly quiet, except for the soft tap of computer keys from Yvonne's laptop.

"Where is everyone?" she asked her assistant who was now sitting in the chair beside her, working away.

Yvonne looked up, surprised. "Hey, you're awake. How are you feeling?"

Jasmine raised her head to test the level of pain. "Better. Are you the only one here?" she asked.

"Yeah, Madie and Maya went to work. Your mom and sister just left to do some grocery shopping. Do you need anything?"

"*Hmm.* No, thank you. I think I'm okay for now," replied Jasmine, moving slowly to sit upright. "How bad is it?"

She pointed to the computer, referring to her very busy calendar that now had to be completely cleared for at least a week, maybe two.

"Don't get mad, Jasmine. But I have an idea," Yvonne stated with a mixture of excitement and apprehension. "I was going to talk to you once I got the job posted."

"What?" prompted Jasmine.

"I really want the opportunity to be the new matchmaker. I know I've only worked here for about six months, but I know I would be good at it. With some training, of course," she rushed to add. "For example, instead of canceling all your new client interviews this week, why don't I go instead? Maybe we can develop a script or checklist of questions I should ask. Then you can help me with the matching."

"Yvonne, I didn't know you had any interest in the position. Why didn't you say something sooner? We could have worked something out," insisted Jasmine.

"Honestly, I didn't want you to feel as though I wasn't happy in my current role. I am! I really like the idea of booking more events and being involved in managing the Web site. But I also think I would be really good at bringing in our new clients."

Jasmine looked at the young, energetic woman who had become essential to the day-to-day management of her tiny business, and tried to envision her working directly with their customers. It wasn't hard to do. Yvonne had the right presentation skills and positive personality. Beyond that, she also deserved the chance to try it.

"Okay, Yvonne. Let's give it a shot," Jasmine finally stated.

"Really? Oh, Jasmine! That is great! I can't tell you how much I appreciate the opportunity," she replied, grinning broadly.

Her enthusiasm was infectious, and Jasmine smiled also. The painkillers were still working, and she only felt the slightest pinch at her injured temple.

"It is a really good idea. I'm just annoyed that I didn't think of it myself," added Jasmine. "So,

I guess that means I need to find myself another assistant."

Yvonne giggled.

They worked together for another hour, reviewing the clients that Yvonne would end up meeting that week. Jasmine also helped her create a thorough list of questions she should ask to create a strong client profile and really understand the key aspects of their ideal mate. They stopped to take a break when Jasmine's head started to ache again. Yvonne went into the kitchen to get the pain medication and some water. When she returned, Jasmine was looking at the phone.

"Why don't you just call him? Or at least reply to one of his text messages?"

Jasmine put the phone down again. She took the pills out of Yvonne's hand and swallowed them with a long sip from the glass.

"It was really good to see you so happy over the last few weeks," continued Yvonne. "It was like you had found the exact thing that you were trying to help everyone else find. And I don't just mean our clients, Jasmine. You're always so ready to help your friends and family find happiness in a relationship. Yet you didn't put any attention into your own love life."

"What are you talking about?" Jasmine mumbled.

Yvonne shrugged. "Before you met Robert Rankin, had you ever been in love?"

The question caught Jasmine by surprise. She looked over at Yvonne, a little uncomfortable with how perceptive the younger woman seemed to be.

"You hadn't, had you?" persisted Yvonne. "Why?"

Jasmine looked away, thinking about how she could respond. It was a question she had asked herself before, particularly once she was spending all of her time finding love for others.

"I don't know, Yvonne. It just never happened for me."

"Do you know what I think?"

"I'm sure you're going to tell me," replied Jasmine with an amused smirk.

"I'm serious, Jasmine. I think you want love to be a rational, logical choice. Like, when you meet a man with all the right credentials and attributes, then you will fall in love with him."

"And? What's wrong with that?"

"Jasmine,"—Yvonne spoke as though talking to a child—"falling in love is not a choice or a factor in a formula. It's a feeling. And sometimes, it's irrational and uncontrollable."

But Jasmine was shaking her head gently in disagreement. "No, I'm sorry. Isn't that what women say when they stay with men that beat them or cheat on them? 'But I love him!' I don't buy it. How can you love someone that treats you badly?"

"That's exactly what I'm saying. If love was a logical decision, why would anyone fall for someone who isn't exactly what they were looking for?" Yvonne shot back with a cheeky grin. "It's all about that 'spark,' that's why. Don't roll your eyes at me. Are you saying that there isn't something intangible and electric between you and Robert? Or does he just look good on paper?"

"Okay, Yvonne. What exactly is your point?"

"My point is that you thought you fell in love with Robert Rankin because he had the right profile. Then, on Saturday, he screwed up. He's not perfect and parts of his life are a mess. So you don't want to call him back because you no longer want to be in love with him. Why would you choose someone who didn't trust you and said horrible things to you?"

Jasmine didn't know what to say. She looked out at the view from the balcony doors, wishing she could make a joke or dismiss Yvonne's words as ridiculous. But what she really wanted to do was cry. Her eyes burned as they gathered moisture. Jasmine blinked rapidly, but was unable to stop the tears from pouring down her face.

"Just call him, Jasmine," pressed Yvonne.

"I can't," she whispered back, covering her face. "I can't!"

Yvonne sat beside her on the sofa and wrapped a comforting arm around Jasmine's back. They sat in silence for several minutes until the tears finally dried up.

"Do you know what else I noticed?" Yvonne added.

"What?" asked Jasmine, clearly reluctant to hear it.

"You didn't deny your feelings for him."

Jasmine snorted.

"I'm telling you, Jasmine. I'm going to be *so* good at this matchmaking thing!"

The conversation coupled with the pills knocked Jasmine out. She stretched out on the sofa again, covering herself with the blanket while Yvonne went back to work. She was in a deep sleep before her mom and sister returned from the grocery store.

By the end of the week, Jasmine was almost starting to feel like her old self. The headaches were less severe and the prescription painrelievers were no longer needed. She stopped napping during the day and was finally able to sleep through the night. The gash at her temple was still bruised but less swollen and raw. Jasmine was encouraged about the healing so far and hopeful there would be minimal scaring.

Gloria was only able to get out of work for a couple of days and went home Tuesday evening, but called every day to check up on Jasmine, promising to come back on the weekend. Jennifer, on the other hand, had plenty of unused vacation time and decided to stay with Jasmine in Miami Beach until the weekend. It gave the sisters plenty of time to talk, something they hadn't done much of recently.

As planned, Yvonne started seeing a few of their clients in her new role as a matchmaker, or what Jasmine had titled Connections Consultant. The first couple meetings were a little rough, requiring some follow-up with the clients to get information Yvonne missed in the meeting. But, overall, Jasmine was pleased with the progress. Now, she only had to find a strong assistant to help them with everything else. They had reached out to a couple of placement agencies in the area, and by Friday, there were four candidates that looked good enough to interview.

That morning, Jasmine was upstairs getting dressed after her shower. She had slept later than planned, still feeling a little more lethargic than usual. Yvonne had a meeting booked first thing, but planned to be in the office by eleven o'clock to help with the candidate interviews. Jennifer was already downstairs getting ready to head out for some errands. She was driving back to St. Petersburg and wanted to pick up a few things for her kids.

When the doorbell rang unexpectedly, Jasmine looked at the clock and wondered who it could be at nine-thirty in the morning. She quickly finished getting dressed, anticipating that it was either Maya or Madison stopping in to check up on her.

As she descended the stairs from her loft bedroom, Jasmine looked around the living room, but no one was there. It wasn't until she walked over to the kitchen and the front hallway that she found Jennifer by the front door about to leave. Beside her was the last person Jasmine expected to see standing in her home, looking like a welcomed visitor.

Chapter 26

While Jasmine spent the week slowly mending, Robert felt like everything around him was quickly deteriorating.

When faced with a problem or challenge, his natural instinct was to confront it head-on. It was the same aspect of his character that enabled him to face down the best shooters in professional hockey without hesitation. Yet, since he drove home from Fort Lauderdale late Saturday night, Robert had not been able to resolve anything about the drama that had become his life. He felt completely handcuffed and helpless.

At first, all he could think about was Jasmine. If he could be certain she was going to be okay, then he could deal with everything else with a clear head. So, as planned, he headed back to the hospital Sunday morning, this time bringing her purse and overnight bag with him.

When he walked into her room, he found her

curled up in the bed still sleeping soundly. Robert put her things in the small closet, then sat in the chair next to her and waited. Over ninety minutes later, after the breakfast cart had come and gone, Jasmine still slept. During that time, a nurse came into the room to check up on her. Robert took the opportunity to ask as many questions as possible about her injury and any potential complications. But once the nurse realized he was not a relative, she would only tell him that Jasmine was doing better.

Finally, he stood up to stretch his legs, and decided to get a cup of coffee from the café he had seen on the first floor. He was getting into the elevator when Maya stepped out.

"Robert!" she stated with obvious surprise. "What are you doing here?"

"Hey, Maya. I came to see how she's doing," he told her in a tired voice.

"Is she awake? How is she feeling?"

He shook his head. "No. I've been here since about eight o'clock and she hasn't woken up yet. But the nurse said she's doing better."

Beside the elevators there was a small waiting lounge. Maya looked over to it, then gestured to Robert that he should go with her.

"Do you want to tell me what's going on?" she asked pointedly once they were sitting beside each other.

He let out a deep, long breath, then let his head fall forward.

"Robert? Because Jasmine said Cara attacked her at your apartment. Then you came to the hospital and broke up with her."

"Maya, I don't even know where to begin," he told her.

"Is it true? Did your sister really assault Jasmine? And for what possible reason?" Maya pressed.

"I don't know; I wasn't there. I arrived home to find her on the floor bleeding."

"Well, what did Cara say?"

He sighed again. Despite everything, the old instinct to protect his sibling was still there. It was so hard to say the words out loud, knowing Cara would have to face the consequences. "She said Jasmine attacked her and she pushed back. And that's how Jasmine fell and hit her head."

"What? That's ridiculous! Jasmine would never hurt anyone," she insisted. "Is that why you broke up with her, Robert? You believe Cara's story?"

His silence was so incriminating, that Maya got to her feet to stand in front of him.

"The last thing Jasmine told me last night was that it was over between you two. I told her that it was just a misunderstanding, that there must be some explanation for why you said the things you did to her. But I see now that the explanation is that you are an absolute idiot." She spat the last few words, then turned to walk away.

"Wait, Maya!" begged Robert, leaping forward to grab her arm. "It's not like that."

"Let go of me," she demanded through clenched teeth.

"Okay, okay. But please, just hear me out for a minute. It's not that simple."

Maya looked at him with obvious disappointment. "I'm listening."

"Honestly, I didn't really believe Cara's version of what happened. But when I spoke to Jasmine in the emergency room, she apologized, said something about hiding something from me and invading my privacy. In that moment, it sounded like she was admitting to the things that Cara told me about her. I just reacted, saying some really nasty things."

They looked at each other for a few seconds.

"Look, I know I made a huge mistake. I knew it didn't make sense from the beginning. But I'm just trying to figure out what really happened. Did Jasmine tell you anything?"

Maya shook her head. "You must know her by now, Robert. She's keeping the details to herself. All she said was that Cara got very angry about something and pushed her. She remembers hitting the wall, and that's it."

Robert threw back his head, wanting to scream with frustration. Somewhere between the load of crap his sister had told him and Jasmine's cryptic explanation lay the truth. Cara obviously lied about Jasmine's involvement with Raphael in order to hide her own guilt, but was everything she said untrue?

"I have to ask you something, Maya, and please

just be completely honest with me. The night before Jasmine's birthday, when you guys went out, did you see her with another man?"

"What?"

"I know that sounds pretty possessive, considering the circumstance. But it's important, okay?"

"No, absolutely not. I was with her all night, Robert. We even took a cab back to Miami Beach together. There was no other man."

It was exactly what he expected her to say, because he knew from the beginning that Jasmine wasn't that type of woman. That was until Cara's words and his own blind loyalty to his sister had allowed a grain of doubt to enter his mind.

"Are you going to tell me what's really going on?" insisted Maya.

He sat back down, feeling emotionally exhausted. Sensing his pain, she joined him again, and put a supporting hand on his knee. Robert wanted to tell her everything, purge himself of the sickening reality that was swirling around in his head and heart. But those protective instincts were hard to overcome. So, he kept the darkest facts to himself.

"It appears that my sister deliberately lied right to my face, accusing Jasmine of things that she knew would make me end the relationship. I knew Cara didn't really like Jasmine from the beginning, but I guess I underestimated how much."

"Is that surprising, Robert? I don't know Cara too well, but it looks to me as though she had a pretty good arrangement up to now. A house on the water, condo in the city, and the freedom to come and go as she pleases. She even got you to hire a housekeeper to act as a nanny for her son," Maya stated bluntly. "I know you tell yourself that she is working for you, helping you out, but do you really believe that? Did you ever ask yourself what she would do if you met a woman, maybe got married again? She would have to get a real job, give up her socialite lifestyle, and take care of her son. That's why she doesn't like Jasmine."

Robert was starting to wonder if everyone around him had seen the truth about Cara living with him while he was blindly in the dark.

"Do you think she will forgive me?" he finally asked.

"Jasmine? I don't know, to be honest. You broke her heart, Robert. She's not the type of woman to give you the chance to do it twice."

It was the truth and it hurt, but he wasn't going to back away because of it.

"We should go check on her now. She's probably awake," he finally suggested.

As he predicted, Jasmine was sitting up in bed while a nurse was doing a routine check of her vitals. Even wearing a hospital gown, and looking bleary with her hair tousled around her, Robert thought she was beautiful. He only wanted to pull her into his arms and hold her close, but the look on her face when she saw him halted him in his tracks in the doorway.

Jasmine stared at him hard for a moment, then turned to Maya who was now standing by the bed.

"What is he doing here?" she demanded in a voice just above a whisper.

"Hey there, we both just wanted to see how you're doing," explained Maya in a soothing tone.

"Make him leave," Jasmine begged with her eyes fixed earnestly on her friend. "Please, Maya?"

Maya looked over at him, and Robert read exactly what she was trying to say. Now was not the time for explanations. If his presence was going to upset Jasmine, he should go.

"I brought the stuff you left at my apartment. It's in the closet," he told them both quickly.

Jasmine ignored him, and Maya lowered her brows disapprovingly. Feeling awkward and inept, he left, and it was a very lonely drive home.

When he walked into the apartment, he was acutely aware that he had not heard back from Cara since leaving her that update message the day before. Robert walked over to the living room window and looked down at the streets below. There was no doubt that he was going to have to confront her about everything he had found out, and he was absolutely certain it was going to be one of the most difficult conversations he'd ever had. But Robert knew it was better to wait until he had a cooler head. Right now, he felt such a sense of betrayal that it was choking him. If he were to speak to his sister at that moment, there would be no holding back. And there was a strong possibility that their relationship would not survive it.

It took a real effort, but Robert went about his day as he had planned prior to Jasmine's injury. Earlier in the week, he had hired an interior designer to help him redo the apartment, and he had arranged for her to come by in the afternoon for couple of hours. It was one of the reasons he had suggested to Jasmine that they spend the weekend at the condo. Robert wanted to get her thoughts on the project, and assumed she would enjoy being part of the process. Though the designer had great ideas, and he signed off on a plan, it wasn't quite as enjoyable without Jasmine there.

The rest of the week was much the same, with Robert doing all the everyday tasks he could think of, including trying to decide on the title for his third novel. He had submitted the manuscript as UNTITLED, but he was going to have to decide on something soon.

Robert also spent a good amount of his time reorganizing his life and thinking about how he would get everything done without Cara's help. As he had told his sister prior to the incident with Jasmine, if his publicist took care of all his marketing and events, everything else was pretty manageable as long has he stayed on top of his calendar. Mary's role was also something to think about, particularly once he knew what would happen with Cara, and therefore Alex in particular.

Robert managed to stay busy enough not to call Jasmine or try to see her. Maya provided a brief update on her recovery by sending him a quick note when she was discharged from the hospital, then later in the week to say she was starting to feel better. He was very grateful for the information, but also very aware that despite their very good professional relationship, Maya's primary loyalty in this situation was to her friend. So he didn't press for anything more.

His one indulgence was the text messages that he continued to send to Jasmine. Like he did from the beginning of their relationship, every day before noon, he sent her a quick note. Robert did not want to be intrusive or disrespectful of her wish not to talk to him, so he kept them very brief. He only wanted to convey that he was thinking about her. On Monday, the text simply said he was glad she was home. On Tuesday, he noted that he hoped she got lots of rest, and Wednesday he asked if her wound was healing well. Thursday's message was: I'm sorry for everything that happened.

Jasmine didn't respond to any of them. While he was disappointed, Robert was not surprised. His actions had led her to believe that he didn't trust her, so it was understandable that she no longer trusted him. But he wasn't going anywhere. He had all the time in the world to prove his feelings to her.

As for his sister, by Wednesday Robert was ready for their talk. But Cara never returned his phone call and tracking her down was proving to be difficult. Scott Archer's surveillance showed that she had gone back to Key West on Saturday, but then left again on Monday. There was no sign of her since.

Robert called his parents, but though Cara had called them earlier in the week to speak to Alex, they didn't know where she was. He called Matthew and got a similar response. Robert didn't want to upset or worry them, so he didn't tell them anything about what had happened over the last few days. And, since Cara was well known for taking off with little notice or details, the rest of the family was unconcerned with her absence, or by Robert's attempts to find her.

Now that he knew more about her secret lifestyle, it did cross Robert's mind that she may be in some other kind of trouble. He toyed with the idea of getting Scott's team to track her down, but dismissed the idea pretty quickly. It was time to let Cara live her life without any involvement on his part. Robert was just going to have to wait until she reappeared.

Chapter 27

Jasmine was completely shocked to find Cara Rankin standing in her apartment. It took a moment to recover, and the two women eyed each other, clearly unsure about what direction the reunion could go. Jennifer seemed oblivious to the tension that filled the tiny space in front of the door.

"Okay, Jay, I will be back later this afternoon," her sister announced with a warm smile.

"Sure," replied Jasmine evenly. "Take your time."

"Good-bye," Jennifer stated politely to Cara, obviously unaware of who she was.

Cara replied with the same farewell in a voice just above a whisper. Then Jasmine's sister was gone, and the other two women were alone. Acutely aware of how close they were standing, and how volatile Cara could be, Jasmine took a step back toward the open area of the apartment.

"What do you want?" she finally demanded.

"I'm sorry. I know that it's not right for me to

just show up like this," Cara stated in a humble tone. "But I really needed to see you."

"Why? Haven't you done enough damage? What could you possibly have to say to me that I would have any interest in hearing?" sneered Jasmine.

"You're right. I have . . ." she admitted, then stepped forward casually.

Her sudden movement caused Jasmine to flinch with alarm, then throw her arms up defensively.

"Stay away from me!" she exclaimed.

Cara's eyes went wide, and she shook her head with silent denial.

As Jasmine stood there, breathing hard and staring at this woman who had deliberately destroyed all the promise and potential she had for a life with Robert, she realized that there was no need to be accommodating or polite. This bitch had no right to step foot in her space and make her feel threatened.

"Get out," Jasmine finally stated, each word punctuated and dripping with disgust.

It was Cara's turn to step back. "Jasmine, I don't want to cause any trouble. Really."

"Get out!"

"Okay, okay. I'm sorry. This was a bad idea."

Cara turned slightly for the door, but Jasmine reached out and grabbed her arm. "You're damn right it was a bad idea, Cara! Do you have any idea what you've done? You ruined everything! Robert and I were perfect, and you ruined that. Why, Cara? Forget me. Why would you do that to your brother?"

"I . . . I . . ." stammered Cara, blinking at the rapid-fire verbal attack.

"What kind of woman would treat her flesh and blood that way? After everything Robert has done for you?"

"I know I screwed up, okay," Cara finally spat. "But it wasn't like that."

"What? Are you for real? What is it like exactly to have your brother's house robbed and deliberately destroy his relationship? It's a concept that I can't grasp, but maybe I just don't understand it. So explain it to me, Cara."

"I didn't know Raphael robbed the house, Jasmine. Not until you told me. I swear!"

"Really? And your reaction to the news was to attack me?" quizzed Jasmine sarcastically.

"I panicked, that's all! But then you slipped . . . You have to believe that I didn't mean to hurt you."

"I didn't slip! You pushed me, Cara. So don't you dare pretend it was just a little accident. You're lucky I don't have you charged with assault."

"I know, I know. It's no excuse. You were threatening to tell Robert about Raphael . . . I just wanted you stay out of it."

"Do you really expect me to believe you had nothing to do with the break-in? It's a coincidence that your acquaintance happens to break into your brother's house miles and miles away?"

Cara bowed her head, clearly uncomfortable to be under scrutiny and attack.

"I owed him money," she whispered. "It was a

long time ago. He went to jail and I guess I just put it out of my mind. Then he showed up, demanding his money, threatening me . . . It was twenty thousand dollars. I don't have that kind of cash."

"Why didn't you just go to Robert?" Jasmine asked.

"I couldn't. I just couldn't let him find out . . . I was afraid he would hate me."

Jasmine looked at the pathetic woman in front of her, so wrapped up in her own problems that she would destroy everything around her.

"Look, all this is really none of my business," Jasmine finally stated, suddenly feeling exhausted. "I don't know what you want from me, and I don't really care."

She stepped forward, and turned the knob on the front door, blatantly suggesting it was time for Cara to leave.

"Jasmine, I didn't come here to explain things. I know I don't deserve your forgiveness," Cara said in a quiet, defeated voice. "I only wanted to give you this."

Jasmine watched suspiciously as the other woman reached into her purse and took out a piece of paper folded in thirds, like a letter. She then swung the door wide open and stood beside it, ignoring Cara's hand still extended with the note pinched between her fingers.

It took a few seconds, but Cara finally walked out of the apartment. But as she passed Jasmine, she made one last appeal. "Take it, Jasmine. It's important."

Jasmine rolled her eyes, but took the letter. She

then slammed the door closed once Cara cleared the threshold. As she walked aimlessly back to the living room, looking around, she tried to remember what her agenda for the day had been before the unexpected visit. But her brain was foggy. Nothing was registering and Jasmine finally sat limply at the bottom of the stairs. The view of the Atlantic Ocean was stretched out in endless blue, but Jasmine didn't see it.

In all of her daydreams about what she would say to Cara Rankin if she ever saw her again, there was the expectation that she would feel so much better afterward. That by venting all of the anger and resentment she felt, Jasmine would be purged of it. Now that it had actually happened, some of what she had expected was accurate. It had felt very good to look Robert's sister in the eye and tell her bluntly what a horrible person she was. But what Jasmine hadn't expected was that once she vented and the anger lessened, it would then just be replaced by aching sadness.

She was still sitting on the stairs when Yvonne arrived for work. Jasmine barely had time to stand up and move to the living area, pretending to be busy so her employee wouldn't catch her wasting even more time looking sad and forlorn. She tossed the paper that Cara had given her on the coffee table and forgot about it.

"Hey, are we all set for the interviews?" Yvonne asked enthusiastically as she walked into the living room.

"Hey, Yvonne. I think so. The first person is

expected in about ten minutes," replied Jasmine with a pleasant smile that she hoped didn't appear forced. "How was the client meeting?"

Yvonne grimaced. "It went okay, I guess. I didn't walk away with a firm commitment, but I think I can still work it."

They then used the time before the first of the agency candidates arrived to discuss the assistant position. Two hours later, they were comparing notes about how disappointing all the candidates had been so far. When the last person rang the doorbell, Jasmine had already lost hope, and was thinking about the feedback she would provide to the placement firm to improve the next batch of interviews.

She was reviewing the information for their final candidate while Yvonne went to let him in. Though she clearly saw the name printed and the experience outlined on the resume, Jasmine was still completely surprised when George walked in, looking as beautiful as he always did at the front desk of the gym.

Jasmine stood up. "George? What are you doing here?" she asked stupidly.

She then looked down at the resume in her hand, titled GEORGE O'TOOLE, and back up at him.

"Hi, Jasmine, how are you?" he asked as he walked up to her with his hand extended politely.

She shook it, still trying to gather her wits.

"How do you guys know each other?" Yvonne asked, looking back and forth between them.

"George works at my gym," explained Jasmine briefly. "You're still there, right?"

She had just seen him there one week ago, but as Jasmine well knew, a lot can change in a very short amount of time.

"Yes, I am. But I've been looking for something more nine-to-five. So when the recruiter at the staffing company mentioned you were looking for an assistant, I wanted to interview for it. I hope you don't mind." he asked Jasmine.

"No, not at all," she replied, slowly warming up to the idea. "Have a seat, and tell us about why you're interested in the position."

Jasmine sat in one of the chairs by the patio doors, while George and Yvonne sat beside each other on the sofa.

"Well, I'm halfway through my degree in kinesiology, and I've been taking it part-time. But the irregular hours at the gym make it hard for me to register for the classes I need. So, I'm hoping that a job with regular hours during the day would allow me to finish school at night. That, and I read an article a few weeks back that said your company was doing really well, providing a new approach to the old tradition of matchmaking," he told them with a charming smile. "It sounded interesting."

Jasmine smiled back, seeing a little ray of sunshine in an otherwise depressing week. As they continued the interview, she tried several times to catch Yvonne's eye and give the younger woman some sort of discreet signal that George was looking more and more like the right fit. But her new Connections Consultant seemed transfixed by his clear green eyes and remarkable good looks, and was unable to look away from him.

"So what did you think?" she asked Yvonne after the interview.

They were sitting beside each other with all the resumes laid out on the coffee table.

"Well, we know the first three candidates are a no. None of them had any personality, not even if you combined them all together. So that really leaves George."

Jasmine smirked, amused that Yvonne was suggesting that he was the right candidate by default.

"So, let's talk about George, then," Jasmine suggested.

"Okay. Well, I liked his enthusiasm. He's very personable, seems easy to get along with. And he's obviously very smart, right?"

Jasmine nodded in agreement. "But is he too gorgeous?" she asked Yvonne.

"What?"

"Yvonne, come on. He's actually painful to look at," quipped Jasmine. "And that's in work clothes. I've see him in only shorts and a tank top. Having him around all day with his perfectness may end up being a little distracting."

"Jasmine, that's ridiculous," scoffed Yvonne. "Yes, I admit he's unusually attractive. But, so what? You're a very professional woman. I'm sure you'll be able to control yourself."

Jasmine snorted, then started to chuckle. "Please,

Yvonne. I'm not worried about me. He's a college kid, nineteen, maybe twenty, years old. Plus, I'm not the one with a puddle of drool staining my blouse."

She then laughed harder when Yvonne instinctively looked down at her top, inspecting it for stains.

"Don't be ridiculous," Yvonne retorted, putting her nose in the air. "And I don't think he's that young. I would say he's at least twenty-two."

"Really, isn't that also your age?"

Jasmine continued to tease Yvonne for some time after, but by midafternoon, there was no question that George O'Toole was going to be their new assistant, if he wanted the job. While Jasmine was on the phone with the placement agency to negotiate salary and other details, Yvonne started to straighten up the living room, and gather all the resumes into a pile.

"Okay, it looks like George is our man," she announced after hanging up the phone.

When she looked from her notes, it was to find Yvonne with a puzzled look on her face, reading a folded letter. "What is this, Jasmine?"

It was at that point that Jasmine recognized the folds of the paper, and realized it was the note that Cara had given her that morning.

"What does it say?" she asked, holding her breath, completely at a loss for what to expect.

But Yvonne only shrugged and passed it over to her. The page only had a few words on it. Across the top, it read: BOOK 3 UNTITLED. Then there were three short sentences in the middle.

Jas•mine
My beautiful, fragrant flower.
I will be forever grateful you are my gift from God.

Jasmine covered her mouth, reading the words repeatedly and it took a while for the significance to sink in.

"What is it?" Yvonne asked again, her face revealing some alarm to Jasmine's reaction.

They were interrupted at that moment when Jennifer came into the apartment laden with shopping bags.

"Hi guys. How were the interviews today?" she asked while putting down her purchases near the staircase. When neither of the other women responded, Jennifer looked up questioningly. "What's wrong?"

Jasmine just stretched her hand to pass over the document to her sister. Jennifer took it, then sat down beside Yvonne to skim the words.

"That's pretty. What is it?" she asked.

"Cara gave it to me this morning," Jasmine stated quietly.

"What?" Jennifer asked.

"When?" demanded Yvonne at the same time.

Jasmine leaned back in her chair and let out a deep breath. "That woman who showed up this morning was Robert's sister, Cara," she explained while looking at her sister.

Both the other women made several exclamations, but Jennifer's was the most insistent. "Why didn't you say something, Jay? You let me leave you alone with that crazy lunatic!"

"What the hell did she want?" Yvonne chimed in.

"She said only to give me that," Jasmine told them, using her chin to indicate the letter still in Jennifer's hands. "I didn't even look at it until now."

"I don't understand," her sister stated. "Is it from Robert? Is it him trying to reach out to you?"

Jasmine felt her throat close up, and tears began to fill her eyes.

"It's the dedication for his third novel," she whispered. "He sent the manuscript to his publisher before my birthday. I guess she wanted me to see how he feels about me."

His intentions and commitment were written clearly in black and white. And in a few short months, it would be published for the whole world to read.

"He loves me," she added, more to herself than the other two women.

"Jasmine, what are you going to do?" Yvonne asked.

"I don't know."

"Well, you can't just ignore his messages now," pressed Yvonne.

"Yes, she can," Jennifer stated simply. "Jasmine, if you can't move past what happened, then don't respond to him. Ignore what he's saying in this dedication. Just move on."

Jasmine was speechless. Over the last few days, Jennifer had given very little advice to her younger sister regarding what to do about the situation with Robert. While Maya and Yvonne remained adamant that she was being unreasonable and too stubborn, Madison was insistent that Robert had shown his true colors and could no longer be trusted. Her mom had stayed neutral, just telling Jasmine to do what her heart wanted. But Jennifer had little to say. Despite her silence, Jasmine just assumed her sister would be in support of Robert and their continued relationship. Now to hear her say the opposite was disconcerting.

"Really, Jen? You think our relationship was too badly damage?" she asked.

"No, I don't think that at all. To me, Robert's actions make perfect sense and are all about loyalty, just loyalty to his sister not you. How can you fault him for that?" she asked simply. "But that's not my point. I don't know Robert, but I know you, Jasmine. And if you can't accept that the person you love is human and might occasionally disappoint you, then you have no business being in a relationship."

Jennifer's blunt words hung in the air as the two sisters looked steadfastly at each other. Finally, Jasmine looked away, grasping the implications of her behavior throughout that week. She had found what every one of her clients were seeking; some-

one she loved and who loved her in return, yet she
had planned to throw it away at the first challenge.

"Jay," her sister continued in a softer tone, "if
you had made a mistake that hurt Robert, don't
you hope that he would love you enough to forgive you? Doesn't he deserve the same thing?"

Chapter 28

On Friday afternoon, Robert was at the Brickell Avenue apartment reviewing some of the fabrics and furniture suggestions that had been e-mailed to him by his interior designer. Now that he had a plan of how the apartment could be updated, he wanted to get it done right away. Once he was finished with that task, Robert's intention was to drive back to Key West for the weekend. If he was going to be miserable, he figured it might as well be while he was out on his boat cruising through the Keys. He had called Mary on Thursday to let her know he would be home, at least for the weekend.

The doorbell rang sometime after two o'clock. He wasn't expecting anyone, but opened the door to find his sister in front of him. Neither of them said anything right away, but Robert eventually stepped back from the doorway so that she could enter the apartment. He closed the door firmly behind her.

"Where have you been?" he asked.

"I've been staying with Aisha for a few days," she told him.

"You could have at least returned my phone call, Cara."

"Robbie, what was I going to say?"

He knew she was right. Everything that had happened was too big to allow for them to have a relationship anything like what they had before. And now with her standing in front of him, and feeling the thick tension between them, it made Robert very sad. It didn't, however, weaken his resolve.

"Look, let's just put it all on the table, Cara. I know everything," he stated coldly.

She closed her eyes, as though her worse fears had been realized.

"I had a nice long chat with your friend Raphael, and imagine my surprise to learn all about the history you guys had together."

"Please, Robert! I am so sorry!" she uttered, choking on the words. "It all seemed so harmless at the time. Like easy money. I never thought anyone would get hurt, and I had no clue how bad it had gotten for Lakeisha. There were rumors among my friends, but I didn't know, I didn't want to believe."

Robert was shaking he head. "I don't care about any of that, Cara. You have your own life, and Lakeisha was a mess. But what I don't understand is why you didn't just tell me the truth? Instead, you did everything possible to cover it up.

It's that deceitfulness and manipulation that I can't forgive."

She looked absolutely dejected, but Robert hardened his heart, refusing to feel sorry for her.

"I know," she whispered.

"So, you have two options. You can go back to Minneapolis so you and Alex can stay with Mom and Dad until you figure out what you're going to do with your life. Or you can stay in Miami. But if you stay here, Cara, you're not taking Alex with you, do you understand? In exchange, I won't tell Matthew or Mom and Dad anything."

"Robert, you can't decide that! He's my son!"

"Yes, Cara, I can. I've watched you ignore him time and time again, but at least I was there to provide some stability. So I didn't say anything. But there is no way in hell I'm letting you continue your reckless lifestyle and expose him to God knows what in the process. Screw up your life if you want; I'm done caring. But you are absolutely not going to take Alex with you. Am I clear?"

"You can't do that, Robert!" she screamed back. "You have no right!"

"Cara, let's talk a little about your boyfriend, Raphael. Did he happen to tell you how he ended up in prison, or what happened to his arm? It's a pretty ugly scar, isn't it?"

She shook her head, her mouth open like a fish.

"No? It's a pretty funny story actually," added Robert.

With great detail, he told her about the night

Raphael got hauled off to jail, leaving her with a cash windfall that would haunt her years later.

Cara listened, shaking her head and quietly sobbing.

"So, you see what I'm saying, Cara? To the police, you look very much like an accessory to robbery, don't you think? They could easily draw the conclusion that you told an ex-con exactly where I live and what was worth taking."

"Robert, please. You wouldn't."

"Yeah, I would. For Alex. Think about it. I'll give you a week to decide."

He let the full extent of his ultimatum sink in and felt only the slightest tinge of empathy for her.

"Do you think you will ever forgive me?" she whispered, wiping away a constant stream of tears.

"Honestly, I don't know, Cara. I don't know who you are anymore. Everything we've been through just seems like part of a lie now," he told her wearily. "But the stuff in the past is water under the bridge. I can let it go. What I don't think I can ever forgive is what you did to Jasmine."

His sister started crying harder, her shoulders shaking as she took big gulps of air.

"I'm sorry," she repeated.

"I know you are, but it just doesn't solve anything. You better get going. I'm leaving soon."

She nodded, then he watched her walk out of the apartment.

Robert was very glad the confrontation was over, and he sincerely hoped that Cara would choose to go back to Minneapolis. As much as he loved Alex and would do anything to make sure his nephew was well taken care of, he didn't like the idea of separating him from his mother. But Robert was absolutely serious about his threat, and only hoped it didn't come to that.

The drive down to Key West was long and tedious. It was a beautiful stretch through the Everglades, then along the Overseas Highway with spectacular views of the ocean. But at the start of a summer weekend, there was constant traffic for most of the way. Four hours later, Robert pulled into the driveway of the house. There was a light on near the front door confirming that Mary was still inside. He could smell something delicious coming from the kitchen.

"Hi, Mr. Rankin, how was your drive?" she asked when he got inside the foyer.

"Hi, Mary. It was long," he told her with a tired smile. "What are you still doing here? It's after seven-thirty."

"It's no problem. I've had a good vacation for the last two weeks, but I was starting to get bored," she told him with a humorous grin. "But it's a good thing I was still here. You have a visitor."

"What? Who?" Robert asked, drawing a blank on who could possibly be stopping by to see him here. He knew his neighbors in passing, and had a few acquaintances from boating and other activities around the Keys, but not anyone who would casually stop by for a social visit.

"Hi, Robert."

He looked past Mary to see Jasmine walk toward them from the area of the kitchen. It was like seeing a mirage in the desert, and he blinked a few times to make sure she was real.

"Jasmine," he whispered, "what are you doing here? Is everything okay?"

Mary looked between them, unaware of their issues but intuitive enough to know that not all was right. She cleared her throat when Jasmine didn't answer right away and the silence around them became uncomfortable.

"Well, I'll get going now," she told them. "Mr. Rankin, there's dinner on the stove if you're hungry, and I've done some shopping so you should have everything you need. I'll be back on Monday morning."

"Thanks, Mary. That sounds good. Enjoy your weekend"

Jasmine mumbled something similar, giving the housekeeper a warm, grateful smile.

Then he and Jasmine were alone.

Robert took a few steps toward her, but then stopped halfway across the room. While he felt a tingle of optimism, he was still uncertain of why she had come all the way to Key West to see him after days of ignoring his notes.

"How are you feeling?" he asked her.

She instinctively, touched the small scar on her right temple. "I'm okay. Still a little bruised, but it's not that bad."

"Good," he told her, but knowing it left so much unsaid.

Jasmine cleared her throat. "I'm sorry to barge in on you like this. I went by your apartment first but you had already left. Maya told me you were coming down here for the weekend, so . . ."

"Jasmine, there's no need to apologize."

There was an uncomfortable silence again, but Robert was perfectly content to wait until she was ready to talk.

"Cara came to see me," she stated.

"Damn it!" Robert spat, immediately fearing the worst. "When?"

"This morning."

"Jasmine, I'm so sorry."

"No, it's okay. Really. She gave me this."

She walked across the room and handed him a folded piece of paper. Robert opened it up with a puzzled looked on his face, then recognized the words right away. It was his dedication of his third novel to her.

"I don't understand," he replied patiently. "Why did she give this to you?"

Jasmine let out a deep breath. "Back when we first met, and we went to Matthew's wedding, Cara told me that she was happy that you were having fun, but then warned me that because of what happened with your wife, I shouldn't expect anything serious with you."

He uttered a nasty curse.

"I was suspicious of her motives. It was pretty

obvious that she didn't like me. But her words were hard to ignore."

"Damn it, Jasmine. Why didn't you tell me? Just ask me if it was true?"

Even as he said the word, he knew it was an unrealistic expectation. There were several times when he wondered if she was still determined to not get married and end up like her sister. But he never asked.

"Robert, what would you say if I did?"

He stepped closer and risked touching her by cupping her shoulder gently.

"I would have told you that I had never felt about any other woman the way I felt for you. And I was in it for as long as you wanted to be," he told her with absolute certainty.

"How could you know that?" she challenged.

"I just did."

"I think that's why Cara gave that to me," added Jasmine, referring to the page he still had in his hand. "I think she was trying to show me she was wrong."

Robert's heart was starting to pound with hope. He slipped his hands up until he cupped her cheeks.

"Jasmine," he breathed, "I am so sorry for everything that happened."

"You don't have to apologize, Robert. You didn't do anything wrong. You had a choice of blindly trusting a woman you've known for a few months or believing the sister you've known for your whole life. You made the logical choice."

"It doesn't matter. In my heart, I knew the truth.

You have to know that," insisted Robert with his head resting gently against hers. "But it doesn't excuse the things I said in the hospital, Jasmine. They were unforgivable, so I'm not asking you to. All I want is the chance to prove that it will never happen again."

They stood like that for a moment.

"Can you do that, Jasmine?" he asked softly, fully prepared to beg if he needed to. Finally, Robert felt her arms wrap around his back.

"Yes," she whispered.

Robert finally allowed himself to breath in deeply, filling his lungs for the first time in almost a week. Then, he wrapped his arms around Jasmine's back, pulling her so close their bodies were completely fused together. The muscles in his throat began to swell with emotion, and he had to fight against choking.

"I missed your note this morning," Jasmine finally said after several long minutes.

Robert smiled, very glad to hear the teasing in her voice. It was the first time he resisted sending her his regular text message. He cleared his throat before replying, hoping that his voice wouldn't reveal his shaky emotions.

"Well, there was only one thing I wanted to tell you today, but I didn't want you to think I was stalking you," he explained, finally stepping back to look down into her stunning eyes.

"What's that?" she asked.

He brushed his thumbs over the delicate ridges of her eyebrows, savoring the simplest touch of her skin. "I wanted very much to say I love you, Jasmine Croft."

He felt her lips quiver as he brushed her mouth with his. The brief contact immediately created a hot spark, and they both jumped back from the shock.

"I love you, too, Robert Rankin."

Chapter 29

Four weeks later, Jasmine and Robert were in Minneapolis to visit his parents and celebrate Alex's eighth birthday. They flew from Miami first thing in the morning in order to arrive in time for the party and pick up Alex's gift on the way.

"It's too bad that Matthew and Rosanna couldn't make it," Jasmine stated while they were in the taxi about a mile from his parent's house.

"Yeah. Matt is swamped with work, but he said they're going to come up for the Labor Day weekend instead," Robert explained

"Does Alex know what you're bringing him?" Jasmine asked with an excited grin.

"No. I spoke to him last night and he still has no clue. He's excited enough that I'm bringing you with me."

Jasmine laughed, squeezing the hand that was linked with his and lying between them. Robert leaned forward and kissed her hard with their mouths open and tongues immediately entwined. She groaned deep in her throat from the intensity, completely forgetting that they were in a public vehicle in the middle of the day.

"See, this is why I insisted we stay in a hotel tonight," whispered Robert. "There is just no way that I can keep my hands off you for one night. And from what I remember, my old bed is pretty squeaky. I don't think my parents would appreciate our activities."

They giggled between hot, wet kisses as the car slowed down on a mature tree-lined street, and finally stopped in front of a pretty bungalow.

"Looks like we're here," he stated when they finally separated.

Her eyes sparkled as she looked up at him.

"Are you sure you're ready to see Cara again?" Robert added.

"Are you?" she retorted with another squeeze to his hand.

He let out a long, deep sigh. "I think I can handle it. We haven't spoken since she came to my apartment last month. But, from what my mom has told me, she seems serious about the move back to Minneapolis. Alex is already registered for school."

"That's encouraging, right?" urged Jasmine.

Robert shrugged. "We'll see."

The taxi driver looked at them in the rearview mirror, clearly wondering what was taking them so long.

"Okay, let's get going," Robert said.

He quickly paid the cab fare before they both stepped out of the car. While the driver took the luggage out of the trunk, Robert reached back into the rear seat and lifted out Alex's gift in a large box wrapped in blue and yellow paper. Holding hands, they walked to the front entrance.

Arnold Rankin opened the door to his home with a big smile on his face. He then enveloped his son in a big hug and did the same with Jasmine.

"You guys are just in time," he stated as he ushered them inside and helped with their luggage. "Everyone is here already. We were waiting for you to arrive before we started opening gifts."

The three of them gave each other knowing looks before heading to the back of the house toward the family room. Delores Rankin met them in the hall, her face glowing with pleasure to see them. She also hugged them both, then looped her arm through Jasmine's to walk her through the rest of the house to the backyard where the party was in full swing. Robert and Arnold followed behind them.

There were about thirty people outside, most of them kids of various ages who were enjoying a variety of activities. Jasmine looked back at Robert.

"Did you do all this?"

He just grinned.

The big backyard was filled with a small collection of inflatable games including a bouncer, giant slide, and a minihoops shooting game. It was a minicarnival and the children ran around laughing and enjoying each of the activities. Robert set Alex's gift down on the ground near the others.

"There he is," stated Robert's mother, pointing out her grandson, who was climbing up a rope ladder to the top of the twenty-foot-tall slide. "Let's start gathering everyone around the table. I'll get the birthday cake, then we can open the gifts."

"Let me help you," Jasmine volunteered, going with Delores back inside to the kitchen. "There are a lot of kids here, Mrs. Rankin. Alex seems to have been able to make a lot of new friends."

"Please call me Delores, dear," she replied, patting Jasmine on the back. "He's doing very well. I'm so glad that Cara has decided to move back home and pursue her education in nursing again. I've tried not to tell my kids what to do once they became grown adults, but I never thought her move to Miami was a good idea. But what can you do? You just have to let them make some mistakes. And, of course, we got Alex, so how can I complain, right?"

Jasmine smiled back while helping stack the dessert plates.

"But it looks like everything will be fine now," continued Delores.

"Well, I'm glad they are both doing well," Jasmine said.

Delores looked over Jasmine's shoulder as someone walked into the kitchen.

"Hi, Jasmine. How are you?"

When Jasmine turned to look behind her, she found Robert's sister standing just inside the doorway. Delores may have sensed something unfinished between the two women and took the opportunity to leave the room, taking the birthday cake and candles with her.

"I'm doing well," Jasmine replied, eyeing Cara cautiously.

"Where's Robert?"

"He's outside helping to get the kids together for the cake cutting."

Cara nodded, then leaned casually against the kitchen counter with one hip. "Is he okay? I mean . . ."

"He's fine," replied Jasmine, knowing exactly what the other woman was trying to ask.

"Good," Cara stated, clearly relieved. "We haven't spoken for over a month."

Jasmine nodded, taking in the other woman's sloped shoulders and the sadness in her eyes.

"It's been really hard," continued Cara. "But it's given me a lot of time to think. About everything. At first, I was so angry with him, with both of you. I guess it was easier than really accepting what I had done." She laughed a little, but it was dry and humorless. "Did Mom tell you that I'm back in school?"

Jasmine nodded to say yes.

"I'm going to spend the year taking a few refresher courses and maybe do a co-op term. Then, I'll be able to get a good nursing job. That's what

I always wanted to do. In a way, by forcing me to return home, Robert has given me back my life," Cara explained, her head bowed. "Even though I know he hates me, and after the way I behaved, he still did what was best for me and Alex."

She finally looked up at Jasmine, and there were tears in her eyes.

"He doesn't hate you," Jasmine replied, feeling strong empathy for the personal struggle that Cara was obviously dealing with.

"Yeah, he does. And you should, too, Jasmine. Do you know why? Because I knew from the beginning how he felt about you. The minute he invited you to Matthew's wedding, I knew everything was going to change. But, instead of being happy that my brother finally found someone that he could share his life with, I only felt annoyed and scared about what it would mean for me," she explained in a tortured voice.

"Cara, it doesn't matter anymore. In fact, that whole incident with you made me take a hard look at myself, too. And Robert and I are fine now. That's what's important," stated Jasmine. "I won't lie to you. I don't know if you and Robert will ever have the same relationship again. But I know he loves you. So, go outside and say hi to your brother. It looks like we're about to cut Alex's birthday cake."

Cara nodded while wiping the last trace of tears from her face. They walked outside together to join the party, bringing the rest of the supplies from the kitchen. Jasmine went to stand by Robert's side, then watched as he saw Cara for the first time. Though he nodded to his sister, appearing unaffected by her presence, Jasmine felt the tension radiating from him, and squeezed his hand in support.

"Jasmine, you made it!"

She turned to find Alex running toward her, then braced herself as he hugged her tight.

"Did you know that I turn eight tomorrow?" he asked after pulling back to look up at her face.

"Yes, that's why I'm here. I wasn't going to miss your birthday party."

"Good. Because this is the best party ever. Did you see the big slide? You have to try it. It's *so* fun. Then I'll introduce you to my new friends, Jamie and Tiana. Tiana's a girl, but she's okay. She can ride her bike almost as fast as I can."

"I'm looking forward to it. Maybe we can do that after we cut your birthday cake and open your presents," Jasmine suggested.

He nodded, then let his mother lead him to the front of the crowd so Arnold could lead the party in singing "Happy Birthday" to his grandson. Once Alex blew out the eight candles and cut the first slice of cake, Cara took him over to where the pile of presents was collected.

Jasmine helped Delores hand out pieces of cake to all of the guests, but she kept her eyes on Alex as he opened each gift with enthusiasm. Finally, there was only one box left, wrapped in blue and yellow paper, strategically placed to hide the big holes at one end. She watched as he read the label out loud.

"From Uncle Robert and Jasmine," stated Alex with a big smile.

He then tore the paper off, revealing a mid-sized pet carrier and the small golden retriever, only eight weeks old and sleeping soundly in its cage. Alex froze for a few seconds, as though he wasn't sure if it was real. Then he was jumping up and down, and squealing with delight. His new puppy was startled awake, shook his seven-pound body, and started barking with equal excitement.

"Uncle Rob, Uncle Rob, I can't believe you got me a dog! Thank you, thank you, thank you!" Alex screamed, launching himself at Robert.

"You're welcome, Alex. Happy birthday, big guy," replied Robert with a tolerant smile.

"It's so small! Is it a boy or a girl?"

"It's a boy. He's still a baby so you'll have to take really good care of him. But soon, he'll be almost as big as you."

"Really?"

"Yup. So, what are you going to name him?" asked Robert.

Alex walked back over to his new pet that was wagging his tail wildly and prancing around the cage.

"I can call him Pokerface, like your speed boat," he suggested. "I think I'll love him as much as I like sailing around with you."

Robert laughed.

"Thanks, buddy, I'm not sure Pokerface is the right name for a dog. But how about Pokey?"

Alex pouted, as though in deep thought. "Okay, Pokey it is," he finally agreed.

Want more Sophia Shaw?
Turn the page for a sizzling excerpt from
Tempted to Touch
Available now wherever books are sold!

Chapter 1

Renee Goodchild was pissed off.

It wasn't the yelling and swearing kind of pissed off either. This was the kind that left her too angry to speak and on the verge of tears. She stood frozen in the front hall of her apartment, still trying to process the evidence in front of her.

The whole situation had started out so small. Insignificant, really.

First, it was a pair of crystal earrings. They were inexpensive, but with the right outfit, they sparkled like one-carat studs. Then it was her favorite travel mug—the only memento from her college days in Pittsburgh that had miraculously survived the numerous moves in the last six years.

Now, several weeks and various other items of increasing value later, it had come to this!

Renee picked up one half of her most prized possession, pinching it with the very tips of her fingers as though she could catch a fatal communicable disease off the surface. Her face revealed a mix of disbelief and outrage as she examined the still-wet, salt-stained leather of her perfectly sculpted, cobalt-blue platform pumps.

No! her mind screamed.

How many times had she walked by that boutique on 52nd Avenue, admiring the pair on display like art and wishing she had the impulsiveness to spend four hundred sixty dollars on shoes just because they were beautiful? And even when the price was reduced to under two hundred dollars in a post-Christmas sale, Renee still had to talk herself into buying them. In the weeks that followed, she had worn them exactly twice, but only inside the office, and only for very special client meetings.

Now they looked as though they had trudged through the dirty slush still lingering on the Manhattan sidewalks: beat up, worn out, and ruined!

Renee finally focused her eyes on the closed door of her guest room. She imagined her childhood friend, Angela Simpson, inside sleeping off another night of reckless drinking, oblivious to the turmoil that her thoughtless actions had caused.

How dare Angela wear her suede shoes without asking, and out in the February weather!

Though it had been well over three years since the women had been in regular contact, Renee had tried to be a good friend by agreeing to let Angela crash at her apartment for a few weeks until she found a job. But it was a bad situation from the beginning. Angela seemed to lack any consideration, discipline, or basic common sense.

At twenty-eight years old, she was older than Renee by about six months, yet she still behaved like she was in high school.

Renee threw down the shoe in frustration, then rubbed at her forehead, trying to calm down. She squeezed her eyes tight to ward off frustrated tears and to stifle the need to scream. Things had just gone too far now, and something had to be done. Angela was going from bad to worse, and Renee was not going to put up with it anymore. It was time for her to get the hell out of the apartment.

But, of course, Renee had no time to address it now. She had a client presentation at nine-thirty, and that gave her about fifteen minutes to pull everything together and another twenty minutes or so for the cab ride into midtown Manhattan. As an interior designer for the small design firm the Hoffman Group, Renee always had to be at the top of her game in the competitive, high-end New York market.

Her newest client, Cree Armstrong, was a middle-aged B-movie actress who could be described as eccentric at best. She had a penthouse condo off 5th Avenue and wanted to revamp the décor in celebration of the recent revival of her career. After a couple of meetings to discuss the design theme, Cree had settled on a new interpretation of 1950s Hollywood glam. The meeting this morning was to finalize the design and decide on fabrics and some of the new furniture pieces.

Despite her sour mood, Renee made it to her client's appointment on time and with a cheerful

smile on her face. Cree Armstrong's mood was also
sunny, but it was soon obvious it was probably drug-
induced. But Cree was agreeable, and Renee left
the apartment with a clear feeling of accomplish-
ment. The project was big, including a redesign of
all eight rooms in the two-thousand-square-foot
space, but did not require any major construction.
Cree's new television role would start filming in two
weeks in Burbank, California, and was expected to
go into late spring. The apartment would be rela-
tively empty for at least three months, and Renee
committed to have the full redesign completed in
that time frame.

With their meeting over by late morning, Renee
decided to run a couple of errands before the
office staff meeting at two o'clock. Almost four
years ago, she had joined the Hoffman Group as
the assistant to the owner, Amanda Hoffman. By
the end of the first year, Renee was leading client
meetings and contributing design ideas for large
projects. Then she started bringing in her own
clients and projects and was promoted to associate
designer before her second anniversary.

Renee loved her job, but Amanda was not the
easiest woman to work for. She was temperamental
and demanding, and not easily impressed. From
what Renee understood, the Hoffmans were a wealthy
family with old money, and Amanda and her
brother had been raised as part of New York's
upper-class elite. But sometime during the early
1990s, much of their money disappeared into bad
investments and extravagant spending. The worst

of it wasn't realized until her playboy father died suddenly. At around thirty years old, Amanda found herself practically broke and with no means or skills to support her lifestyle. She started Hoffman Designs in 1996 after doing several successful renovations and design projects for family friends. It eventually grew to the Hoffman Group with the addition of four associate designers.

By the time Renee was hired, Amanda was mainly doing magazine features and was a regular contributor to several local talk shows. Now there were four full-time designers, including Renee, who did regular client projects. Two years later, Renee was still the most junior designer on the team, but she had a good, well-established reputation and a growing client list. She also had the freedom of managing her own time and doing the bulk of her planning work at home. Her trips into the office were mostly for weekly Monday-afternoon status meetings, large team projects, or the occasional one-on-one meeting with Amanda.

The Hoffman Group was located on the second floor of a restored 1940s building on Lexington Avenue near 41st Street, right in the heart of midtown Manhattan. Renee made it there by 1:30 P.M. with a large spinach salad in one hand and a selection of new upholstery fabric samples in the other. She had just enough time to eat and return a few phone calls before the meeting.

"Hey, Renee," announced the receptionist, Marsha Adams. She had been with the firm almost from the beginning and was the source of almost all of the details Renee knew about Amanda Hoffman.

"Hi, Marsha," Renee replied with a warm smile as she walked by the front desk.

"Wow, is that a new hairstyle?" Marsha asked, clearly taken aback.

Renee stopped walking long enough to touch the top of her head, lightly exploring the unusual texture of her short and spiky hair. She smiled shyly. "Yeah, I just got it done on Saturday. I'm still getting used to it."

"It makes you look so much younger! And the color is perfect. I love it!" declared Marsha.

"Thanks. I was worried that it was too light. My stylist wanted to go blond, but thank God I talked him into light brown highlights instead."

"It looks a bit like a Mohawk, doesn't it?"

Marsha had already stepped out from behind her desk and was up close inspecting the hairstyle with fascination. Renee was not offended by the reaction. Though Marsha had worked in the interior design industry for about ten years, she was still a very conservative middle-aged woman from New Jersey, and all things African American remained new and intriguing to her.

"It's called a 'faux-hawk,' actually," Renee told her with a light giggle. "It's just styled like a small Mohawk with a bit of gel, but it's really just a short cut."

"Well, you just look stunning, my dear. It really brings out those big, beautiful cat eyes."

"Thanks, Marsha," she replied bashfully before continuing the walk to her desk.

Apparently, the change of her hair from a boring, shoulder-length cut to a funky, spiky crop was more of a statement than Renee had anticipated. Everyone she passed in the office stopped to comment and compliment her, though a couple of her coworkers were actually speechless for a few seconds. By the time she started eating her lunch, there was less than ten minutes before the staff meeting. When her desk phone rang, she picked it up quickly without thinking, her mouth half full of salad.

"Good afternoon, this is Renee Goodchild," she stated.

"Good afternoon, Miss Goodchild," the female caller replied in a cool, professional voice. "I'm calling on behalf of Mr. Trent Skinner. He was referred to you by a colleague and would like to book a meeting with you for Wednesday afternoon if you are available."

"All right. Is this for an interior design project?" Renee asked. The name didn't sound familiar, but she was excited to meet any new clients. She quickly opened the calendar on her computer to check her schedule.

"Yes, I believe he is looking to redecorate a room in his home."

"This Wednesday, right?" she asked.

"Yes, ma'am. Mr. Skinner is free at two-thirty P.M. and would like you to meet him at his residence in Greenwich."

"I'm sorry, did you say Greenwich? Greenwich Connecticut?"

"Yes, ma'am. If two-thirty works, I will send a car for you at one-thirty."

Renee paused with surprise and was about to ask more questions until she realized that her meeting was in less than five minutes. She scanned her schedule and saw that there were a couple of meetings booked in the morning, but they should be done by at least one o'clock.

"Okay, I think that will work. And it was Trent Skinner, right?"

"Yes, ma'am," the woman confirmed.

"Did he mention who had referred him to me?"

"I'm sorry, no, he didn't. Now, I'll get your address for the car and we'll be all set."

They spent a few more seconds on the phone, then Renee had to run to the boardroom, leaving half her lunch on her desk.

The staff meeting went smoothly. Amanda seemed a little distracted, listening to each designer give a status update of his or her project without adding any questions or comments. Once the team had finished its review, Amanda had an announcement of her own. She was going to Aruba for a month for some relaxation and to work on a client's vacation home. The news was a little surprising, since Amanda rarely took time off, but she assured everyone that she would stay in touch daily and would be easily reachable by e-mail or phone if needed.

Renee was just as startled as everyone else but had struggled to stay focused for most of the

meeting. She kept replaying the mysterious phone
call regarding the new client meeting and pondering how odd the whole thing seemed. The
idea of a new project was exciting, but the call
had been so strange and formal. Who was Mr.
Trent Skinner, and why couldn't he call her himself
to set up a meeting? Why would someone she
didn't know want her to do a design all the way in
Greenwich, much less send a car for her just for the
first meeting?

The minute she got back to her computer, Renee
did a Google search on her new prospect. According to a professional networking site, Trent Skinner was a senior funds manager with Goldwell
Group, a private equities firm in Greenwich. There
wasn't much else. She went through several pages
of search results but could not find anything else
that seemed relevant.

Eventually, Renee put the mystery in the back
of her mind and got back to work. Rather than
pack up early and restart at home, she decided to
stay in the office to complete a long list of calls to
suppliers and stores to check on orders or works
in progress.

She had three major projects under way, including the job for Cree Armstrong, all at various stages
of completion. One was a small redecoration for a
long-standing client, Margaret Applebaum, who
just wanted to redecorate her guest room. Renee
was only waiting for the upholstery and fabric work
to be completed; then she would paint and finish

the room. It was scheduled to be finished in abou
four weeks.

The other was a large renovation of a classi
New York brownstone. It was for new clients, Wayn
and Rachel Gibson, a couple with a young son
and they were redoing the second-floor bedroom
and bathroom. The structural changes were cur
rently in progress, and Renee was still working with
the clients to decide on furniture and finishes. Sh
spent about two days a week working on the desig
and managing the contractors. Cree's projec
would take an additional two days a week unti
completed, so Renee felt comfortable that she coul
take on another small commitment. This Connecti
cut client might be ideal if the project wasn't to
complicated.

Finally, at about six-thirty, she packed up and lef
the office. The subway ride uptown took only a fev
minutes, but it was enough time for her to remem
ber the situation that was waiting for her at home
Since it was almost dinnertime, it was pretty likel
that Angela would be in the apartment, watching
television and waiting to see what Renee brough
home to eat or volunteered to cook. But Rene
vowed to herself that it wasn't going to be like tha
anymore. She wasn't as angry about the shoes any
more, but the situation was still unacceptable. Sh
and Angela were going to have a long talk, and i
wasn't going to be pleasant.